Sowing in the Morning

Sowing in the Morning

Robert Dunn

VANTAGE PRESS
New York

Cover design by Susan Thomas

FIRST EDITION

Published by Vantage Press, Inc.
516 West 34th Street, New York 10001

Manufactured in the United States of America
ISBN: 0-533-14101-X

Library of Congress Catalog Card No.: 01-129294

0 9 8 7 6 5 4 3 2 1

To the courageous men who served in the Iowa Regiments during the Civil War. Iowa recruited more federal soldiers per capita than any other state, and their horrific sacrifices went far beyond the call of duty; yet, these brave men remained largely ignored by the mainstream media even to this day.

Acknowledgments

The people listed below were instrumental in bringing this book to fruition. I wish to thank them and acknowledge each one for their individual contributions:

Lois Meacham of the Grinnell Iowa Historical Society for the wealth of information about life in Grinnell during the 1860s, the dangers faced by those bold enough to support the Iowa Underground Railroad, and the hardships endured by the soldiers of the 40th Iowa Volunteers.

Molly Dorsey Sanford, my great-aunt, for writing her wonderful journal which kept track of not only her family's and her own activities during the 1850s, but also the episodes involving her precocious little sister, my great-grandmother, Dora.

My father, Joseph, and my aunt, Phiddie, for sharing with me all of the stories about their grandparents, Sam and Dora, as I was growing up.

Gordon Sandviken of the Palm Desert, California, Library who uncovered information about the Iowa Regiments during the Civil War, including depictions of battles that had literally been lost for generations.

Dennis Strahl, my editor, for his patience and help in keeping me on schedule and bringing everything to a successful conclusion.

My wife, Barbara, for her assistance in gathering research material, and helping me determine what should or should not be included in this book.

Without the help of these people this book would lack the historical accuracy found on the following pages.

Prologue

The region west of the Missouri River was Indian Country, from which all white settlers were forbidden by law prior to the Kansas/Nebraska Act of 1854. The act, which was one of the points of controversy between the North and South, provided a unique opportunity for Americans of courage and vision. One hundred and sixty acres of land could be purchased for a much lower price here than in the settled states. The Preemption Law of 1841 had already made it possible for the settlers to select land from the public domain and purchase it for one dollar and a quarter per acre, once the government had offered it for sale.

Land ownership was a powerful attraction for the men who migrated westward in the mid-1850s. The more fortunate ones came in covered wagons or riding on horses. Some came by mule. Others simply walked. It was not unusual for a man to travel west with only the clothes on his back and a few days' stores and provisions, plus a rifle or pistol.

In the new settlements, due process was often decided by a committee, then enforced by the men's skill with firearms. More than a few young ladies discovered an opportunity to earn money by trading on their professional improprieties. The lives of these women and those of many of the bachelors centered in the saloons that had sprung up on every main street throughout the new territory.

Families also arrived. They built schools and churches and provided a more stabilizing influence as well as some degree of law and order in the emerging communities.

It was during this time that the two families depicted in this story began making preparations for journeys that would change their lives forever.

1

April 1855

James Harris relaxed his grip on the reins and allowed his chestnut mare to take a short drink out of the creek; then he wheeled the horse around and rode up to the top of the rise. There, from the shade of a red cedar tree, he surveyed row upon row of newly plowed fields. To his left, near the creek, Harris's son Samuel was supervising his two younger brothers, James Agnew and William, as they built the family's new home. Just beyond the construction site, in a brush arbor kitchen, Harris's wife, Mary Ann, and three of their daughters were preparing the noonday meal. His two youngest daughters were picking wild plums just a few hundred feet upstream. The worried frown that Harris displayed was in all ways contrary to the peaceful scene that stretched out before him.

Relocating to this new territory had not been an easy decision for them. The family had strong bonds tying them to Butler County, Pennsylvania. The town of Harrisville had been founded by James's father, Ephriam Harris, and James's wife, Mary Ann, was the daughter of Judge McKee, the founder of McKeesport. To venture out west the Harris family would have to abandon their relatives and lifelong friends, as well as the Harrisville Congregational Church, where the couple had been married and where each of their children had been baptized. There were good reasons to stay in Butler County, but there were even better reasons to go. It was a simple matter of priorities. The best opportunity Mama and Papa Harris had of keeping their family together was to moving to the newly opened territory. Two of their boys and five girls still remained at home. Three of their boys had already left Harrisville.

Their eldest son, Ephriam Harris II was studying medicine at Allegheny College, with future plans to set up his own practice somewhere out west. When gold had been discovered at Sutter's Creek, near San Francisco, their second son, Thomas McKee Harris, had taken his wife, Prudence, along with their baby daughter to open a hotel for the newly rich gold miners. The third son, Samuel, was a skilled carpenter who was in Iowa building homes for new settlers. He had written his parents several letters urging them to move out west and join him.

For generations both the Harris and the McKee families had produced offspring of high energy and a restless nature. The same emotions that were driving their children to explore the newly opened territories still beat within the hearts of James and Mary Ann. It was time for them to take their remaining children, pull up stakes, and move westward. They decided to join Samuel in Iowa, then try to persuade Ephriam to join the family there after he finished his medical studies.

Before they could leave, Harris needed to divest himself of his two farms and the smelting furnaces that he used for manufacturing pig iron and smelting ore. He had no trouble selling his farms but found no buyers qualified to operate the furnaces and was forced to abandon them. There was something peculiar about the ground around the furnaces. Every time it rained, the pools of water were covered with oil that was tinged with iridescent hues. People came from miles around to drink the oily water, believing it had some beneficial medicinal effect.

The family said their good-byes, sold what they were willing to part with, packed their personal belongings, and boarded a riverboat. They went down the Allegheny to Pittsburgh, then boarded the steamboat *Diadem* and traveled on the Ohio River toward Cairo. While aboard the *Diadem* the family ran into their first encounter with people who had strong political beliefs that differed from their own radical abolitionist views. The incident happened one afternoon when eleven-year-old Joanna was walking around the decks of the *Diadem* singing softly to herself. Passengers had already complimented her on her lovely voice, and on that day some of them asked her to sing. She, of course, sang the songs with which she was most familiar and at this time sang the following words to the tune of "Oh! Susannah":

"I'm on my way to Canada,
That cold and dreary land.

The dire effects of slavery
I can no longer stand.

"My soul is vexed within me so
To think I am a slave,
 I'm now resolved to strike the blow
For freedom or the grave."

Antislavery members of Joanna's audience applauded vigor-ously. Others who had different views about slavery turned on their heels and stormed away. The child had no idea of the social signifi-cance of what she had sung, nor the hostility it had created. Kentucky was on the south shore of the river, and citizens of that state, along with passengers from other slave states south of Kentucky, went to the captain and protested. Mama Harris told Joanna not to respond to any more requests to sing. Tempers eventually cooled down, and the rest of the trip on the Ohio River passed without event. After reaching Cairo the Harrises disembarked from the *Diadem*.

The last portion of their river trip was spent aboard the *New Englander* steaming up the Mississippi River to Keokuk, Iowa. At Keokuk they purchased wagons and supplies and began their search for a suitable piece of land. They finally found an area they liked and purchased a relinquishment. The place they had chosen was about halfway between the Mississippi and Skunk rivers. It seemed at the time to be an excellent choice. The soil was dark and fertile, ideal for growing corn, soybeans, sweet potatoes, and other vegeta-bles that the family could eat or trade. Forests of oak, hickory, and cottonwood lined rivers that were abundant with perch, largemouth bass, and blue gill. There were plenty of wild turkeys, pheasant, and deer in the woods to satisfy the family's appetite for meat, along with several fur-bearing animals for their other needs.

There was a nice little town called Farmington about seven miles away from their relinquishment. At least it had seemed to be a *nice* town at the time. It wasn't long after the family was settled that Harris discovered that his closest neighbors were Copperheads. That was the name an abolitionist like himself would give to a pro-slavery sympathizer. In Harris's mind, he had settled his family in a whole nest of Copperheads. To make matters worse, word had spread throughout the township that the Harrises were radical abolitionists.

The town was no more sympathetic to the Harris family's convictions than the Harrises were to the town's political views. There were some people in town who were more neutral on the subject, but it was an uncomfortable situation for a family that was used to being surrounded by friends and family who were of the same ideology.

As Harris gazed out across the prairie toward town, he saw a growing cloud of dust moving toward their farm. Some men on horses were coming to see them. From the amount of dust being kicked up it appeared to be a large group, and they were moving at a fast pace. There could be some good reason for this unexpected visit, but none came to his mind right at this time. He reined his horse around and galloped down the hill to where his sons were working. When he was still several feet away he yelled, "Samuel, get your brothers and head for the main tent! Some riders are coming!" Then he rode up the creek toward the spot where he had last seen his two younger daughters.

Sam Harris stopped his work, stuck his hammer into his belt, and looked toward the growing cloud of dust, then yelled at his brothers. "J.A., William, drop what you're doing and head for the tent!"

When Harris reached the plum tree thicket where his girls were gathering plums, he reached down, scooped up Joanna, and plopped the startled girl right behind him on his horse. With another quick motion he grabbed little Mary and placed her in front of him.

By the time Harris and his girls reached the tent, his three sons, his wife, and one of his older girls were already brandishing weapons.

"Do you think someone wants to cause us trouble?" Mary Ann asked her husband.

"I hope not, but we'd better be ready just in case. Samuel, you and James Agnew take your rifles and take positions behind the woodpile. William, you take your rifle and go just inside the sleeping tent. Susan, give me that pistol. You and Jane take Sarah and Joanna and lay down behind the supplies here in the kitchen. Your mother and I will stay here. Everyone stay low and keep your guns ready until I find out what these people want."

Susan grumbled, "I'm a better shot than William."

Once each of his family was in his or her assigned spot, Harris called out, "Don't anyone fire your gun unless I say so! We don't want an unnecessary incident! The people in town dislike us enough as it is!" Harris pushed the pistol into his belt and took out another rifle.

For several minutes the family crouched in their positions and watched the men approach.

Harris stared intently through a pair of field glasses until the riders were within a couple hundred yards, then turned to his wife. "They're a group of men that I've seen hanging out at one of the saloons in town. They probably got drunk last night and made plans to come out here and cause the abolitionists some grief."

"How many of them do you see?" Mary Ann asked.

"Five men on horses and two on mules. I have to say they're a pretty rag-tag-looking bunch."

"Seven of them altogether. What kind of weapons do they have?"

He put the binoculars back up to his eyes. "I see one musket, and some of them have holstered pistols," Harris said.

"Some of them?"

"Two of them are just carrying clubs."

"Not a well-organized scheme," Mary Ann said.

"Still, they could be dangerous. They might not have enough sense to know how many guns they're facing. Three of the horsemen are carrying some kind of cans."

When the group of riders rode into the clearing between the tents and the construction site, a skinny man with a large red nose and a pockmarked face yelled out, "Come on out, Harris! We got some things to talk to you about!"

"Do you know him?" Mary Ann asked.

"I've seen him around Farmington a couple of times. If I'm not mistaken, he's spent a few days in the town jail." Harris called out just loud enough for his family to hear, "Samuel, you and James Agnew bring your rifles and come with me!"

All three men pointed their rifles toward the visitors as they walked out to meet the group. One of the horsemen was an old man who appeared to be hungover. The two mule riders were obviously brothers, if not twins. Neither of them looked very bright. Harris guessed that there had might have been some inbreeding somewhere back down their family line. From the surprised looks on the men's faces, they hadn't expected anywhere nearly this much opposition.

7

The skinny man looked around to make sure all of his friends were backing him up, then said, "My pardners and me rode out here to let you know that you ain't welcome round here."

"We've known that for some time," Harris replied. "I detect the smell of kerosene from those cans you're carrying, and that puzzles me. Why would you men bring something flammable out to our farm when you just wanted to give us a message?"

The leader of the group looked nervously toward the guns Harris and his two sons were carrying. "Thar's about twelve more of our gang coming along soon. So I wouldn't try nothin' funny if I was you."

"What's your name?" Harris asked.

"Name's Filpot. Why do you want to know?"

"Because I'd hate to kill a man without even knowing his name. Now I'm going to give you just one chance to explain the purpose for bringing that kerosene out to our property."

Filpot stared at his shoes.

"OK, we all know what the kerosene was for. You figured that all you had to deal with was a man, his wife, and some kids. You came to burn us out. I want to show you men just how wrong you were." Harris held up the rifle he was holding. "This is a seven-shot repeater rifle. You can load it on Sunday and shoot it all week. Not counting the three guns that you see right here, there are two more pointed right at you as we speak. Do you men realize what a mess you've gotten yourselves into? Now, Filpot, let's not try to kid each other. We know that that this sorry bunch of misfits that you brought with you are the only friends you have in the entire town, and they hardly constitute a gang. You've made a serious miscalculation of our strength. Whether or not you die today pretty much depends on how angry my family is about someone coming out here to set our place on fire. That musket and those pistols you have aren't nearly enough to stand up against us."

"Nobody in town likes you, Harris, and that's the truth."

"You're probably right about that, but most people in Farmington abide by the law. Although if you were to disappear, I doubt if anyone in town would be too upset about it. It's a cinch that the townspeople won't support you in what you're doing today. Now I'm going to tell you just once: I want all of you to get down off your horses and those two mules. Then, drop your gunbelts, that rifle, and those stupid clubs onto the ground."

The men looked at their leader, then at the rifles that were pointed at them. One by one they climbed down from their mounts, sheepishly staring at everything but the armed men confronting them. The skinny man was the last one to climb off of his horse.

"You didn't think this operation through too well, did you, Filpot?" Harris said. "I wouldn't be surprised if your own buddies run you out of town after today."

Harris turned to his son Samuel. "What do you think we should do with these fellows?"

Sam smiled and shook his head. "It would be a shame for them to carry that kerosene all the way back to town. Maybe we should let them build a fire before they leave."

"That might be not a bad idea. What do you suggest they burn?"

"Well, from where I'm standing it smells like their clothes are beyond salvaging."

"Hmm," Harris said, and stroked his chin. "I'm not sure your mother and sisters want to see these buzzards naked."

"I don't think I want to see that, either," Sam replied. "Why don't we leave them in their underwear?"

J.A. remarked to his father and brother that riding back into town in their underwear would be very embarrassing for most people, but that those roughs most likely had no reputation to protect anyway.

"OK, gentlemen, you heard what my sons said." Harris pointed with his rifle barrel to a bare spot of ground. "Stack your clothes here in a nice little pile."

The skinny man said, "You ain't fooling me. You ain't really goin' to shoot anybody."

Harris raised his rifle to a point just below Red Face's belt. "Do you me know well enough to take that risk, Filpot?"

The man quietly mumbled a string of expletives and began to undress. The rest of the men followed suit. The cans of kerosene were emptied onto the pile of clothes, and in short order a bonfire was blazing. Sam and J.A. emptied the cartridges out of the men's pistols and returned the guns to their owners.

Sam aimed his rifle at a wild turkey that was about fifty yards away and said, "I hate to bring my gun out here without even firing

9

it once." He pulled the trigger and the unfortunate fowl emitted a loud squawk and dropped to the ground as feathers flew into the air.

The hungover old man sprang into action when the shot was fired. He climbed back on his horse quite hastily for a man of his age, whirled the horse around, and took off back toward town. The other men followed.

As the dust cloud moving back toward Farmington grew smaller, the Harris family gathered in the main tent. Appetites for their midday dinner were now mixed. Sam and his two younger brothers were ravenous. Harris ate a couple bites of fried pork and half a biscuit and then pushed his plate aside. Mary Ann and her daughters had lost their appetite, too.

"Do you think we might have started a war?" J.A. asked his father.

"No. Those men have no support in town. We may have some political differences with the townspeople, but they aren't criminals. Those boys just drank too much whiskey last night and thought they were invincible."

"What are we going to do?" Mary Ann asked. 'It's not very pleasant living in a town where nobody likes you."

Joanna spoke up. "The pastor of the church says he likes us, and I have some nice friends at school."

"The pastor says he likes us but doesn't agree with our politics. Others aren't so benevolent. I'm afraid that your mother is right, Joanna. Our family should find a more suitable place to live than Farmington."

"We've sunk a lot of money into this land," Mary Ann said.

"I know. When we're finished eating Sam and I will take a ride into town and see what we can work out with the bank."

"You think that's a good idea?" J.A. asked.

"If you're referring to those men who were just here, I'm sure that if they see us coming they'll run and hide."

"Just be careful," Mary Ann said.

When James and Sam Harris rode down Main Street in Farmington, some of the people acknowledged them, but no one smiled or shouted a greeting as would have commonly occurred back in Harrisville. The town's barber, who was sitting on a bench in front of his shop, nodded politely, then looked the other way. The blacksmith seemed too absorbed in his work to look up. Two women walking down the street suddenly became interested in the merchandise displayed in a nearby shop's window.

"Remind me not to run for mayor of this town," Sam told his father.

As they passed the saloon, a young lady crossed her legs, fluttered her eyelashes and smiled seductively at the tall, black-haired younger of the two men riding past.

"It looks like you might get at least one vote," Harris said.

They rode on past the post office and the livery stable and tied their horses to the hitching post in front of the bank. Each of them had a holstered gun on his hip.

When the stocky gray-haired banker saw the two men coming through the door he looked up at them over his spectacles and without a trace of a smile said, "Good afternoon, Mr. Harris. Good afternoon, Samuel. What brings you two into town today?"

"Howdy, Mr. Jenkins. We're just fine. Thanks for asking. I'm thinking of buying some more land outside of town. I thought maybe you could tell me who I can get to handle the paperwork."

Harris had heard that the banker was a pretty good poker player, but if that was true, he wasn't wearing his poker face today. His mouth turned down at the corners, and his shoulders slumped visibly. He took off his eyeglasses and rubbed his hand across his forehead.

"You already own a hundred and sixty acres. How much land can you and your family farm?" the banker asked.

"Oh, it's not for me. Mary Ann and I have a lot of friends back home who would certainly love this part of the country. I'm thinking about starting a new township. That's what my father did in the earlier part of this century."

The banker scratched his head and looked perplexed. It was obvious that the thought of a mass migration of abolitionists into Farmington was not a happy one for him. "Do you really like it that well around here?" he asked.

"Of course I like it. Who wouldn't? The soil is great for farming. There are fish in the rivers and more than enough game in the woods. I'd say this area is about as good as anyone could ask for."

"What about the local people?"

11

Harris appeared surprised at the question. "They seem about the same as anywhere else."

"Listen, Harris, I don't have anything against you personally. If circumstances were different maybe you and I could even be friends. However, I'm sure you know that most folks around here are against the federal government forcing the abolition of slavery down people's throats. It's an extremely sensitive issue these days. I would think that you would be more comfortable living around people of your own persuasion."

"Well, I don't think that political differences should be any reason that people shouldn't get along with their neighbors. Besides, Mr. Jenkins, there will probably be a lot of new people moving in soon. Who knows what political bent they might represent?"

Jenkins shuffled papers around on his desk and then pulled out a map and unrolled it. He pointed to a spot a couple hundred miles northeast of Farmington. "Have you ever heard of a town called Grinnell?"

Harris looked at his son. "Do you know anything about Grinnell?"

"I've heard of it, but I've never been there," Sam replied.

"Let me tell you about it," Jenkins said. "This town was founded about two years ago by a fellow named Josiah Grinnell. It's as nice a spot as you could find anywhere. Anyway, Grinnell was a United States congressman and the pastor of a Congregational church in Washington."

Sam and his father looked at each other wondering if Jenkins had somehow found out that the Harris family were Congregationalists.

The banker continued, "It seems that Grinnell preached an antislavery message to his congregation and it didn't set too well with them. Some said he had quit preaching and started meddling. I would have to agree with them. He lost his pastorate. That's when he resigned from Congress and came out here to Iowa."

"Most of the churchgoers we knew back home were against slavery," Harris commented.

"I guess every place is different. You know I've never owned any slaves myself. I'm not saying I won't ever have any, and I'm not saying that I will. I just don't think that it's right for the government to be telling people what they can and can't do. This is supposed to be a free country. If we allow the government to tell a man he can't own slaves, what will be the next freedom we lose? Besides, it's the right of the states to make the laws, not the people back east in Washington."

Harris's face reddened and his fists clenched.

When Sam saw his father struggling to contain himself, he spoke up, "We didn't come here to discuss politics, Mr. Jenkins. We just need to know who we should talk to about buying some more land."

"I guess that's the point, gentlemen. I like you and your family, but Farmington might not be the best choice of places for you to live. I think that before you get too settled into this area, you might want to consider some other options."

"Even if I agreed with you, it's too late for that," Harris said. "Do you have any idea how much money and work we've put into our place? Besides, the next ten families that move in might feel pretty much like we do. No, I think we'll stay right here, thanks. Now, about finding someone to help us with our legal work."

The old banker sighed deeply. He didn't want to lose this argument, and he clearly didn't want a pack of abolitionists taking over his town. "What would you say if I told you that I could put together a group of men who would buy your land at a nice profit to you?"

"I'm not sure. I guess I might at least look at your offer, but it would have to be a mighty good one for me to consider selling out right now. Why can't we just let matters stay the way they are?"

It was getting close to dusk as Sam Harris and his father left town to return to the ranch. People were lighting their lamps in the stores and the small cottages, and the Harrises could hear loud music coming from the saloon. The men who had paid them a visit earlier in the day were now nowhere in sight.

"I wonder what happened to our visitors?" Harris commented.

"My guess is that they'll hide out somewhere until dark and then come out and scrounge around for some clothes. They'll probably land in jail, charged with theft, before tomorrow."

"If they aren't any more adept at stealing clothes than they were at intimidating settlers, that's just what will happen."

"So, when do you want me to leave for Grinnell?" Sam asked.

"You might as well leave in the morning. There is no use continuing work on the new house. We're not going to be around this area much longer."

"Do you think Jenkins will come up with a good offer?" Sam asked.

"Probably not. He's not as dumb as he's acting. I'll bluff him up as high as I can, then sell out to him. We won't come out too bad though."

The father and son rode along quietly for a while. Each one was absorbed in his own thoughts. Then the elder Harris spoke up: "Assuming that what the banker said was true, we'll get along fine with the citizens of Grinnell. The important thing you need to do is make sure that the land is as good as Jenkins described."

"And that there is still good land available," Sam added.

2

Just after dawn the following morning Sam Harris began his journey to Grinnell. He had charted his course from the same maps that his family had used on the trip from Harrisville to Farmington. First he would ride along the Des Moines River northwest for approximately seventy-five miles; then he would head straight north for another thirty miles. Up until now it had been a mild spring, and there were no signs that the weather would change much in the three days he had allotted for his trip. His destination for tonight was Ottumwa, which, along with the other towns along his route, was no more than a mere name on a map to him.

He chose a black stallion, better known for his endurance than his speed. Sam took some food, a couple changes of clothing, a bed-roll in case he needed to camp out, a repeater rifle, a pistol, and enough money to pay for food and hotels along the way. As he finished securing the last of his gear behind the saddle, he turned and addressed his horse: "It looks like we're going to be traveling quite a long ways in the next few days." The horse didn't appear too concerned, which Sam took as a good sign.

About three and a half hours out of Farmington, Sam rode past the remains of an ancient Indian village set alongside a crystal-clear lake. Just past the lake was the town of Keosauqua. At the port of Keosauqua he was able to board a ferry and cross the Iowa River. In between towns, the road narrowed to a cart path and then to nothing more than a trail. When the train began to widen again, he knew he was nearing another town.

As evening approached, he became aware that there wouldn't be enough daylight hours to reach Ottumwa, which was the next town on his map, so he began looking for a spot to camp for the night. A thick wooded area had followed the course of the river for several miles, and he couldn't see any break in the foliage up ahead. The woods usually meant animals, which would have been welcome if he was hunting. In this situation he felt he would sleep better knowing that there was some open space around him. Just before dark he crossed a sparkling little creek winding its way down toward the river. The horse and rider left the trail and followed the creek down the hill until they found a sandy area with some large rocks.

Sam asked the black stallion if this campsite was satisfactory to him. The horse didn't object, so Sam dismounted and tied his horse to a nearby tree, where there was ample grass for him to munch on. Sam remembered seeing a couple of pheasants not too far back where the trail had dipped down near the river. The thought of going back and shooting one of them was tempting, but he rejected the idea. Hunting, cleaning, and cooking one of these fowls would have been an enjoyable experience if he was with a traveling companion, but he couldn't summon the resolve to go to that much effort just for his own meal. Instead, he built a fire, fried some bacon, boiled some coffee, and warmed up some biscuits and beans.

After dinner he leaned against a rock, gazed up at the stars, and wondered what Grinnell would be like. He had been in the process of constructing a house near the Missouri River when he'd received the letter from his father saying that the family had decided to follow his suggestions and move out west. As soon as the house he was working on was completed he had joined them in Farmington. Now his goal was to help the family find a place as desirable as Farmington, but with citizens who shared their political and religious convictions. The sounds of the creek flowing past soon made him drowsy. He laid his bedroll down between his campfire and the creek and retired for the night.

At daybreak Sam climbed out of his bedroll and stretched the kinks out of his neck, back, and shoulders. He restarted the campfire, fried three eggs, warmed up a couple of day-old biscuits, and promised himself that tonight he would be eating and sleeping at a hotel.

Less than thirty minutes from his campsite, Sam began seeing ditches, denuded tree stumps, and fences. Soon he crossed a bridge over a narrow river and passed a farmhouse. The river widened and sandy beaches began to appear along the shore. If his map was correct, he was already approaching Ottumwa. The town was located on both sides of the Des Moines River, with a ferryboat anchored on the far shore across from where he was riding. It appeared that the buildings were about evenly divided on each side of the river. When he got to the main section of town, Sam caught the aroma of bacon and eggs frying and fresh coffee brewing. He could have enjoyed a hot dinner and comfortable bed last night, had he ridden just a little farther. As it was, he went inside, had a quick cup of coffee, then got back on his horse and headed up the road. Determined not to make the same mistake that night, he informed his horse that they wouldn't stop riding until they reached Oskaloosa.

Sam's second day was pretty much like the first. The sun was directly in his face for most of the morning. Open plains broken by an occasional cropping of purple and yellow wildflowers stretched out as far as the eye could see. The wooded area wound out in front of him like a long snake charting the course of the river and his route. It was only midafternoon when Sam again began seeing signs that he was nearing another town. Instead of riding late into the evening to get to Oskaloosa, he was going to have time to kill.

From the outskirts of Oskaloosa he could see that the locals took pride in the appearance of their town. Fields were planted in neat rows. Fences, barns, and houses all looked freshly painted. He rode past a Quaker meeting house, a school, and a mule cemetery. He stopped for a few minutes at the latter to make sure that he wasn't imagining what he had seen. This would be something to tell everyone about when he got back home.

Once he was in the corner of town, Sam took his horse to the livery stable; then he grabbed his traveling bag off the back of the saddle and headed for the hotel.

Inside the hotel parlor a tall, thin man with light red hair was standing behind the desk. He introduced himself as Matthew Boone and told Sam that he was the owner of the hotel. Boone watched Sam sign his name on the register, then surprised him with an unexpected remark: 'You look to me like a man of God, Mr. Harris."

Sam looked down at his dirty black pants, black coat, and black vest and said, "I'm not a preacher, Mr. Boone."

"No, I didn't think you were. You just look like a man of high moral character."

"Well, I believe in God and I go to church as often as I can. Do you only rent rooms to people who are religious?"

Boone laughed. "No, I just wanted to know how to address you. What church do you attend, Brother Harris?"

"I'm a Congregationalist. Does that make any difference in what you're going to charge me for a room?"

"No, but I might try to talk you into settling here. I'm a Quaker. My wife tells me that I'm too bold in the way that I talk to strangers."

Boone checked his guest in, escorted him to a room at the top of the stairs, and asked if there was anything that Sam needed. Sam requested some hot water.

In a few minutes two preteen girls, both with red hair, arrived with kettles of hot water, towels, and some soap. Sam did his best to sponge off two day's worth of road dirt, then shaved, put on clean clothes, and walked downstairs to the hotel dining room.

It wasn't long before Sam understood the reason for the personal questions that he had been asked when he checked in. Two young ladies with light red hair were having a discussion with a third red-head near the kitchen door. The hotel owner joined the group and pointed at the girl who looked to be the oldest. She smiled triumphantly at her two younger sisters and came over to Sam's table. She was not an unattractive woman. She had green eyes, a face sprinkled with freckles, and a generous bosom bulging underneath her gingham dress. She looked like she might occasionally sample some of the pies in the hotel kitchen, but overall she didn't look like she needed her father's assistance to find a man.

"My name is Ann. Father said you were just visiting us for one night," she began.

"That's right. I'm just passing through town. What are you serving for supper?"

"We have roast beef or we can fry a steak for you if you'd prefer."

"Roast beef is fine."

"I'm sure my father has already told you about all the advantages of living in Oskaloosa." Her face had turned a shade of pinkish red that people with darker complexions couldn't hope to duplicate.

"No, he hasn't got to that yet, but I'm sure he will."

"You'll have to forgive him; he has seven daughters and he's already worrying that we're all going to become spinsters."

Sam looked at Ann's two sisters serving some dinners on the other side of the room. All three of Boone's daughters looked attractive in a robust, full-bodied kind of a way.

'I think he's worrying about a problem he doesn't have."

"We try to tell him that. If he asks will you tell him that I flirted with you?"

"Only if you do."

She smiled and rolled her eyes at him. "After dinner we gather around the piano and sing some songs before dessert. Would you like to stand next to me when we sing?"

"Does this kind of thing go on every night?"

"Only on Saturdays."

"OK, I'll tell him you flirted with me."

"No, I mean it. Will you *please* sing with me and have dessert with me afterward?"

"I guess if I want to have some dessert, I'm going to have to sing, so we might as well do it together. Before you leave, could I ask you a question, Ann?" She smiled and he continued, "Back in Pennsylvania our towns were named after the people that founded them. Were these towns named after Indian chiefs?"

"Maybe some of them. Oskaloosa was the name of the Indian village that was here before the white man arrived. It was named after a Seminole chief's wife. It means, 'The Last of the Beautiful.' " Ann smiled and winked at Sam and marched back toward the kitchen. He saw her stick out her tongue at her two sisters as she hurried past them. He figured that if the other four of Boone's daughters grew up to be as high-spirited as the ones who were serving dinner, he would have no trouble at all getting them husbands.

Sam reviewed the events of his previous night as he rode out of Oskaloosa on the last leg of his trip to Grinnell. Ann had turned out to be more of a coquette than Sam had expected and probably much more than her father knew, given his strong religious convictions. After they'd spent some time singing and had eaten their dessert, she had offered to show him the town. As they were walking down Main Street, her hand found its way into his. Then, just before they reached the hotel, she suddenly whirled around, stood on her tiptoes, and placed a firm kiss on his lips. She had walked with him all the way to the door of his room and then seemed reluctant to say good night. When he had finally disengaged himself from the strong grasp of Annie Boone, Sam closed his door and then leaned back against it to catch his breath. He had observed over the years that the aggressive girls usually got the men faster than the more attractive ones.

19

Add that to the preponderance of men over women in the new territories, and Brother Boone's daughters would have their choice of suitable men.

Although the distance from Oskaloosa to Grinnell was about the same as what Sam had traveled yesterday, it took him three and a half hours longer. First he had to cross the Skunk River; then he ran into a more rugged trail than he had encountered in the last two days. Next he swam his horse across a narrow part of the Skunk River North.

It was almost dark on Sunday evening when Sam first began to see evidence that he was getting close to Grinnell. Denuded hillsides took the place of undisturbed woodland. Fences appeared, then farmhouses with their lamps just coming on. The horse and rider crossed a covered bridge over a crystal-clear stream flowing down over glistening rocks to a forest in the distance. "The banker was right. This is nice country," Sam told his horse. The horse did not respond. Perhaps he had a different point of view.

When Sam saw a church with a white steeple on top of a hill, he knew he was on the outskirts of town. The church looked quite similar to the Congregational church in Harrisville that his family had attended. The sound of congregation singing told him that it was between seven and seven-thirty. He knew the formula well. The service would begin right at seven with the congregation singing hymns. This would go on for about twenty-five to thirty minutes After that, there would be the pastor's prayer and maybe a testimony meeting. Customarily a couple of the church elders would pass the offering plates around; then, after the offering, the preacher would begin his sermon. The message would take between forty and ninety minutes, depending on his tendency toward the loquacious.

The road Sam was traveling wound around to within a hundred yards of the church and afforded him an opportunity to listen to the words of an old hymn as he rode by. "*Love divine, all loves excelling, Joy of heav'n to earth come down.*" Sam was surprised how much better the music sounded from this distance, or maybe it was being outdoors that made the difference. "*Fix in us Thy humble dwell-ing: All Thy faith-ful mer-cies crown.*" He decided that when he was inside of a church the sound of his own voice distracted from the beauty of the song. That and his habit of flirting with the prettiest girls in the choir rather than thinking about the meaning of the words he was singing. As he rode down the trail toward the main part of town, the music became fainter: *"Je-sus, thou art all com-pas-sion; Pure un-bounded love thou art."* Then he rounded a curve in the trail and again there were only the sounds of the river and the wind blowing through the trees.

He pulled himself up straight on his horse and let the reins hang loosely from his fingers. He was tired from his three-day ride, but nothing that a good night's sleep wouldn't cure. Getting his clothes wet in the two rivers he had crossed, then having the horse kick up a coat of dust on them before they were dry, made him feel like he needed another hot bath and one more change of clothes. When he reached the main street of Grinnell everything was closed except for the hotel. He tied his horse to the hitching post, walked through the door of the hotel, passed an empty bar, strolled through a dark restaurant and a billiard room, and approached an older man who was sitting on a high stool behind the desk in the hotel parlor.

In the dim light Sam thought the man might be sleeping until he said, "Good evening, sir. Do you need a room for the night?"

"I'll need a room for at least three days or four nights. Also, I'm going to need a place to take a shower and shave."

While Sam signed the guest registry the old man watched and said, "We don't have any bathing facilities here and the bathhouse isn't open on the Sabbath, but I'll bring some hot water up to your room to get you by for now. You can go down the street to the bathhouse and the barbershop in the morning."

"I see that the dining room is also closed. Where can a man get a meal on a Sunday night?"

"I'll bring some food to your room, too. Will biscuits and gravy be all right?"

"That will be fine. I went by the livery stable, but it was closed. Will my horse be OK tied to the hitching post overnight?"

"It would be better to keep your horse inside. When church lets out someone will be at the livery stable. If you like, I can take your horse over there for you."

"Well, I certainly can't complain about the service here. I am pretty tired, so I'll take you up on that offer."

Sam scrubbed up the best he could and ate a surprisingly good plate of food that one of the housekeepers brought to his room.

When he was finished he climbed wearily into bed and fell asleep almost immediately.

Grinnell, Iowa, put her best foot forward for Sam's first day in Iowa. The air was crisp and cool, and the sky was a brilliant shade of blue. By ten Monday morning, Sam had eaten a hearty breakfast at the hotel, downed several cups of coffee, and spent the better part of an hour scrubbing the road dust off his body at the bathhouse. By the time he was slouched comfortably back in the barber chair in Ira's Barbershop he was feeling pretty good. Sam had told the barber a little bit about his reason for coming to Grinnell. Now, fully lathered and with a man he'd never seen before guiding a straight razor up his neck, Sam felt that it was in his best interests to let Ira do the talking.

"From what you tell me, I'm sure your family will find Grinnell much more to their liking than the southern part of the state. There aren't many Copperheads around these parts." He put his hand under Sam's chin and said, "Tip your head back a little more." As the barber guided the long sharp edge over Sam's Adam's apple, Sam began to wish that the barber would concentrate more on the task at hand and leave the description of Grinnell for later.

"You can go six or eight miles in any direction and you'll find yourself some prime land that Grinnell will sell your family for two-fifty an acre. You can buy an acre or two at the grove for about ten dollars. That should give you enough timber for building, fencing, and fuel. Just north of town is a place we call the Long House. It's not much more than a big shed, but people often use it for shelter when they first come to Grinnell. Until you get your own place it's better than living in a tent. Several of us local citizens started out in the Long House."

Sam breathed more easily when the barber cleaned his face with a hot towel and began trimming his hair and sideburns. Finally the barber pulled off the apron, gave it a shake, and shook his hands with Sam.

"Good luck in your search for land," Ira said.

"Thanks. How much do I owe you?"

"The first cut is free. Next time you come in it'll cost you fifteen cents."

"Thank you, Ira. I'm sure I'll be back."

Sam walked past a couple of dry-goods stores and made a mental note to buy his mother a present before he left Grinnell. He was going to miss being home for her birthday, but he knew a gift, although a belated one, would be appreciated. The locals seemed quite friendly. Most of them smiled and nodded. A few of them wished him a good morning. Two young ladies in sun bonnets offered up flirtatious smiles as he walked past, then giggled when the tall, dark stranger tipped his hat to them. He strolled past the office of the justice of the peace and a bank, then crossed the street to pick up his horse from the livery stable.

When the barber had told Sam about new settlers staying at the Long House north of town, his first thought was that since most people follow the line of least resistance, the majority of newcomers would purchase their relinquishments out in that same direction. Following the same theory, he guessed that there would be more prime land still available on the south side of Grinnell. His first day in town would be dedicated to seeing if his hunch was right. He had seen the land southwest of town when he rode in last night, so he headed down the road northeast of Grinnell. A few miles from town Sam located the Long House. It was set near a grove of cottonwood trees, just up the hill from a creek. From the direction the water was flowing, Sam supposed that it was the same one he saw last night on his way into Grinnell.

The barber had been absolutely right. Staying at the Long House was much better than tenting. It was a broken-down but comfortable-looking building with vines growing up the walls. Sam got off his horse and walked inside. It was easy to see why people called it the Long House. The structure was only about fourteen feet wide, but Sam guessed it had to be at least sixty feet long. The ceiling was around seven feet high, made of green oak boards, and looked like it would offer little protection from the elements. There was even a cookstove and some crude furniture.

He rode up the hill away from the Long House and surveyed the area. His theory had been right. Farmhouses and barns stretched into the distance in every direction. He hadn't seen nearly as many farms on his ride into town. As tempting as the Long House looked, Sam knew that the Harris family would be tenting again. They would purchase their relinquishment on the other side of town. He remembered a nice-looking piece of ground that he'd seen just a few miles before he had passed the church last night.

It was late in the afternoon when Sam rode back down Main Street into Grinnell. He would need to hurry if he was going to do some shopping before the stores closed. The downtown was small enough that it could easily be covered on foot, plus he was tired from riding the better part of four days, so he first took his horse back to the stable. He then went directly to a store he'd seen that morning where he thought he could find a gift for his mother. Behind the counter, a tall, thin young woman with light blond hair looked up as Sam entered. She smiled and fluttered her eyes at him. "Good afternoon, sir. What can I show you today?"

Sam noticed her quick appraisal of him and had a feeling that this was a woman who didn't miss much. He hoped he had passed muster. "I'm looking for a gift for a lady."

"For your girlfriend?" she asked.

"No, for my mother. Tomorrow is her birthday."

She smiled. "Do I know her?"

"No, we live about eighty-five miles south of here."

"Then you won't be celebrating with her on her day?"

"Unfortunately not."

"I don't know you, either," the girl said. "My name is Jenny Hamlin."

"I'm Sam Harris."

"Are you just passing through town, Sam?"

"Actually, I'm looking for land to purchase for my family."

"For your family?"

"For my parents and my brothers and sisters. We've decided to settle here."

Jenny flashed Sam another big smile. "Then you will need someone to show you around. I can also introduce you to some people who you'll want to know."

"I've already met a few local people, but I'd appreciate any help you can give me."

"You'll have to come to my house for supper tonight. My dad is the pastor of the local church."

Sam had the feeling that he was being talked into something, but on the other hand, why should he worry? Jenny was an attractive girl, and it would be an opportunity to get acquainted. "Were you at church last night?" he asked.

"I was there, but you weren't. I would have noticed you," she said, and nudged his arm. "Why do you ask?"

"I heard you sing."

"You heard my solo?"

"No, but I heard the congregation singing as I rode into town. It was a beautiful sound."

"Really?" Jenny said. "I've heard all those songs so many times I wouldn't care if I never heard them again. When are you planning to move to Grinnell?"

"It will probably be a couple months. First, I've got to pick out the right parcel of land. Then, we have some business to take care of in Farmington before we leave. My family moves pretty fast when they get an idea into their heads."

"How about you, Sam? Do you move fast when get a notion in your head?"

Sam grinned at this disarmingly frank young lady. "I guess that might depend on what kind of obstacles I might encounter."

"I'm sure that there won't be any obstacles that can't easily be overcome. Now, what do you think your mother might like for her birthday?"

3

March 27, 1857

The subdued conversation between Charles and Lois Dorsey, along with the absence of banter from their younger children, gave notice that tonight's supper was different from the many others that the Dorsey family had enjoyed in their home in Indianapolis. This one would be their last. Eighteen-year-old Mollie looked worried. Sixteen-year-old Dora appeared unconcerned. Both seemed to be lost in their thoughts. Only baby Charlie playing with his food in his high chair was unaware of the changes that were rapidly approaching.

It had been only a few weeks since Dorsey had announced, first to his wife, then to his children, that he was selling their house and that the family would be relocating to the newly opened Nebraska Territory. Lois wasn't sure that they were doing the right thing. She would have preferred staying in Indiana rather than going to some strange place that she knew nothing about. Mrs. Dorsey understood the importance her husband placed on providing the opportunities for their sons that they could find only out west, and she had to agree with him that if their two younger daughters grew up to anywhere near as popular as Mollie and Dora, they would have their choice of suitors wherever they went. Still, everything was happening too fast for her to be comfortable with relocating their family.

Dorsey's oldest daughter, Mollie, had also expressed her reservations about leaving Indianapolis. Mollie was an attractive and intelligent young lady, who had already turned down proposals of marriage from two ardent suitors. Dora, sweet sixteen, a warm-hearted and impulsive beauty, considered the move an exciting adventure and could hardly wait to go. For the last couple of years Mollie's beaus had been bringing their friends to see Dora when they came courting. Dora flirted with each of the boys and teased them, much to Mollie's chagrin, but never formed any serious attachments.

Fourteen-year-old Anna and twelve-year-old Sam were also consumed with excitement about the journey into the new territory. Ada, Will, Dent, and baby Charlie were all too young to understand all of the implications of the family's impending relocation.

Dorsey shared some of the apprehension that his wife and oldest daughter had expressed but was still confident that he was making the right decision. The opportunities that Nebraska offered for himself and for his boys far outdistanced anything that Indianapolis would have to offer in the foreseeable future. Dorsey was a carpenter by trade. He planned to work in Nebraska City while looking for a suitable piece of land. Once he had purchased his property, he would build a house for his family, plant a crop, and then divide his time between working his farm and building houses for other newcomers to the Nebraska Territory. His wife, Lois, was not a strong woman; however, Mollie, Dora, Sam, and Anna were all dependable workers who could help with the farm in the early years.

Shortly after dinner, the Dorsey family retired for the night. Their trunks were packed and their clothes laid out for their journey. Tomorrow they would board the train that would take them from Indianapolis to Saint Louis on the first leg of their journey.

The following morning the family began the task of loading trunks, suitcases, and personal belongings into the larger of the two wagons parked alongside their home. The other wagon would carry the family to the train station. When the wagon was loaded, the older children began scrubbing and cleaning to get the house ready for the new owners. Dorsey had sold his horses, wagons, milk cow, chickens, and furniture along with the house. The new owner and his son were to arrive later in the afternoon to take the family and their cargo to the depot.

That evening the Dorsey family bounced back and forth in one of the passenger cars of the night train to Saint Louis. Dorsey, his wife, and Mollie found it difficult to get comfortable as the train swayed and shook down the tracks. Dora, Anna, and their brother Sam ignored the discomfort as they sat in window seats straining their eyes to see every bit of the moonlit countryside along their route. The bumping and jostling that the older family members found annoying had already rocked the younger children to sleep.

Dorsey laid his head back, closed his eyes, and tried to wash his mind clear of any thoughts. He needed to grab some rest whenever he had the chance. He figured that the next few days would prove to be the most complicated part of the trip. He would have to supervise the transfer of his family and their cargo from the train to the hotel and then from the hotel to the boat that would take them up the Missouri River to Nebraska City. The family's boxes and trunks were stored in a baggage car toward the rear of the train. His greater concern was the suitcases that contained the clothing everyone would wear on the trip. Before they had boarded the train he had given each person, except the baby, the responsibility for his or her own personal baggage. Even as Dorsey had said the words, he knew that he would have to oversee them closely. A flood of tears from one of his children was not what he cared to see during their journey.

Not long after dark the lights in the passenger car were dimmed. One by one the remaining members of the family fell asleep. Finally weariness overcame Charles Dorsey and he joined his family in slumber as their passenger car rumbled, jolted, and banged down the tracks. None of the family was awake to see the train cross the state line into Illinois, nor when they raced through the small farm towns on their way toward Missouri.

The morning sun shining through the window awakened Charles Dorsey. He took out his pocket watch and saw that it was a little before six. Nine hours of their trip had passed. It would be another eight hours before their scheduled arrival in Saint Louis. Last night, just before they had boarded the train, his family had eaten supper at a restaurant next to the station. Today their breakfast and afternoon snack would both come from the picnic basket Dora and Mollie had prepared for them yesterday. They could look forward to a hot supper at the hotel that night. Dorsey wondered why food took on so much more importance when one was traveling.

Mrs. Dorsey began to squirm and rub her neck. He moved her hand aside and gently began to massage her neck and shoulders.

"How are you feeling, dearie?" he asked.

"It feels like every bone in my body aches."

"You've worked awfully hard the last few days. We should be able to get some rest when we're on the boat."

"I'm not quite sure whether this pain is from the work or the tumbling around in this seat while I was sleeping."

Mollie opened her eyes and said. "I feel like I've fallen out of a four-story window." She rolled her head in a circle and stretched her neck. "I had a dream that there weren't any churches where we're going."

Dora heard Mollie's remark and taunted her without opening her eyes, "We're going to New-brasker to live with the heathen."

"Don't say that!" Mollie wailed. "It might come true."

Dora opened one eye and grinned mischievously. "It's OK with me as long as they're tall and handsome."

Mollie looked pleadingly at her mother, who patted her on the shoulder. "She's just teasing you. Don't get upset."

The younger Dorsey children were awake now, and little Will asked, "What kind of dogs do they have in Nebraska?"

"I imagine that they have all breeds, Willie," his father answered. "What kind do you want?"

"I want one of every kind."

His father nodded, "We'll see when we get there."

"I'm hungry," Anna said.

A chorus of children saying, "Me, too," prompted Mollie to pull the food basket out from under her seat.

Leaning back comfortably in his deck chair with his feet propped up on the railing, Charles Dorsey surveyed the scene around him. To the west, the last orange rays of sun reflected across the wake of the boat and the glassy Missouri River beyond. A bronze glow flatteringly enhanced the faces of the passengers who occupied the other deck chairs as well as those strolling the deck. Fussy old ladies were protecting their poodle dogs, and mothers were scampering after their children in mortal terror of one of them falling overboard. In front of one of the ship's saloons, Dora and Mollie were surrounded by bachelors who were competing to see who could impress them the most. At the same time, these men were attempting to avoid any kind of contact with the frolicsome children.

The inactivity Dorsey was now enjoying was especially welcome after his chaotic days in Saint Louis. He had searched for and found a traveling bag one of his boys had misplaced under his seat in the train. Dorsey had also located a couple of boxes of household items left in the baggage car. Then he had transferred every piece of the family's possessions from the train to the hotel. The next day he had to make sure that everything was in the cargo hold of the boat or in the family's stateroom. Lois Dorsey and her two older daughters had also been busy in Saint Louis, spending almost the entire time in and out of shops and stores. They had purchased a large cookstove, a new set of dishes, a barrel of sugar, and other provisions, and of course each one had come back to the hotel room with a new bonnet. They all had earned a rest.

Dorsey leaned back in his deck chair, sipped a cup of coffee, and sighed. His family would be confined to this boat for twelve days. He would have all that time with nothing better to do than relax. Almost two weeks of inactivity, and then? Well, plenty of time to worry about that when the time came. For now he was going to make the most of this interlude from his responsibilities. He was bone tired but not too tired to enjoy activities on the deck as long as they didn't require him to get out of his chair. His wife was in their stateroom resting. The younger children were in the care of Sam and Anna. Dora and Mollie were vigorously flirting with the growing crowd of young men around them, as well as some others who were not all that young.

Dorsey watched the captain going from one passenger to another, shaking hands and welcoming each of them on board with a wide, friendly smile. It was obvious that he was proud of his boat, *Silver Heels*, as well as he should be. When the captain reached the place where Dorsey was sitting, he pulled up a deck chair and, settling into it, asked. "Are you and your family comfortable in your quarters, Mr. Dorsey?"

"Our quarters are fine, but this chair I'm in right now is even better. I have to say that I'm quite impressed with the size of your ship. I've been told that you are also the owner."

"That's right. I had the *Silver Heels* built for me in Louisville, Kentucky. I named it after the race horse."

"I figured that's how you came up with the name. Tell me, what's the diameter of those waterwheels?"

Captain Barrows smiled. "You've noticed that they're oversized."

"I'm a builder myself."

"They're twenty-nine feet. We can move along at a pretty fast pace if I need to get someplace in a hurry."

"Just like its namesake."

"That's right."

"Do those two ladies who are getting all the attention belong to you?"

"I'm afraid so."

"Well, you might as well be prepared. It won't end when you get to Nebraska City. There are at least twenty-five bachelors for every single woman."

"Those two were getting more than their share of attention when we were in Indianapolis."

The captain pulled two cigars from his coat pocket and held one out to Dorsey. "Care for a smoke?"

"A comfortable chair, a beautiful sunset, and a good cigar. What more could a man ask for?" Dorsey looked over his shoulder and saw a disapproving glance from Mollie. "On second thought, maybe I'd better pass up that cigar."

Captain Barrows lit his cigar as an attendant refilled Dorsey's coffee mug. A Cajun minstrel strolled past, adding his melodic voice and music to the ambience. The two men talked until almost dark. During that time the captain gave his passenger a brief overview of the business opportunities and the best places to look for land in the new territory. One piece of valuable information that Dorsey learned from the captain was that his home-building skills would command a substantially higher price than what he could have charged in Indianapolis.

When Captain Barrows excused himself and resumed mingling with the other passengers, Dora broke free from her sister and their group of admirers and settled into the chair the captain had just abandoned.

"Good evening, Dora. I can't believe that you'd rather talk to your father than all those young men."

"They were starting to bore me. Don't you think Captain Barrows is a handsome man?"

"Captain Barrows is a fine-looking man but way too old for you."

Dora shrugged.

"That brings up a good point. From what I hear, you are going to have your pick of suitors when we reach Nebraska City. Just what kind of a man does interest you?"

"A rich one," Dora said, and glanced over her shoulder at Captain Barrows.

"That sounds rather shallow. I thought that your mother and I instilled some noble Christian values into our daughters."

"I haven't read anything in the Bible against having money."

"That's true, but I'd rather have you judging men by their integrity and good name rather than how much money they have."

"Well, since you say that I will have my choice of men, I'll start by eliminating all of the poor bachelors, then pick the qualities I want from the ones who are left."

Dorsey leaned over and kissed his daughter on the forehead. "What am I going to do with you, sweetheart?"

"Don't worry, I'm only sixteen, and I'm going to take plenty of time before I settle on any one man."

For the next several days the Missouri River showed its ugly side. Cold, blustery winds and drizzling rain kept passengers confined to their parlors and staterooms. Finally, on the fifth morning out of Saint Louis, the winds calmed, the sun came out, and gray skies turned to blue. Passengers' spirits lifted as people abandoned their isolation and crowded the decks of the ship. The *Silver Heels* pulled into port at a small town called Werton. Farewells were said to the passengers who had reached their final destinations. Even though new friendships had hardly had time to blossom, there was much well-wishing as people said good-bye to others who were on the same type of quest for new opportunities.

At dusk, pleasant aromas from the ship's saloons signaled to hungry passengers that supper would soon be served.

Dora and Mollie had spent a good deal of time in the family's stateroom fixing their hair, primping in front of the mirror, and making sure that they were dressed in their most fetching outfits. At five in the evening the two sisters strolled down the deck of the ship and received their rewards for their efforts. While the bachelors were giving them smiles and looks of appreciation, Dora and Mollie were quietly discussing which men they might encourage into a shipboard romance. Suddenly the Dorsey sisters completely lost their audience.

Bedlam had erupted on the port side of the ship. All of the bachelors and some of the married men were rushing to the ship's rail. Young mothers, with hands over their youngsters' eyes, were running in the other direction. Curiosity got the better of Dora and Mollie, and they went to the ship's rail to find out the source of the excitement.

Set among a grove of pine trees was an Indian encampment. Women were roasting meat over open fires, while groups of braves sat in huddles watching the ship go by. This idyllic scene might have garnered some attention, but what was happening at the river's shore was what had caused all the commotion. Four young women were walking out of the water up onto a sandy beach. The glow from the setting sun on their naked skin was awe-inspiring. After much yelling and waving from the men on the ship, one of the women turned and casually waved back. This gesture immediately received a loud cheer from the men. The Indian women seemed completely innocent about the way their unclothed bodies were affecting the men on board the large ship.

For a moment Mollie seemed unable to catch her breath. Finally she said, "I've never seen anything like that in my life. Those girls are completely shameless."

"I think they look beautiful. Wouldn't it be fun to swim naked like that?"

"You don't really mean that, Dora. You just like to shock me."

Dora chuckled. "If it makes you feel any better, I most certainly wouldn't do it if all these men were watching."

"I wouldn't do it at all," Mollie added.

"Maybe when you have a husband you'll feel different."

Mollie thought for a moment, then conceded, "Maybe."

Some men leaned so far over the railing to get one last glimpse of the girls that Dora and Mollie feared someone might fall overboard. Finally the ship rounded a bend and the men began to walk away. They all seemed to be talking at once as they each described in detail what they had seen as if no one else had seen exactly the same thing.

"Well, Mollie, I guess that shows how good we are at keeping the men's attention."

Mollie put her arm around her sister and they both started to laugh.

"At least we found out what men like," Mollie said.

"As if we didn't already know."

The ship's bell sounded at exactly six o'clock, signaling that everyone could go to their assigned saloon for supper. Tonight the captain served roast beef and cabbage boiled in beef broth, with biscuits and gravy.

Later that same evening Dora and Millie each made their selection for male companionship for the remainder of the trip on the *Silver Heels*. Dora looked over the entire dining room, then settled on a young merchant named Armstrong. She rolled her eyes at him just once and that was enough. He quickly came to her table and introduced himself to Dora and the family.

Mollie thought the matter over a little more carefully and chose a tall, dark, indolent planter from Mississippi. His name was Purcell. She induced him to come over to the Dorsey family's table with only a slight cock of her head and a little smile.

As the days passed by and the big ship proceeded up the river, it turned out that Armstrong liked nothing better than to talk about himself. Dora played the wide-eyed demure type and for a few days became the perfect listener. To Mollie's horror, Purcell turned out to be a pro-slavery sympathizer. The two of them spent most of their time walking the decks and arguing.

On the last night of the boat trip both sisters received proposals of marriage. Dora explained to Armstrong that while she thought him to be a fine gentleman whom some young lady would be fortunate to have as a husband, she was much too young to seriously consider marriage at this time. Mollie pleaded that she and Purcell's political and religious differences would prove to be an insurmountable obstacle, adding that she wished him well in finding a girl who shared his views. Thus Dora and Mollie would arrive in the new territory unencumbered by romantic attachments.

Later that night the *Silver Heels* slipped quietly past Brownsville. The Dorsey family's long journey was nearly over.

At sunset on Wednesday the ship docked in Nebraska City. It soon became apparent to those on board that the arrival of the *Silver Heels* was considered to be a major event for the town. The ship and its passengers were greeted by a loud boom of artillery and then a robust cheer from the crowd waiting on the levee. Most of those watching the ship come in were men and boys who hoped that for once, more single ladies than men would be disembarking.

The Dorseys said good-bye to the passengers who were traveling on to Omaha and Sioux City. Mollie looked at Purcell's gloomy face and felt compassion for him. She tried to muster up some tears for him but failed. Armstrong settled for a kiss on the cheek and a promise that Dora would never forget him. Any sadness that the Dorseys felt in parting from their new friends was completely overshadowed by the excitement of finally arriving at their intended destination.

The lamps were just coming on as the passengers walked down the plank toward the dock and got their first look at their new home. Each member of the Dorsey family, except the baby, was still carrying his or her own bag or suitcase. Nothing had been lost or misplaced along the way. Dorsey smiled and breathed a sigh of relief. His mission had been a success.

4

"Nebraska City. It's a nice name, but not much of a city." Mollie remarked as they disembarked from the *Silver Heels*. What she was looking at was the spot where the town had originally been founded. It was composed of nothing but crude cabins and unplastered shanties and was actually called Kearney City. The town proper was located about a mile above the river and already contained a church, stores, two hotels, a post office, and several saloons.

Dorsey rented a carriage and within a short time the family arrived at Allen's Hotel in the center of the main town.

As Dorsey marched his family into the hotel parlor and up to the desk to register, the hotel owner, Mrs. Allen, approached them. She was a talkative middle-aged woman who within a few minutes told them more about the town then they could digest in a month. She went on about how the town was full of gamblers, topars (losers), and toughs of every description but added that they hung out primarily in the saloons. Her hotel, she announced, was more family-oriented, including even her own saloon. When Mrs. Allen stopped to take a breath, Dorsey asked her about the availability of rental houses around town. She told him that there were a few available but not to expect too much. According to the hotel owner, every stable and barn in town had been turned into a place to rent. That was good news for his chances of getting a job building houses, however, not too thrilling for his family and their immediate housing needs.

When they were all settled in their room, Dorsey had a short conference with his wife, then announced the plans for tomorrow. Mrs. Dorsey, Dora, and Mollie would go house hunting. Anna and Sam would stay at the hotel and look after the younger children, while Dorsey would begin looking for employment.

When the family awakened, the morning sun shone brightly through the hotel window. It could have been a nice day for the ladies except for the cold wind that was of sufficient intensity to make searching the town for a rental a daunting task. None of them wished to have their skirts blown up in front of gawking men who seemed to always be watching them from the time they had arrived.

After they all had breakfast in the hotel dining room, Mrs. Dorsey gave some quick instructions to Anna and Sam regarding the care of the children; then the ladies bundled up in warm clothes and left the hotel in search of suitable accommodations for the family. The first rental they looked at was directly across the street from the hotel. It didn't take long for the Dorsey ladies to agree unanimously that these quarters were not at all suitable.

Over the next several hours they examined numerous converted barns, small clapboard shanties with dirt floors, and even some tent-and-shanty combinations. Thoroughly discouraged, they ended up renting the first place they had looked at. It was a dilapidated log structure with one small room, plus a three-cornered kitchen. The rent was a shocking fifteen dollars a month. Lois Dorsey sat down on a dusty chair in their new quarters and put her head in her hands.

"This is only temporary, Mother," Dora said. "Father will build a nice home for us soon."

Her mother shook her head despondently.

Mollie surveyed the two rooms and commented, "I think we can make this place quite comfortable."

Mrs. Dorsey was not convinced.

During supper at the hotel, the younger Dorsey children asked several questions regarding the place they would be living. Anna and Sam listened to encouraging comments from their older sisters and balanced them against the distressed expressions being exhibited on their mother's face.

When supper was over, the Dorseys carried their personal belongings across the street to their new home and the tears began to flow. The younger Dorseys, who hadn't seen the alternate sites that were for rent in town, couldn't understand why they were moving into a barn. "Not here!" "We can't move into this place!" were the pathetic wails that were heard. Dorsey tried to look cheerful, but his wife could hold back no longer. She burst into tears.

Dorsey and Sam retrieved their cookstove from the storeroom of the hotel and set it up in one corner of the room. There wasn't room for any furniture except a few chairs, so they set up the largest packing crate for a table. Beds were made on the floor, and the younger children were tucked into bed. Then the rest of the family discussed their new living arrangements. After several disparaging comments from those who hadn't seen the other rentals in town, Mollie countered the objections with a short dissertation: "This is only the beginning. The end will be better. Tonight I will say my prayers with a thankful heart, acknowledging my blessings and accepting the misfortunes as belonging to mortals here below."

"You composed that speech for your diary," Dora said.

"What if I did?" Mollie answered.

Dorsey looked fondly at his two oldest daughters. "Don't pick on Mollie for her efforts to make her journal more interesting. Someday we'll all enjoy reading it as we look back at what's happening to us now."

"If she ever lets anybody read it," Dora added.

Spirits were lifted at sunup when Sam opened the back door and everyone discovered the view from their tumbledown shack. Just down the hill behind the house a clear, sparkling stream was reflecting the morning sun. Its water spilled over rocks and green mossy logs as it wound its way toward the Missouri River. Purple and yellow wildflowers lined the grass-covered banks of the stream, and a grove of cottonwood trees towered in the distance. Just behind the shack there was a flat area big enough for a brush-arbor kitchen. The family decided that they would convert the kitchen into more living area and eat outside whenever the weather allowed.

In short order, the aroma of Mollie's bacon and eggs sizzling and Dora's freshly ground coffee brewing filled the morning air.

After breakfast, Dorsey left to meet with a local builder named Tucker. It was a lead Mrs. Allen had given to him.

The scrubbing and cleaning had just begun when Will discovered a dollar gold piece while sweeping outside the door. This inspired the younger children to begin an unsuccessful treasure hunt. It also kept them out of the way while the others cleaned the cabin. Dora, Mollie, Sam, and Anna cleaned and scrubbed, sometimes on their hands and knees, until the shack grew more presentable and the cleaning crew became more grimy.

About midmorning there was a knock at the door. Each one of them looked at the others; no one made a move toward the door.

Mollie's eyes opened wide. "What are we going to do? We can't answer the door looking like this."

"Sure we can," Dora said. She brushed her hair down across her face with her right hand, picked up a wet mop in her other hand, and opened the door. A heavy, balding man with a gray-and-black beard stood outside holding his hat in his hand.

"Are you Mr. Dorsey?" he asked.

"Oh, lawdy, no," Dora answered. "I'm Miz Dorsey's maid. She's taking herself a carriage ride with the guvner this morning."

The man looked puzzled. "I manage the Planters Hotel up the street. I heard some young ladies moved in here and I just wondered if anyone needed a job. I can pay up to six dollars a week."

"Well, sir, you can see that I already have a job, and the Dorseys are all very rich, so I guess the answer is no."

When the hotel manager left, Mollie and Anna took turns scolding Dora about her rude behavior.

At midafternoon, the house was still a made-over barn, but it was clean and a few nice personal touches had been added. Freshly picked flowers adorned their crate table, clean dishes were stacked on the shelves, and a makeshift room had been added by hanging a curtain from the ceiling in the main room.

A fire was built in the cookstove and water was heated for bathing. Since Mollie and Dora had seniority, they took washbasins behind the curtain and bathed first. When they felt like they looked presentable they put on some clean clothes and headed out to see the town.

Before they left, their father returned with some good news. Captain Barrows had been right about the shortage of carpenters in the new territory. Dorsey had not only secured a job, but Mr. Tucker had also given him an advance just to make sure he didn't get a better offer and sign up with another contractor.

Mollie and Dora visited several different shops. They got acquainted with some of the male clerks, as well as checking out Nebraska's versions of the new spring fashions. When they became tired of shopping without being able to buy anything, they decided to walk over to Allen's Hotel and have another chat with the owner. The shortest distance to the hotel would take them right past two saloons. They had walked past the first saloon and were nearing the second when loud noises caused them to stop. A woman yelled an obscenity, followed by the sound of breaking glass. Next there was a bedlam of loud male voices and the sounds of scuffling. The Dorsey sisters crossed to the other side of the street and kept walking. When they were directly across the street from the bar, a woman inside the bar screamed. The sisters hurried their pace as fast as they could go without breaking into a run.

When they walked into the hotel parlor, Mrs. Allen was talking with a short red-haired gentleman. The young man was wearing a black vest, a black bow tie, and a white shirt with the sleeves rolled up to his elbows.

"Well, hello, ladies," Mrs. Allen said. "These are the Dorsey girls, Mollie and Dora. This is my bartender, Dick Gregory. These girls have just arrived in town, Dick. Aren't they beautiful?"

Judging by the expression on Gregory's face, his boss's last question was unnecessary. He was grinning unabashedly.

Mollie and Dora exchanged pleasantries with the bartender; then he excused himself and went into the dimly lighted and almost-empty bar.

"Mr. Gregory opens the bar in the morning, but we never get busy until the supper hour."

Dora thought about all of the commotion across the street and asked, "Is your bar very busy at night?"

"The bar doesn't generate much money, if that's what you mean. The saloons down the street are where people go to do any serious drinking, and that's the way we like it. Most of our customers have one drink or a cup of coffee and play cards or talk. We have some patrons who play the piano and others who like to sing. I pride myself on the fact that there are more business deals put together here than anyplace else in town. Why don't you two come over this evening and I'll introduce you to some of our local citizens?"

Dora waited patiently for Mrs. Allen to finish her dissertation, then accepted the invitation. Mollie frowned at her younger sister, and Mrs. Allen caught the disapproving glance.

"You come, too, Mollie. I'll have the cooks bake a chocolate cake for you."

Mollie looked uncomfortable but agreed to come with Dora.

At half past seven both bachelors and married men turned their heads as the Dorsey girls walked into Allen's Hotel. Dora's jet-black hair was piled atop her head. Her normally olive skin was even more bronzed by the days aboard the *Silver Heels* and was set off by a bright yellow dress. Her light blue eyes quickly surveyed the room and observed the admiring looks.

Mollie looked equally attractive, though more conservatively attired. She wore a tan dress with a white scarf. Her thick black hair was woven into a braid that hung down almost to her waist.

Mrs. Allen motioned them toward her table, which was closer to the piano than the bar. A young gentleman who was seated with the hotel owner rose and helped first Dora, then Mollie into their chairs. Dick Gregory waved to them from behind the bar.

"Mollie and Dora, I would like to introduce you to my good friend Byron Sanford."

Dora smiled at Sanford, then turned her attention toward Mrs. Allen. Mollie's eyes met Sanford's and neither of them looked away for several seconds. Dora saw the attraction between her sister and Sanford and gave him a more thorough appraisal. As Mrs. Allen's voice rattled on about how Mr. Sanford had also moved here recently from Indiana and was involved in several business deals here in town, Dora decided that he was a rather attractive and probably decent person. He was above medium height, with wide shoulders and a lean frame. His calm blue-gray eyes appeared to signal intelligence. His beard was a little full for Dora's tastes, which made her wonder what he looked like under all the hair. She had a feeling from the way Mollie was reacting to Sanford that she would be seeing a lot more of this man in the future.

Each time Mrs. Allen turned toward Mollie or Sanford, Dora stole glances around the room, but she was careful not to give their hostess the impression that she didn't have her complete attention.

Finally Sanford caught Mrs. Allen between topics and began asking Mollie some get-acquainted-type questions. This gave Dora a better opportunity to look over the other single men who were present. It was difficult to focus too long on any one of them, because each time she did she was greeted by a broad grin and a friendly nod. Several men and just a few women were playing cards at the tables around them. She decided that the only safe way to get acquainted with any of the men would be through a proper introduction by someone she trusted.

Two men walked from the dining room into the bar. One was carrying a violin, and he followed the other one over to the piano. After some shuffling around with music sheets, they selected a song and began playing. Soon two couples walked over near the musicians and began twirling around to the rhythm.

Of course Mrs. Allen filled Dora and Mollie in on the dancing couples. She identified one couple as Mr. and Mrs. Tucker. He was a local builder, and she ran a boardinghouse. Mrs. Allen said that the Tuckers were both active in the local church. She tossed in some local gossip, too: "The Tuckers don't really need the money Mrs. Tucker makes from her boarders. Most people think that she just likes having a few young men around. Nothing bad, of course. She just enjoys the company of men her own age."

The other couple was a man who worked for Waddell Shipping Company and a housekeeper from another hotel down the street. Mrs. Allen explained that the latter couple had recently been keeping house together without the benefit of the justice of the peace.

Dora wondered if she wouldn't be learning more about the town from Mrs. Allen than she could find out from the local newspaper. In spite of Mrs. Allen's talkative nature, it was impossible not to like her. She gossiped more than a little, but not in a critical or judgmental manner.

The next man to enter the bar caught Dora's attention. His clothes looked more like what you might see at a fashionable gathering back east than at a small hotel in the Nebraska Territory. He was clean-shaven. A bright gold chain hung across his silk brocade vest, and his polished boots looked like they had never seen a cow pasture or a dusty road. His thick blond hair was neatly combed but receding at the temples, with touches of gray streaked through.

"Oh, how wonderful!" Mrs. Allen exclaimed. "Mr. Dailey is back in town."

"Does he travel a lot?" Dora asked.

"He has business interests that take him as far east as New York, but he calls Nebraska City his new home. Wait; I'll call him over to meet you."

As Mrs. Allen was securing Dailey's attention, Dora whispered to Mollie. "He's mine."

Mollie frowned and whispered back, "He's too old for you."

"Just watch."

When Mrs. Allen caught Dailey's eye, she smiled gratuitously as people frequently do with the rich. She waved and beckoned him to their table. When he saw the two black-haired beauties with the hotel owner it didn't require any coaxing.

"Mr. Dailey, I would like to introduce you to my new friends. This is Mollie and Dora Dorsey."

Dailey smiled and nodded to Millie, then turned toward Dora. His eyebrows raised perceptibly, and his smile widened. Dora was wearing an unmistakably flirty grin.

"Won't you join us, Mr. Dailey?" the hotel owner asked.

He nodded his head in the affirmative and, without taking his eyes off of Dora, reached for a chair at the table behind him. His lack of concentration on this relatively minor task caused him to stumble over Sanford's large boot and lose his balance. Apologies were exchanged, with both men insisting on taking the blame for the near mishap. Dailey finally placed the chair next to Dora and sat down.

By this time Dora was faking a cough to cover up her laughter. Mollie kicked Dora's shins under the table, resulting in a high-pitched squeal from her younger sibling. This caused a more evenly distributed loss of dignity all around.

Mrs. Allen detected the attraction between the two couples and mercifully became a listener while Mollie and Sanford and Dora and Dailey got better acquainted. Generally, when either of the Dorsey sisters set out to charm a man she was successful. Tonight would be no exception. The sisters flirted, danced, and both became intensely interested in hearing all about the history of the two men they had met.

Mrs. Allen pretended to have business to take care of and left the couples alone for long periods. Finally she appeared with two members of her kitchen staff. One held a beautifully iced cake; the other one had a pot of coffee in one hand and tea in the other.

After they had eaten their dessert, the musicians announced that this would be their last number and urged everyone to dance. Dick Gregory left his bar duties and gallantly asked Mrs. Allen to dance.

The musicians played a slow waltz, allowing the men to hold the ladies closely in their arms.

At the end of the evening, Dailey and Sanford walked the Dorsey sisters to the door of their cottage and said good night. Both men indicated that they would come calling very soon. Neither sister had the slightest doubt that this was true.

Dora's and Mollie's beds were on the floor. In the crowded little cottage, their two pillows were not more than a foot apart. They had been under the blankets for a few minutes when Dora whispered, "Are you asleep?"

"No."

"You really like Mr. Sanford, don't you?"

"By's OK."

"By?"

"It's short for 'Byron.' He asked me to call him that."

"How sweet."

"Why do you always have to tease me?" asked Mollie.

"I just said it was sweet."

"It was the way you said it. How do you like Mr. Dailey?"

"I like him a lot. He seems to be a fine gentleman," replied Dora.

"And he's *rich*." Mollie emphasized the final word.

"What's the matter with being rich?"

"He's way too old for you."

"He's mature. A young person like me could use a steadying influence."

"At least you're right about that."

From behind the curtain that hung between the senior Dorseys and their children came a loud, "Shoosh," then an equally loud whisper from their mother: "Be quiet, you two. You'll wake up the children."

Dora got in one final teasing remark: "How can you tell what By-yie looks like with all that hair on his face?"

Another, "Shoosh," came from behind the blanket.

Dora waited for Mollie to answer and, when she saw it wasn't going to happen, pushed herself up on her elbows and leaned over and kissed her sister softly on the forehead. "I love you, Mollie," she said.

5

June 5, 1857

There was a feeling of excitement in the air when the Dorsey family climbed out of bed. It was well before dawn, but no one complained about the early hour. Today was the day they had all been waiting for. Charles Dorsey had finished the house on the Little Nemaha and was moving his family into their new home. Thanks to the persuasive powers of his two oldest daughters, there were more men than they needed to pack the wagons and transport the family across the prairie. If Dorsey had not already hired a teamster to drive one of the wagons, he would have allowed the volunteer help to handle that chore, too.

The last few days had provided more rain than normal for this time of year, so everyone applauded when the sun came up revealing clear blue skies. John Dailey, the wealthy New Yorker who was in love with Dorsey's daughter Dora, had actually gotten his hands dirty and worked up a good sweat carrying boxes from the cottage to the wagons. Byron Sanford, who was subtler about his feelings but seemed to be enamored with Mollie, was likewise soiled and damp.

Dora and Mollie had been cooking beef stew and baking pies and biscuits for the last few days in anticipation of feeding all the moving party. Normally the distance between Nebraska City and the new Dorsey homestead could be traversed in a single day. The slowness of the heavily packed wagons, plus the possibility of muddy roads caused by the recent rain, made that time schedule questionable for this trip. They had made plans to camp out for one night if necessary.

Shortly after sunrise, the wagons were packed and the caravan started down the road. Dorsey drove one wagon with his wife, Lois, and the younger children. Byron Sanford drove a two-seated wagon with Dora and Mr. Dailey in the back. A tow-headed teamster named

Hemphill drove the largest wagon, loaded with the family's household belongings.

The first crisis the family faced was when little brother Willie rounded up his pack of stray dogs for the trip. Dorsey told Willie to pick out his favorite, which turned out to be a big yellow mastiff, and he was tied to the back of Dorsey's wagon. The deserted canines were tied to a fence post to keep them from following along. Protesting their abandonment, the dogs erupted in a chorus of whining and barking as the wagons pulled away.

The sun was warm and the prairies were soft and green, with thousands of wildflowers dotting the landscape and perfuming the air. At times the road was as level as Main Street in Nebraska City. At other times the wagons plowed through gullies and ruts, tangled grass, and muddy sloughs. Settlers stood at the doors of claim shanties and waved at the Dorsey caravan as it passed by.

The first fourteen miles of the trip were pleasant and uneventful. Dorsey even entertained the idea that with any luck they might reach the Dorsey farm by nightfall.

About high noon the wagons reached the first branch of the Little Nemaha River. They found a clearing and set up two makeshift tables. Dailey and Sanford gathered some dry wood and built a fire while Dora gathered some wildflowers. Dailey found a rusty old tin can, and Dora arranged a bouquet for a centerpiece. Then Dora and Mollie heated the beef stew and served it with biscuits and honey.

When they resumed their journey the going got much tougher. From the spot where they had first reached the river the land was all open territory with no traveled road. For the first couple of miles they could see the line of timber that marked the river near their farm. Then the timber disappeared behind grass too tall for even a man standing on top of a wagon to see over. After a few miles of veering around sloughs and thickets, no one in the party was even sure whether they were heading toward their destination or away from it. They wandered through the deep grass until dusk, then decided to camp for the night and make a fresh start in the morning.

A search for firewood turned out to be fruitless, so supper consisted of cold leftovers and hot tea boiled over a blaze made out of dry grass. However meager the fare, a few of the men did compliment Dora and Mollie on the pungent flavor of the tea. Anna was clearing up the dishes when she pulled the soiled dish rag used in cleaning the dinner dishes from the bottom of the teakettle and held it up. "Maybe this explains the unusual flavor of the tea," she said.

Mollie looked horrified. Dora started to giggle. Dailey, who was never too far away from Dora, heard her laughing and came over to investigate the cause.

Before Mollie could stop her, Dora held up the greasy rag and repeated Anna's statement. Dailey didn't seem at all amused. He wisely suggested that this event should remain a secret.

While Anna and Sam finished the dishes, Dora and Mollie unpacked blankets and quilts and anything they could find to make sleeping on the ground more comfortable. Mrs. Dorsey and her daughters slept on bedrolls under the wagons, while the men and boys slept out in the open with only blankets and grass piled under their heads.

Toward morning a stiff wind began to blow and a few raindrops fell on the campers. Dorsey decided that it would be better to be on the move again if they were going to have to deal with inclement weather. In the darkness, with no road to follow, Dorsey carried a lantern and marched on ahead of the wagons in the direction he prayed would lead them to their new homesite.

As daylight approached, the clouds blew over, revealing another day of clear blue skies. Within a short time they broke out of the deep grass, and the timber surrounding the Dorsey farm came into view.

Since Dorsey had returned to Nebraska City to move his family to their new home, he had been faced with a myriad of questions about Little Nemaha. His stock answer was, "Wait and see." When the moving party finally reached the cabin, he turned to watch everyone's reaction. The smaller children cheered, and Mrs. Dorsey began to smile and cry at the same time. Dora hugged Mollie and said, "It's absolutely beautiful. I had no idea that there was country as lovely as this in the Nebraska Territory."

About two hundred feet below the cabin the clear water of the river peeked through giant elm trees as it wended its way past steep banks overhung with creeping vines.

First everyone inspected the cabin. It was about twenty feet square and made from hewn logs. There were two windows, one door, and a clapboard roof. If there wasn't enough room inside the cabin, there was ample space right outside. It was unanimously decided next to remove the cookstove and the table and chairs from the wagons. This was set up in the brush-arbor kitchen, and in minutes Dora and Mollie had the fry pans sizzling. Bacon was spitting grease and several eggs were dancing around the frying pan. The aroma of the food and of fresh coffee brewing filled the air. Some squirrels ran up nearby trees and looked down at the odd creatures that had invaded their forest.

When all appetites had been satisfied, the moving party broke off into groups, each pursuing their own varied interests. Sam and Anna took the smaller children and Willie's yellow mastiff and went toward the dense foliage beyond the clearing to chase squirrels. The senior Dorseys went inside the cabin to plan living and sleeping arrangements. Mollie and Sanford disappeared into the woods.

Dailey asked Dora if she would like to walk down to the river. He seemed to know his way around this area.

As they strolled down the path toward the river, he asked, "How do you like the Little Nemaha?"

"What can I say? It's beyond anything I could have imagined. Why do I get the feeling you've been here before?"

"You're very perceptive. I've purchased a hundred-sixty acres adjacent to your property."

For some reason this made Dora feel uncomfortable. "When did this happen?"

"Just a couple of weeks ago. I knew where your father was building his house and I had some free time, so I rode up here to see if I could give him some help."

"I didn't know that you did carpentering."

He laughed. "I don't do it too well, I'll admit. I was mainly looking for land."

"So how did you help my father?"

"Well, like I said, I'm not too good with a hammer or saw. I'm more adept at finance."

"Did you finance our property?"

"No, of course not. I did loan your father a small amount of money to buy a cow and some chickens." When he saw that Dora didn't appear pleased by this news, he added, "It's only until he gets paid for the house he's working on in town."

When they reached the river they found a spot where it had widened out.

"This looks like a good spot for a swimming hole," she said.

"That's what I had in mind."

"I beg your pardon?"

"I mean I . . . " He looked flustered. "When I first saw this part of the river I thought that maybe your family would like to swim here."

She laughed. "It's all right. I understand what you meant. That's probably just what we'll do."

Dora found a large, flat rock a few feet from the water and sat down on it. She lifted one foot and took off her shoe. Dailey's eyes widened. She slipped off the other shoe and then removed the stockings. His face started to redden. She hoisted her skirts up around her knees and waded out into the water. "Oh, that feels so wonderful. Come on in. The water isn't cold."

He didn't need any urging. He quickly shed his shoes and waded toward her but stopped when the water was up to his ankles. "I thought you said it wasn't cold."

Later she sat on a smaller rock and dangled her feet in the water. He had put his shoes back on and was sitting on another rock facing her.

"Have you lived in Nebraska City very long?" she asked.

"I purchased some land near town about a year ago. I also have some rental properties back east that keep me pretty busy."

"What exactly do you do for a living?"

"I buy and sell real estate. Sometimes, when I get a commercial building that has good income potential, I hire a manager and keep it."

"How long have you been doing this?"

"Since I got out of school. Before my father died, he and I were in business together."

Dora noticed that he'd avoided telling her how long it had been since he'd left school. She picked up a flat rock and sent it skipping across the water.

"I'm sure you know why I'm here, Dora. Helping people move isn't part of my normal activities."

She picked up a bigger rock and arched it through the air and splashed it into the water. A silver-colored fish darted away from the rippling disturbance.

"Ever since the first night we met at Allen's Hotel I haven't been able to think about anything but you."

"I'm only sixteen."

"I know that I'm much older than you, but I can give you things that most younger men could never offer."

"Is this a proposal, Mr. Dailey?"

"It is."

They sat for a time listening to the water spilling over rocks and logs, hearing the sounds of squirrels chattering and birds singing their songs in the trees.

"I don't want to get married until I'm older."

"I'll wait for you. I'll stay in Nebraska City and run my business by mail."

"It could be years before I'm ready."

"If you're saying yes, then I'll wait however long it takes."

"I'm not saying yes, but I will think about it."

Brother Sam and sister Anna, who had been escorting their younger siblings on a tour of the area, found their way to where Dora and Dailey were sitting.

Eight-year-old Will came running up to them. "Sister, sister, we saw a big snake."

Dora wrinkled her nose. "A snake!" she repeated.

Dailey grinned. "There are plenty of snakes around here, but most of them are harmless. There are a few rattlers, though, so you have to be careful."

"Father told us that there are wolves, too," Anna said.

"That's right," Dailey said, "but if you leave them alone they won't bother you."

"Did everyone hear that?" Dora said. "If you see a wolf, stay away from it. They might look like a big dog, but they're wild animals. Don't try to pet one of them."

Will looked skeptical.

Dora lifted her feet out of the water and reached for her shoes and stockings. "I think it's time to go back to the house," she said.

Toward evening everyone gathered under the brush arbor. Mollie fried several fish that she and Sanford had caught. Dora dipped some hard bread into a batter and fried it to a golden brown. Anna prepared stewed gooseberries she had picked from a bush near the house.

Supper was a time of celebration. The smaller children prattled on about their adventures in the woods, while the adults heaped praise on Dorsey for his choice of spots to build the family's new home.

It turned out that Dailey had also built a small bungalow on his property on the side closest to the Dorseys. After dinner, when the fire began dying down, Dailey, Sanford, and the teamster Dorsey had hired left for Dailey's house to spend the night.

After the men were gone, Dora asked Mollie to stay in the brush arbor with her for a little longer while the rest of the family was getting ready for bed. The air was crisp but not too cold. A bright three-quarter moon shed its light through the trees and lit up the area around the cabin. The girls huddled close together next to the cookstove and began recalling the events that had transpired since they had left Indianapolis. When that subject was exhausted, Dora asked how everything was progressing between her sister and Byron Sanford.

"By and I get along well enough. I found out that he had a girlfriend back home, but he said they stopped writing to each other months ago."

"How well do you like him?" Dora asked.

Mollie thought for a few seconds. "You know, Dora, I think one of the things I enjoy most is he doesn't try to impress me with a lot of silly compliments. So many men seem desperate to be liked. From the beginning, By let me know how much he likes me, and he seems to assume that I like him as well."

"And that's what you want?"

"I guess so, but there are other things, too. I like the way he tells me what's on his mind. He doesn't play games. Also, the way he looks at me is different from anyone I've ever known. Sometimes he just stands there and smiles at me in a way that makes my knees feel weak."

"I've seen the way he looks at you." Dora leaned closer to her sister and lowered her voice. "Mr. Dailey asked me to marry him."

Mollie looked shocked. "Dora, he's much too old for you. He must be close to forty, at least."

"Maybe, but he's good-looking and kind and generous."

"Please tell me that you didn't accept his proposal."

"I told him that I'd think about it."

"Do you like him that much?"

"Why shouldn't I like him? It's as easy to fall in love with a rich man as it is to fall in love with someone who is poor. I haven't seen any bachelors in town that would be a very good catch."

"But you're not in love with him now."

"I told him that I didn't want to get married now. He said that he would wait for me."

"OK, you're talking about getting engaged, but you're not talking about getting married, at least for a while."

"That's what I'm considering."

"What I would worry about, little sister, is that once you agree to marry him, he will start pressuring you into setting a date. From what I've seen of Mr. Dailey he is a man who's used to getting what he wants."

Dora took her sister's hand and squeezed it. "Do you know how much better I feel after I talk with you?"

"Just be careful, dear."

Dora and Mollie sat close together until the last bit of wood in the stove had burned down to the embers.

"The air is so lovely here I'll think I'll sleep with my head out the door," Mollie said.

"From what I've been hearing, you'll either get bitten by a rattlesnake or get eaten by a wolf."

"Or By Sanford will drag me away."

"Mollie!"

Mollie looked pleased that for once in her life she had actually shocked her precocious little sister. She took Dora's hand and said, "Let's go inside the cabin and see what kind of place they've fixed for us to sleep."

6

December 24, 1859

The rider hunched over on his saddle and pulled his coat collar up around his neck to protect himself from the icy wind. A bright moon appeared from behind the clouds and reflected off the snow lighting up the countryside until it was almost like daylight; then it disappeared behind another black cloud, throwing the trail back into darkness. Cold air and dark clouds moving across the sky foretold that another storm might be on the way. An increasing number of fences and a few scattered farmhouses indicated that he was nearing a town. He began hearing the music before he saw the church. *"Oh, holy night, the stars are brightly shining. It is the night of the dear Savior's birth."* As he rounded a bend in the trail, he saw the lights from a church up the hill just a few hundred yards away from the trail. It was Christmas Eve, and the singing brought back memories of a gentler and simpler time in his life.

He knew that the church would be warm and he supposed that the people were friendly. It was always that way on Christmas Eve. They would most likely serve something hot to drink after the service, too, maybe even some food. It was certainly tempting. He pulled up on the horse's reins for a moment and gazed at the brightness of the white sanctuary against the black-and-gray sky. He listened for a time to the old carol; then tipping back his head, in clear tenor tones he added his voice to the chorus. *"Long lay the world in sin and error pining, till He appeared and the soul felt its worth."* After the song was completed, he pulled a flask from his coat pocket, tipped his head back, and took a long drink. Then he resumed his journey.

Pine logs blazing in a black pot-bellied stove in the front corner of the sanctuary provided enough heat to keep the chill off of the parishioners who were gathered in the Community Congregational

Church of Grinnell. Through the frost-rimmed windows icicles were visible hanging down from the eaves. Pine boughs, garlands of flowers, and festive ornaments decorated the platform. A winter storm had moved down from the north earlier in the week, guaranteeing that the town of Grinnell would have a white Christmas.

Sam Harris was sitting two rows away from the hot stove, and he was struggling to keep his eyes open. This was the only church within fifty miles of Grinnell, so all of the pews were full. Many of the worshipers were people who didn't attend regularly. Some of them had traveled quite a distance to attend the service tonight. This forced the pastor to have the choir remain in their seats on the platform and limited Jenny Hamlin to just shooting warning glances at Sam. At a regular Sunday evening service Sam's ribs would have been subject to one of Jenny's sharp elbows the first time his head even nodded. It wasn't that Jenny actually listened to her father's messages; she just thought that propriety demanded that one should at least stay awake.

Without any threat of bodily harm, Sam had sung Christmas carols, stayed alert through Jenny's solo rendition of *"Hark the Herald Angels Sing,"* and stayed awake through the town founder's annual Christmas dissertation.

Prior to coming west and establishing this town, Grinnell had been one of the most outspoken antislavery members of the U.S. Congress. The ex-congressman had Sam's full attention as he once again recited the story of his eviction from the church pastorate and his disillusionment with the Washington establishment that had caused him to come to Iowa. Sam listened with interest as Grinnell told of his firm conviction that if slavery wasn't abolished soon, that the South would form their own confederation of states and would soon become a boil on the backside of our nation. His voice rose to its highest pitch when he predicted that a free state would never and could never coexist with a slave state. His voice literally exploded with the words, "Before that happens our young men will be going to war." He ended his message with the statement, "If the South prevails in these hostilities, then the United States of America will never again be a great nation."

When Josiah Grinnell sat down, Pastor Homer Hamlin stepped to the pulpit and began his sermon. He compared the slavery of one man being owned by another with the slavery of an unrighteous man's soul belonging to Satan. This, of course, led into his Christmas message about God sending His Son into the world to deliver men from the slavery of sin. Grinnell had spoken for just over ten minutes and had greatly inspired the assemblage. Twenty minutes into Pastor Hamlin's sermon, he had also made some excellent points. The crowd nodded their approval, and a few "amens" were voiced. It would have been a wonderful place for Jenny's father to stop preaching and pronounce the benediction, but unfortunately, he was just getting started. It wasn't that Sam had no interest in the account of Jesus, Mary, and Baby Jesus; it was just that he had heard it so many times that he could have done a reasonably good job of telling the story himself.

He fought to keep his eyes open but failed. In that moment between sleep and consciousness, Sam's head fell forward while his whole body jerked visibly. Parishioners sitting nearby turned to see what had happened, and a small boy put his hand over his mouth and snickered. Sam glanced quickly toward the choir and caught Jenny's withering stare. He straightened up, cleared his throat, and then pretended to be completely absorbed in what Pastor Hamlin was saying. He noticed that several other men seemed to be less than wide awake, including the town's illustrious founder, Josiah Grinnell.

Sam's body was now under control, but his mind immediately began to wander. He had been seeing Jenny exclusively since he had first arrived in town. It wasn't a case of his looking around at the available young ladies, then selecting her for his female companion as much as it was her staking her claim on him. Early on, she had warned the other town girls to stay away from him. Since she was the pastor's daughter, they obliged her, although some more reluctantly than others.

That evening, while the women were still upstairs getting ready for church, Sam and his father had engaged in an important discussion. At that time, Sam had shared with his father that he felt that he would have better opportunities building new homes for settlers farther west. He added that he would be leaving Grinnell for Nebraska City right after the first of the year.

Sam's father was disappointed but not surprised. Instead of trying to persuade his son to stay, he told him that he fully agreed and wished him well.

Then Sam moved to a subject of a more personal nature. "I believe you know that some people expect Jennie and me to get married."

"I've heard that."

Sam hesitated for several seconds, then asked, "Did you ever have any doubts? I mean . . . before you married Mother . . . "

"If you're wondering if I had any doubts that your mother was the right woman for me? None whatsoever."

Sam looked worried.

"Son, I did have a few minor attachments before I knew your mother, but once I met her, I knew that I'd found the person with whom I wanted to spend the rest of my life. Even after all these years she's still the most exciting woman I've ever met."

Sam heaved a big sigh. "I don't feel that way about Jenny."

"I was fairly certain that you didn't. You'll have to tell her how you feel. The longer you wait, the harder it will be."

"That isn't as easy as it sounds. A few weeks ago I told her that I was leaving Grinnell and that we needed to have a talk. She said that she would rather talk about it some other time. Since then, every time I bring it up, she refuses to discuss it. She keeps acting like nothing has changed."

"Then she knows. I would guess that she's hoping that you'll change your mind."

Sam began to make another comment but stopped when his mother and sisters came down the stairs.

Homer Hamlin slammed his fist down on the pulpit, bringing Sam's mind back to the present. The speaker raised his voice a few decibels as he decried the way that so many people had forgotten the true meaning of Christmas.

Jenny smiled sweetly at Sam from her chair in the choir. Anyone noticing might have suspected that she and Sam were planning to announce their engagement this Christmas. Sam looked at her happy face and wondered if perhaps he was thinking too much about himself. Maybe, after all, he should just ask her to marry him and move out west with him. If she wasn't willing to leave Grinnell, she would turn him down. That would help absolve him of this gnawing guilt he was feeling.

Apparently the speaker had asked the congregation to rise, because Sam suddenly realized that he was only one in his pew who was still seated. He jumped quickly to his feet and added his voice to the others singing *"Joy to the World."*

After the service had ended, everyone quickly gravitated toward the hot stove. Christmas wishes and affectionate hugs were exchanged freely. A few married men embraced the prettier single girls a little longer than seemed necessary, but none of the wives seemed to mind. The holiday spirit was in the air.

Sam told Jenny to wait inside the church while he went to get the horse and wagon. She slipped on her gray outercoat and wrapped a red scarf around her neck. Her large hazel eyes peeked out from beneath a white knit cap. He had never seen her look this pretty nor this vulnerable. He could do a lot worse than marrying Jenny. It's true that Jenny could be a bit too controlling at times and she was a little fragile for his taste in women, but overall Jenny would make some man a very good wife.

As they rode away from the church, she put her mittened hand on top of his and snuggled close to him. The wheels of the wagon made a swishing sound as they rolled across the newly fallen snow. The black horse pulling the wagon was spotted with white flakes. A three-quarter moon shone through a break in the black clouds.

It began snowing harder, so Sam put his arm around Jenny to keep her warm. He had an impulse to say what she wanted to hear, to make her happy, to just do what all of their friends expected him to do.

She seemed to sense the moment and turned to him and smiled. What kind of man could hurt a woman like this, especially on Christmas Eve?

"You have something that you've been wanting to ask me?" Jenny said, and snuggled more closely.

He couldn't remember saying that he was going to *ask* her anything. Apparently she had misunderstood him.

She looked up into his face. "Now I'm ready, Sam."

There it was. The door was open and all he needed to do was step through and ask. *"Jenny, will you marry me?"* There would be no guilt for him to deal with, no hurt feelings, and no surprises. He would just do what everyone expected him to do. "I'm leaving town in one week for the Nebraska Territory, and" —he felt her body stiffen in the middle of his sentence—"I thought that we should talk about it. I don't know if this is the best time or not."

"I don't understand why you didn't say something sooner. What do you think you can find in Nebraska that you couldn't have here?"

The truth was that Sam didn't know himself. The excitement of riding into new undeveloped territory. Going places that he had never been. Finding opportunities that more timid souls could only dream about. If you didn't feel it deep within your being, then comprehension was impossible. How could he explain such a passion? So he just said, "The hardest thing is leaving people that I care about."

"Then don't do it."

Her demeanor had suddenly changed from soft and expectant to more controlling and argumentative. This was easier to deal with.

"You know that I'm very fond of you, Jenny."

"That's what people say when they're breaking up." She was sitting stiffly next to him. Their bodies were no longer touching.

For several seconds there were only the sounds of the horses' hooves and the swishing of the wheels through the snow. He was relieved that her main argument was for him to stay. She hadn't mentioned going with him. At least not yet.

Finally she broke the silence: "I thought that you cared about me."

What could he say? Jenny was a wonderful girl, but he would never feel for her the same passion that his parents felt for each other.

"I'm not going to wait for you," she said.

Sam didn't comment. The horse and wagon rounded a bend in the road.

"I'm almost nineteen. I'm not going to be a spinster."

"You'll never be a spinster. You could just snap your fingers and get any man in town."

She started to cry. "Every one except the one that I want."

Sam had dealt with the display of affection. He had coped well with her anger. He didn't know what to do about these tears.

She put her mittened hand on his arm and looked pleadingly into his face. "Sam, you could make this the happiest Christmas of my life. All you have to do is say the words I want to hear."

For a brief moment he almost gave in. "Jenny . . . I . . . I can't promise you anything. I . . I just . . . "

She jerked away, angry again. He felt relieved.

"You don't know what you want. You think some perfect girl is going to come along and you'll hear bells and chimes. You're twenty-eight years old, and it hasn't happened yet. That's because it never will; life isn't that way."

They both were silent the rest of the way to her house. The snow began to fall even harder, and she snuggled up close to him again. It was like their conversation had never taken place. When they arrived, he walked up on the front porch with her. At the front door, she turned and kissed him on the lips, then took his hand and pulled him toward her front door. They both knew quite well that it would be at least an hour before Pastor and Mrs. Hamlin had talked to the last of the stragglers, put out all the lamps, locked up the church, and come home.

He pulled his hand back. "I think I better start home. It looks like the storm is getting worse."

She looked surprised. "You're not coming into the house?"

"I better not."

She smiled and her expression went from surprised to seductive. "You'll be sorry, Sam."

"I probably will, but I think I better get home."

She kissed him again, looked closely into his face, and saw that he meant what he had said. She took both of his hands, looked up into his face, and said, "Sam, I lied when I said I wouldn't wait for you. If you have to go away, I'll wait for you no matter how long it takes for you to return."

As he rode from Jenny's house, Sam felt like he had been through a battle and had prevailed. He knew that she would be choosing his replacement just as soon as he left town. With this thought in mind he grinned and told his horse, "It looks like this is going to be a pretty good Christmas after all."

The horse didn't respond. Perhaps he had other matters on his mind.

Now that Sam and Jenny had resolved their plans, or lack of them, he spent the next few days making preparations for his trip westward. He withdrew enough money out of the bank to see him through a couple of months of unemployment, just in case there wasn't as much work in Nebraska City as he had thought. He serviced the wagon that he planned to take with him, packed his best clothes, and gave the others to his younger brothers, James Agnew and William.

Early in the morning on January 2, 1860, Sam Harris climbed onto the seat of his wagon, picked up the reins, shook them once across the horse's back, and left Grinnell heading west. He estimated that the trip to reach the Missouri River and Nebraska City would take him five or six days. It wasn't the best time of year to travel, but he was anxious to get on the road and no snow had fallen since Christmas Eve. If another storm blew into the territory before he reached his destination, he could stop at the next town he came to and wait it out.

7

Yesterday the mild weather that Sam had enjoyed for the greater part of his trip began to deteriorate. Dark, threatening clouds, accompanied by a brisk chilly wind, had warned him that his good luck could be running out. He had climbed out of his bedroll before sunup, eaten a quick cold breakfast, and ridden away from what he hoped would be his last campsite before reaching Nebraska City.

Now, as he rode into town, the snow was beginning to fall and shopkeepers were lighting their lamps along Main Street. Sam's first stop was the livery stable, where he made sure that his horse would be fed and cared for during the night. Then Sam asked the stable manager for a recommendation for a hotel for himself. Ten minutes later he walked through the door of Allen's Hotel and up to the desk. He signed the guest register and told the clerk that he would be needing a room for at least three or four nights.

After checking into the hotel, he took his bags up to the room, quickly washed off the worst of the road dirt, and went out looking for a place to get a hot meal. He only had to look as far as the bottom of the staircase. The hotel dining room was just beginning to serve supper. Sam took his time savoring the first steak dinner he had eaten in several weeks, then paid his check and wandered into the saloon. Men and women were seated at round tables sipping both hot and cold beverages. He noticed that less alcohol was being served than you would normally find at a saloon. A man was playing a piano, and a woman and two men were joining their voices in an old song. Sam found the music mediocre, not bad enough to laugh at or good enough to enjoy, certainly not of the quality usually found in church choirs at either Harrisville or Grinnell.

The bar itself was almost empty. He had learned from experience that a man tending bar would know more about the townspeople than almost anyone else in town. He walked over to the bar, climbed up onto a stool, and introduced himself to the bartender, "My name's Sam Harris. I just rode into town a couple of hours ago."

The bartender stuck out his hand, and the two men went through the age-old ritual of gripping and grinning.

"The name's Gregory. Dick Gregory. What can I get for you?"

"A cup of coffee, hot, black and strong."

"My coffee is so strong that I have to watch that it doesn't walk across the bar and pour itself." The bartender filled a mug and placed the dark, steaming liquid on the counter in front of Sam. "You just passing through, Harris?"

"No, I plan to stay around here for a while. In fact, I need to get a job and find a place to live."

"What kind of work do you do?"

"I'm in construction."

"Well, you won't have any trouble finding work around here. We have more homes to build than we have workers to build them."

Sam sipped his coffee, then set it on the counter. "Do you know anyone that I could talk to about a job?"

Gregory leaned over the bar. "You see the third table from the door?"

Sam turned and looked at the table Gregory had indicated. Four men were engaged in conversation.

"The big man on the right with thinning hair, that's Nathan Tucker. He's a contractor. Got more work than he can handle. You see the two women at the table back in the corner. The young one is Tucker's wife. The other one is my boss, Mrs. Allen."

"Tucker's wife looks like she could be his daughter."

"Yeah, but she ain't."

"Who are the other men with Tucker?"

"Young fellow on Tucker's left, that's Byron Sanford. He owns some lots in town and works sometimes as a blacksmith. Right now he's managing a dry-goods store down the street."

"Jack-of-all-trades?"

"You might say that. Sanford is a good man, though. He'll always find a way to make money. The middle-aged guy sitting next to him wearing the fancy clothes, that's Mr. Dailey. The other man is Charles Dorsey. He works for Tucker. Dorsey's got two of the prettiest daughters you've ever seen. Sanford is engaged to the oldest one. They're getting married sometime soon. Dailey is engaged to the younger one, but she keeps stalling him every time he tries to set a date."

Sam had come to the right place. Like most bartenders, Gregory knew everyone's business and liked nothing better than passing that information around.

"Dailey is engaged to the younger one? How old is she?"

"Dora's just turned nineteen."

Sam started to say that Dora must be interested in Dailey's money, then thought it was more prudent to say nothing.

Another man walked up to the bar and took a seat several stools away.

Gregory said, "After I help this gentleman, I'll take you over and introduce you to Tucker."

Tucker's voice could easily be heard over the others in the lounge as Sam and Dick walked toward his table.

When all of the introductions had been completed, Tucker told Sam to pull up a chair and join them. "So you build houses," he said. "Where are you from?"

"Originally from Pennsylvania. The last few years I've been working in Grinnell, Iowa, a couple hundred miles east of here."

"And you came west because you heard there was more work and higher pay in the Nebraska Territory." Tucker looked at Sam's wide shoulders and heavily callused hands and said, "Well, you weren't wrong about this place. What-all can you do?"

"I've built a few houses by myself, so I can do about anything you need."

"We're just finishing up one job. We'll be starting a big home up the hill the middle of next week. One of the local saloon owners has made so much money it's starting to burn a hole in his pocket. I can use another experienced man."

Sam nodded. "I'd like to talk to you about that. When is a good time for you?"

"We're all putting in a long day tomorrow. How about Sunday afternoon? Are you a churchgoing man, Harris?"

Sam hesitated. The last time a man had asked him that question, he had some daughters he was trying to pawn off. "Is going to church a prerequisite for the job?"

Tucker tipped back his head and erupted in a big booming laugh and said, "No, I just thought that if you were going to church, we could meet you there, and then, if you like, you might want to come over to our place for dinner."

Tucker's voice wasn't unpleasantly loud. It just carried well. Mrs. Tucker looked up from across the room at Sam and smiled.

"That sounds like too good an offer to pass up."

"I have to warn you, though, my wife likes to have a few boarders, and we just had an opening occur. She tells me that we can always use the extra money, but I think the real reason is she likes to have some young, handsome men around to flirt with. There's no doubt she'll try to get you to move in."

"Thanks for the warning." Sam thought, *Tucker's wife likes to flirt, and he's OK with that. Interesting.*

"This man boards with us when he's not at his farm." Tucker motioned toward Dorsey. "You'll be there for dinner Sunday, won't you?"

Dorsey shook his head. "Mollie and Dora are coming into town. They've already made other plans."

Mrs. Allen's curiosity finally got the best of her, so she and Mrs. Tucker came over and joined the group. For the rest of the evening the loquacious hotel owner provided Sam with more information about the citizens of Nebraska City than anyone could assimilate in one evening.

Sometime during the night a strong wind came up. The morning dawned bright, clear, cold, and windy. After a hearty breakfast and a few cups of coffee at the hotel dining room. Sam went to the stable to check on his horse. His horse didn't complain about the service he'd received, so Sam assumed that the animal was in good hands.

Next Sam headed toward the barbershop for a shave and a haircut. Although the sun was warm, there were several iced-over puddles for him to avoid. As he crossed Main Street, a tall, slim girl was crossing in the other direction. Because of the hazardous footing, neither Sam nor the young lady looked up until they were just a few feet apart. Sam saw her out of the corner of his eye and glanced up just as a strong gust of wind blew off her bonnet, leaving it dangling from a ribbon around her neck. Her dress flapped tightly against her legs, and her glossy black hair, which had been so neatly arranged, plunged down across her face. Sam was no expert at reading lips, but he could have sworn that she uttered an expletive normally reserved for the opposite sex.

Between the young woman's battle with her dress and the struggle with her hair, she didn't see the frozen puddle directly in her path. When her foot hit the ice she went into a skid. Sam quickly stepped forward and slipped his arms behind her waist just in time to keep her from falling. Her arms flew around his neck as she tried to pull herself to an upright position. When he attempted to steady her, his boot hit the ice and he automatically tightened his grip on her. Feeling him start to slide frightened her, causing her to hug him even tighter.

Sam and Dora were locked in a close embrace right in the middle of Main Street in broad daylight. When he was sure that they were on solid ground, Sam looked down into the most beautiful blue eyes he had ever seen. They had both regained their balance, but for a moment neither of them released the other. They merely stared at each other. Finally she stepped back and began trying to rearrange her hair.

"Excuse me . . . I mean . . . I'm sorry, ma'am. I didn't mean to . . "

"No . . . it was me. What I mean is it was *very nice* . . . that you were here, that is. I could have fallen."

"Thank you," he said.

"No . . . thank *you*."

As he proceeded toward the barbershop, he looked in both directions. It appeared that no one had observed what had just occurred.

Once inside the shop, he found out that he and the young lady had not completely escaped observation.

The barber grinned at Sam. "I don't know who you are, but you're a very lucky young man. Getting Dora Dorsey to hang on to you like that was really something. A lot of men in town would give a year's wages—"

Sam interrupted the man, "That was Dora Dorsey?"

"Yes. Do you know her?"

"I've met her father." Sam didn't mention that he had also met her fiancé.

After his shave and haircut, Sam got his horse from the stable and spent the day familiarizing himself with Nebraska City and the area around the town. There was quite a group of large new homes up the hill just south of Main Street and more under construction.

Sam's problem began that night in his room at the hotel. Every time he closed his eyes, he saw her face looking up into his. When he fell asleep, he and Dora Dorsey were back out in the middle of Main Street, only this time they were kissing each other passionately. He woke up, got out of bed, sat on a chair, and looked out the window down at the darkened street. Finally, he went back to the bed, slammed his fist into the pillow, and tried to get back to sleep. It was going to be a very long night.

On Sunday morning, Sam leaned toward the mirror that hung on the wall next to the door of his hotel room. Steam rose up from the pan of water that was sitting on the table in front of him. The white foam from his fully lathered neck and cheeks strikingly contrasted with his dark skin. His black eyes intently followed the course of his straight razor as he guided the sharp blade around his neatly trimmed beard. Sam's room at Allen's Hotel was barely large enough for a bed, a table, and two wooden chairs. His black long-tailed coat, pants, vest and white shirt were laid across the bed. Nathan Tucker had said that the morning service started at ten. Sam wanted to get there early enough to get a back-row seat. In all of the small churches that he had attended, the pews filled up from the back to the front, forcing latecomers to walk down the aisle in full view of the congregation and take a seat down front. This wasn't his idea of the best way for him to make an entrance.

He ordered a breakfast of bacon, eggs, biscuits, and gravy in the hotel dining room, then asked the waitress how he could get to the community church. Her directions were simple enough: "Go down Main Street one block, turn left, and you'll see the church up on the hill." She looked at his long legs tucked under the table and added, "You should be able to walk there in ten minutes."

He took his gold watch out of his vest pocket and saw that he had ample time to enjoy his meal and still get to church a little early.

On his way out of the dining room, Sam saw Dick Gregory setting up the bar for another day's business. He gave him a quick wave.

Mrs. Allen was standing behind the desk in the parlor counting yesterday's receipts. "Good morning, Mr. Harris. Why the suit and tie?"

"I'm going to church."

"Good for you. Say a prayer for me while you're there."

Strolling down Main Street, he looked toward the river and saw smoke rising from the chimneys of the shanties in the lower town. The shops near the hotel were all closed, but some of the store windows were already displaying their new spring finery. Two carriages passed him, transporting families in the direction of the church. He glanced at his watch and began striding faster. As he trudged up the hill, he began wondering if Dora Dorsey would be at church. He hoped that she would. He was convinced that when he saw her again he would be able to overcome his first impression and see that she was just another ordinary young woman.

Two shaggy-haired young men on sorry-looking mules passed him, headed back toward Main Street. They appeared to be hungover. His guess was that they were heading for another day of drinking at one of the saloons.

He went up the church steps two at a time, walked quickly through the door, and headed for the last aisle seat available in the back row. By the time the service started, forty to fifty worshipers were crowded into the small sanctuary. Nathan and Mrs. Tucker were about halfway down on the middle aisle. Dailey was not there, nor was Mr. Dorsey. More importantly, for Sam's peace of mind, neither was Dora. That is, she wasn't there until the choir came in and took their seats. Three men and nine women walked in from a door on the side of the platform and sat down in the two rows of chairs behind the pulpit. Dora was sitting in almost the same spot that Jenny had occupied in the church at Grinnell just a few weeks ago. Next to Dora sat another attractive young lady whose resemblance was such that Sam knew she had to be Dora's older sister and the fiancée of Byron Sanford.

As soon as the choir sat down, Sam began his project of ridding himself of his infatuation: *To begin with, she looks a little too saucy and self-reliant. Maybe there is something else I didn't notice yesterday. Her face is certainly pretty but awfully tan. Nothing like the fashionable ladies back east who avoid the sun, in order to keep their skin pale. Not at all like Jenny, either. Dora looks like she would be more at home riding a horse bareback than sipping tea and playing bridge with the ladies. She looks like a girl you could take fishing. A girl who would camp out and not complain of the inconvenience. More of a playmate than a lover. Well . . . maybe a lover, too. Face it, Sam: she's a girl a man could spend the rest of his life with. This strategy isn't working. OK, so she is pretty nice. She's engaged to be married to a rich older man. She must be shallow. More interested in money than in character.*

A young lady from the congregation walked up on the platform and sat down at the piano. A plain-looking woman who, from her authoritative manner, Sam guessed to be the pastor's wife stood up and faced the choir. She held her hand out, palm up, and then raised it slightly. The choir stood to their feet. She pointed to the pianist, who started playing. The choir began singing. "*Sowing in the morning; sowing seeds of kindness; sowing in the noontime and the dewy eve.*"

Sam watched fascinated as Dora's full red lips formed the words. She seemed to open her mouth much wider than the other singers. Wider than really seemed necessary. He visualized how it would feel to kiss those soft lips. He was losing ground fast. If he wanted to sleep well anytime soon, he had to get control of himself. He remembered something his father had told him years ago and silently reviewed his father's words: "*Never, never get attached to a girl who isn't interested in you.*" *That's it. She hasn't even glanced my way. If she recognizes me at all, it's apparent she's not interested. Why should she be?*

As Sam continued to stare at Dora, her head slowly turned until she was looking right at him. She stopped singing in the middle of a phrase. Her lips were still parted like she was holding a note, while the rest of the choir had moved on. Her eyes widened. *Is it my imagination or is she looking at me the same way I'm looking at her?* He straightened up, took a deep breath, and forced himself to look away. *It doesn't matter how I feel about this woman or even how she might feel about me. She's taken—she's off-limits—and that's the end of the matter.*

For the rest of the service, Sam carefully avoided looking in Dora's direction. When the service ended, a few people introduced themselves to him; then he walked directly to the back of the church, where a smiling Deborah Tucker was waiting for him. She slipped her arm through his and guided him out the door to where Nathan Tucker was waiting in his wagon. This would be Sam's first home cooked meal since he left Grinnell.

By early that afternoon, Sam had lined up both a job and place to live. He would be renting an upstairs bedroom from Deborah Tucker, building houses for Nathan Tucker, and working alongside of Dora Dorsey's father.

8

During the week before her wedding, Mollie Dorsey had been a whirlwind of activity. She had sent out the last of her invitations, finished sewing her wedding dress, then Dora's and Anna's brides-maid dresses, and finally given her attention to preparing food for the wedding guests. Dora, Anna, and brother Sam had done their best to stay out of Mollie's way, while at the same time taking on the chore of making the house and garden look as perfect as possible for the festivities.

One thing that Mollie saw as an imperfection in herself was not as easy to handle as the chores around the house. Since the family had left Indianapolis she had spent long hours in the sun. Working in the fields and the garden, walking in the woods, and, worst of all, swimming in the river and sunning herself along the shore had made her skin darker than she felt was appropriate for her very special day. Somewhere she had heard that mudpacks would bleach the skin. Earlier in the day she had enlisted Dora to try out an experiment with her.

Now Dora and Mollie were wearing makeshift bathing attire not suitable to be seen by others and lying on their backs on a blanket next to the river. Their faces were coated with mud and were turned up toward the sun.

"I hope nobody sees us," Mollie said.

"Why would it matter? They wouldn't recognize us under this mud."

Mollie looked at her sister. "With as little as we're wearing, I'm certain that no one would mistake us for our brothers."

Dora, who would have normally laughed at her sister's comment, didn't respond. In her exuberance over the upcoming event,

Mollie had failed to notice that Dora had not been her usual charismatic self. So, still unaware of Dora's mood, Mollie began chattering about the wedding, the honeymoon, and her future husband.

Dora listened quietly until there was a break in the dialogue, then said, "I broke my engagement to Dailey."

Mollie straightened up and looked at her sister through small slits in the mud. "When did that happen?"

"Yesterday."

"I've wanted you to do that from the beginning, but why now?"

"Because I don't love him."

"I never thought you did, but what's changed now?"

Dora told her sister about the incident with the stranger on Main Street and about seeing him at church the next day.

"You're not telling me that you've fallen in love with someone you don't even know?"

"I guess that doesn't make any sense, does it?"

"None at all."

"OK, then, it must be an infatuation, but I know that when I was in his arms I didn't want him to ever let me go. I could tell that he felt something, too. That's when I knew that I could never marry Dailey."

"I'm glad for that, anyway. What does this man look like?"

Dora rolled her eyes back and made a circle with her mouth. It was a comical sight. Mollie burst out laughing. Dora looked hurt, which presented another amusing spectacle.

Mollie put her hand on her sister's bare mud-covered shoulder. "I wasn't laughing at what you said, honey. I was laughing at how silly we look. You've only seen this man twice?"

"I see him every time I close my eyes."

"Describe him to me."

"He's tall and very dark, and his eyes and hair are black."

"His eyes are black?"

"Either black or so dark they seem black."

"I think you should meet him and find out more about him."

"How can I do that?"

"When have you ever had trouble meeting a man?"

"This one is different."

Early in the evening, Dorsey rode up to the farm to spend a few days with his family. After dinner, Mollie asked her father to go for a walk. As they strolled along the path by the river, she related the incident that Dora had shared with her.

"His name is Samuel Harris. He works for Tucker Construction and boards with the Tuckers. I work with him every day and have dinner with him every night, except when I'm here."

Mollie looked incredulous. In her superstitious mind nothing in life ever happened by accident. "You work with this man and you live in the same house?"

"That's right."

"How can you be sure it's the same person?"

"I got a haircut this week. The barber told me about Harris and Dora clutching at each other in the middle of the street."

"What kind of a man is Mr. Harris?"

"He seems like a nice guy. He's a good-looking son of a gun, but I don't think he's vain. He likes to kid around a lot. Keeps us all laughing."

"Do you think you could get him to come to my wedding?"

Dorsey smiled. "I don't know if I could take losing two daughters at once, but I'll see what I can do."

Allen's Hotel was the gathering place for many of the townspeople. Saturday night was the hotel owner's birthday, so a bigger crowd than usual was sitting around the lounge. Shortly after dinner that night, Tucker had asked Sam if he would escort Deborah to the hotel. He claimed he had some paperwork to do and didn't want his wife to miss the festivities. Sam figured that it was more likely that Tucker preferred sitting at home with his feet propped up in front of the fireplace, reading. He didn't blame him. Doing hard labor and managing a business was challenge enough without trying to keep up on all the social events that his younger wife wanted to attend.

Sam had been seated at the bar visiting with Dick, but now they were taking a recess from their own conversation, and listening to an enthusiastic discourse that was going on at the table close to the bar. A newcomer to town was addressing a group of men, telling them how they could all become rich with just a minimum of effort on their part. "Yep," the man said, "there's so much gold in Denver that you can just stake a claim and start hauling it away. Some pick it up out of the streams that run down from Pikes Peak. Others dig mines and strike veins of gold all over the hills around Denver. If you men want to get rich in a hurry, you'll pick up and head for Colorado just as soon as you can."

"What do you think about this guy?" Gregory asked.

"I think the man's selling something."

"You don't think there's any gold in Denver?"

"I'm sure there is, but if it was that easy to find, this fellow behind me would be out there digging right now. He figures that he can make more money selling supplies or wagons or maps or whatever it is he's selling than he can searching for gold."

"It sounds like you've had some experience along these lines."

"One of my older brothers, McKee's his name, took his wife and baby girl out to San Francisco a few years ago, just after they'd discovered gold at Sutter's Creek."

"McKee had a pretty bad experience, I'd guess."

"Not at all. He never went for the gold. He opened a hotel and a restaurant. He does quite well for himself."

"Would you go to Pikes Peak?"

"As a matter of fact, I'm thinking of doing just that."

"What will you do when you get there?"

"I'm not sure exactly, probably build houses, but even if one person out of twenty *is* striking gold, there's going to be a lot of money flowing around that town."

Mrs. Allen had three tables pushed together, where a gathering of ladies had been laughing and talking and celebrating the passing of another year in the life of the hotel owner. As Sam and Dick watched, a waitress from the dining room carried a cake blazing with candles across the lounge and placed it in front of her employer. Two cooks and another waitress stood outside the kitchen door watching everyone's reaction. Another waitress, who was filling everyone's coffee cups, began singing a birthday jingle and the entire room joined in.

"Do me a favor, Harris," the bartender said. "If I ever tell you my birth date, don't spread it around."

"You have my word."

While the waitress was slicing the cake, Mrs. Allen looked in the direction of the bar and said something to the ladies.

"Look out!" Gregory said.

"For what?"

"It looks like we're going to be asked to join the party."

73

"It will be a tough offer to refuse."

"There's no use even trying. Look out for Tucker's wife, she's been watching you all evening."

"It's because I'm her ride home."

"Whatever you say."

The hotel owner was all smiles as she ushered the two men over to her table. Deborah Tucker stood up, pushed her chair to one side, pulled a chair from an adjoining table up next to her, then motioned for Sam to sit in the empty chair.

There was a place on a knoll about a hundred feet above the Little Nemaha River where a giant elm spread its branches high above the green undergrowth. A person could sit under this tree and look across the river to a high bank that was covered with flowering vines. Dora often came to this spot when she wanted to be alone.

It was late in the afternoon as she sat leaning against the tree, idly throwing rocks at some smaller trees a few feet away. The scene was tranquil, but her mind was in conflict. *Dailey looked so shocked when I told him that I wasn't going to marry him. He is a good man, and I made him wait for over two years, thinking I would set a date for our marriage, and then I backed out. What did he expect, though? I was only sixteen when I accepted his proposal. I knew nothing about love then. And now I suppose I do? I know that I didn't do this because of the man I met on Main Street. At least I don't think I did. That would be stupid, to break an engagement because of someone I know nothing about. So, why do I think about him constantly? Mollie says that I come here to commune with God. I feel that I come here to sort things out, only now nothing seems to be making any sense to me.*

She sat morosely looking at the river winding its way downstream, always knowing where it was supposed to go, never veering off course. She turned her face up and looked at the leaves turning a brilliant shade of green from the afternoon sun. Taking a deep breath, she closed her eyes. *OK, God, my sister says that You help her when she doesn't know what to do; so her story goes. I don't know You as well as Mollie does, but maybe You could give me some kind of a hint as to what I'm supposed to do now.*

She looked into the sky. Nothing was changed. No voice. No sudden revelation. Not even any new ideas came to mind. *See, Mollie, it doesn't work. Mollie isn't going to answer me because she isn't here, but I already know what she would say: "Of course God isn't going to talk to you if you don't know Him."*

Dora closed her eyes again and leaned her head back against the tree. *If my sister is right, if there is a way to know You better, please show me.* What happened next took her completely by surprise. A sudden rush of exhilaration went through her body, almost like an electric shock. She started to laugh and to cry at the same time. She felt as if an enormous weight had been lifted from her shoulders. It hadn't happened in a church, but Dora knew that God's spirit had visited her and that something very special had happened to her today.

The words weren't spoken audibly, only a Bible verse going through her mind, but she knew that she had her answer: *"Those that wait upon the Lord shall renew their strength. They shall mount up with wings like eagles; they shall run and not be weary; they shall walk and not faint."* She was to do nothing but wait. Whatever was supposed to happen would happen. She jumped to her feet and started running back toward the cabin to find her sister. She had to tell Mollie what had happened to her. It was all she could do to contain her excitement.

Sam Harris and Charles Dorsey had put in a long hard day's work. Starting at eight in the morning, they hadn't laid down their tools until almost dark. The big two-story Victorian house they were building was to be the new home of the proprietor of the biggest saloon in Nebraska City. The tavern owner's establishment made money from liquor, gambling, entertainment, and also from the bedrooms upstairs. Men paid two dollars for a ten-to-twenty-minute romance with one of his three bar girls. He wasn't the most popular man in town, and he didn't appear particularly to care. He didn't intend to run for any office.

When the contract was signed, Tucker had said, "I build homes for people who can pay for my services. If I start being selective about who I work for, where it is going to end?"

Sam and Mr. Dorsey walked the short distance from the construction site to the Tucker residence. The aroma of chicken sizzling in a frying pan and a pastry baking in the oven almost overwhelmed the two hungry men when they entered the house.

"You two get cleaned up as soon as you can," Deborah said. "Supper will be ready in about fifteen minutes."

Sam washed his face and hands, splashed some water on his hair and combed it back, then put on a pair of warm wool pants, a soft flannel shirt, and a pair of well-worn boots. He made it to the dining room just as Deborah was setting the food on the table.

His landlady looked him up and down and said, "How can you make yourself look so handsome in such a short time?"

He didn't have any answer, so he just said. "Thank you, ma'am," and sat down in his usual spot. Tucker and Dorsey came in too late to hear the exchange.

The dinner conversation was first dominated by the men as they talked about business. Deborah waited until her husband and her two boarders were caught up with what was happening with Tucker Construction; then she began questioning Dorsey about his oldest daughter's approaching wedding.

When Tucker finished his meal, he pushed his plate aside, looked at Dorsey, and said, "I saw Dailey this afternoon. He told me that Dora has called off their engagement."

Sam's chicken leg slipped through his fingers, bounced on the edge of his plate, then flipped onto his lap. He put his napkin over his mouth to hide the big grin that had appeared and plucked the piece of chicken off the front of his trousers.

Tucker gave Sam a puzzled look. The man had just gotten a grease spot on the front of his pants, and for some reason he seemed pleased about it.

Deborah was much more perceptive. Her big brown eyes looked quizzically at Sam for just a moment; then she smiled and winked at her husband. This brought a frown and furrowed eyebrows from Tucker but no apparent comprehension of what had happened.

Dorsey watched Sam's mishap and his happy expression when he had found out about Dora's broken engagement. His face betrayed no hint of any prior knowledge about any feelings between his coworker and his daughter. "Mollie told me about the breakup. I wasn't surprised."

"Neither am I," Deborah said. "I never did think that she was actually in love with him."

"Apparently she wasn't," Tucker added.

Deborah said, "She's such a beautiful girl. When she's ready to be married, she'll have her pick of suitors." This time she smiled and winked at Sam, who was now wearing his most innocent look.

"Just like you, dearie," Tucker said, and patted his wife's hand. "Remember all of your beaus that I had to fight off to get you?"

Deborah blushed and said, "Oh, Nathan, how you do carry on."

"I hope all of you are planning to come to Mollie's wedding," Dorsey interjected.

Tucker looked like he was making some difficult calculations. "Let me see; the wedding is next Tuesday? I'm not sure that I'll be able to get away, but Deborah will be there for sure."

Deborah laughed. "The last wedding that Nathan went to was his own, and some people were betting he wouldn't show up for it. If it was at four in the morning at our own house, he would find some excuse not to be there." She looked at Sam. "You'll be my escort, won't you?"

"It would be my honor," Sam answered.

"I guess I'd better keep my eye on you two," Tucker remarked.

9

Tuesday, February 14, 1860

The morning that Sam was due to escort Deborah Tucker to Mollie's wedding dawned clear and sunny. There were still patches of snow on the ground, but no new snow had fallen for several days. With any luck, Mollie's wedding would have good weather for this time of year in the Nebraska Territory. Dorsey had left town a couple of days previous in order to make arrangements to accommodate all of the wedding guests, a few of whom would be staying overnight. The road conditions between the town and Dorsey's farm had improved during the last couple of years; however, the trip from Nebraska City to the Little Nemaha, plus the time it would take for the wedding, would not leave enough daylight hours for guests to travel home the same day. Sleeping arrangements had been made at two neighboring farms. Dailey had left on a business trip to New York, but he had given the family permission to use his house, too—a magnanimous gesture under the circumstances.

Sam had heard Tucker's horse ride away from the house just after daybreak. Apparently he intended to take no chances of being roped into going to the wedding by some last-minute stratagem by his wife. Sam had already bathed and was shaving when he heard Deborah pouring water for her bath in the bedroom next to his. He looked at his pocket watch. It was seven forty-five. He had never traveled to the Little Nemaha, but Dorsey had assured him that the trip wouldn't take over four and a half hours. The service wasn't scheduled until two, but Sam wanted to leave himself enough time to see if he could get Dora alone for a while prior to the exchange of vows. However, maybe she would be too busy helping her sister with the last-minute preparations to give him any time. He wondered if Dora would even recognize him. He was going to need to be at his best if he planned on making any impression on her in the limited amount of time he had.

His black pants were pressed and lying on his bed next to his black coat and vest. He had polished his boots to a high gloss the night before and planned to complete his outfit with a high-neck white shirt. He was confident that his clothes would look presentable when he and Deborah boarded his wagon. After four and a half hours of bouncing down a dusty road, he wasn't so sure. Judging from what he had seen of Mr. Dailey at Allen's Hotel, his chances of impressing this young lady with his sartorial splendor were not all that good in any event.

At eight forty-five, Deborah came down the stairs in a lavender dress and a matching bonnet. Her hand was on the front of her low-cut dress, and it looked like if she let go, it would fall to her waist. She turned around, revealing her bare back. "I'm sorry to have to ask you to do this, but I can't seem to get these buttons fastened." He fumbled with the buttons, trying hard not to let his knuckles come in contact with her skin, and finally got the dress secured.

She turned around and asked, "How do I look?"

"Very lovely," Sam said, and meant it.

"I wonder what the sleeping arrangements will be?" she asked.

Sam gave her a blank look.

"Did you think we were coming home tonight?"

"I guess that would be impossible. I just hadn't thought about it."

When Sam helped Deborah into the wagon, Mrs. Burnham, her next-door neighbor, called over to them, "You two certainly look splendid together!"

Deborah beamed. Sam nodded and gave the reins a shake, and they began their journey to the Dorsey farm.

A short distance down the road, Sam said, "I'm going to give you a pretty good workout before this day is over."

Deborah appeared startled. "I beg your pardon."

"Sorry, I was talking to my horse."

Deborah took a small fan out of her bag and began fanning her now pinkish red face.

In the well-organized mind of Mollie Dorsey, nothing much was ever left to chance. That's probably why she kept her journal up-to-date and documented the events in her life each day as they transpired. By the morning of her wedding, Mollie's wedding dress, plus

Dora's and Anna's bridesmaids dresses, were neatly hung in the bedroom of their cottage. The food that was to be served to the guests had been prepared in advance, and the wedding cake was proudly displayed on the kitchen table. Their Uncle Milton, who was an ordained minister, had arrived in town a few days ago and was ready to perform the ceremony. Only one thing was missing: the groom.

Byron Sanford was due at the Dorsey farm at eight in the morning. Eight o'clock came and went. Then nine and ten and eleven. No sign of the errant Mr. Sanford. Some of the women began sympathizing with Mollie, while a few of the men began making jokes. The owner of a neighboring farm told Dorsey, "Some of these chaps can be slippery. I never did trust that man."

Another man partially defended the groom with these words: "The fox is a sly but noble animal. Sanford is a good man." Then he added, "At least I thought he was."

Mollie just kept smiling and assuring everyone that once her loved one arrived, he would explain the reason for his tardiness. Dora knew that her sister wasn't as confident as she was pretending to be.

Forty-five minutes before the ceremony was due to begin, a cloud of dust appeared down the road toward Nebraska City. As the horse and wagon got closer, everyone could see that there were two passengers. Dora held Mollie's hand as the wagon drew nearer. When the couple were close enough, Mollie saw that the man was too tall and too dark to be her wayward lover. She let go of Dora's hand and rushed into the house.

Dora stood almost mesmerized as she recognized the man's face. It was the man she had run into on Main Street. And why was he with her father's landlady? Dora knew that she should be feeling disappointment that it wasn't her sister's husband-to-be, but all she felt was elation.

Sam helped Deborah down from the wagon, then turned to Dorsey and said, "I hope we're not too late."

"No," Dorsey answered, "you're right on time, Sam. Sanford hasn't arrived, though."

Mrs. Allen came over to greet the new arrivals: "I'm glad you two came. I was thinking that maybe Dick Gregory and I were going to be the only townspeople here."

Deborah slipped her arm through Sam's in a somewhat possessive manner and said "I wouldn't miss Mollie's wedding for anything."

Sam looked over the two buildings that Dorsey had constructed. The larger one looked like it had just received a new room addition. "You did a good job," he remarked to Dorsey.

"Thanks, Sam, that's a nice compliment coming from you. Let me introduce you to my family and some of our neighbors." He made the introduction, saving Dora for last. "Dora, I want you to meet my good friend Sam Harris. You already know Mrs. Tucker."

"Dora and I have run into each other once before," Sam said.

"That's what my barber told me," Dorsey commented.

Dora's head was whirling. First the man who had occupied her dreams for the last several weeks had arrived, then her father had introduced him as a good friend, and next someone had seen the episode on Main Street.

Dorsey noticed that Deborah Tucker still had a firm grip on Sam's arm and it looked like she didn't intend to release it anytime soon. "Deborah," he said, "I've told you so much about the Little Nemaha, now I have a chance to show it to you." He pried her hand away from Sam's arm and placed it through his own. "Dora, why don't you show my friend Sam our place?"

Dorsey guided Deborah toward the house, leaving Sam and Dora suddenly alone. They stood looking at each other awkwardly for a few moments, then Dora asked, "Is there something going on here that I don't know about?"

"It certainly appears that way," Sam replied, "but I'm just as surprised as you are."

"Where would you like to start?" she asked.

"It's your place; you tell me."

"Let's walk down by the river."

Dora led the way down the well-worn pathway that her family had used since their move to the Little Nemaha. No words were spoken. Neither Sam nor Dora knew where they stood with the other.

As they neared the river, Dora said, "The water here is very pure. My brothers keep the water barrel full."

"It's nice that you have four brothers."

She felt that her remark must have sounded dull and stupid. He felt the same way about his reply.

"We catch some great fish here!"

"What kind?"

"Oh, there are perch, trout, and some other kinds occasionally." She pointed to a wide spot up the river. "Over there is where we go swimming."

"It looks like a nice spot. It's certainly kind of you to show me around."

They became silent again as she walked ahead of him along a narrow part of the path that ran up the river. When they came to a clearing she said, "I guess I owe you my thanks for catching me that day I slipped on the ice."

"I'm glad I was there."

"I'm glad, too."

Sam had never been a man of caution, and he figured he might not get any better chance than this to say what he came here to say. "Something unusual happened to me that day." He watched her face for a reaction and saw none. "Maybe it wasn't the same for you."

She didn't answer, but she did reach out and take his hand. "There is another place that I want to show you."

"If I said the wrong thing, forgive me."

"Follow me, Sam." She started up another path in the direction of the house.

As Sam followed along, he thought, *I've completely misjudged her. Right now she's thinking about how she can let me down without hurting my feelings.*

She led him to the knoll that overlooked the river, and they sat together and leaned back against the giant elm tree.

There was a small pile of stones next to him. He picked one up and asked who had brought them there.

"I did," she said. "I gather up rocks on my way here, and then I throw them at a tree or at rocks."

"Can you hit anything?"

She picked up a rock, drew back her arm, and sailed it up against a tree about twenty-five feet away. "Can you do that?"

"It looks like you've had some practice." He picked up a larger stone and launched it high over the trees, splashing it to the middle of the river. "Can you do that?"

She gave him a saucy smile. "I could if I wanted to."

They sat without talking for a while, throwing Dora's collection of rocks at different objects.

"I guess I was too presumptuous imagining that what happened to us meant something to you, too."

Again he was met with silence. "Shall we go back to the house?" he asked.

She grabbed his arm, preventing him from getting to his feet. "Let's stay here for a little while longer."

"Why don't you just tell me if you didn't feel anything the way I did?"

She leaned forward and turned her head to look directly into his face. "I broke up with a man I'd been engaged to for two years after being in your arms for only a few seconds. Doesn't that say something about the way I feel?"

He took hold of her shoulders and grinned down at her. "Then you . . ."

"Of course," she said. "I'm sorry; I thought you could tell."

"So, what do we do now?"

"We have to get to know each other better."

"I agree."

They sat quietly again. This time they were both smiling.

"I have an idea, Dora. After the wedding, why don't you come home with Deborah and me for a few days? There's an extra bedroom at the Tuckers'."

"I know, I've stayed there before. I could say that I want to visit my father for a while."

"Then it's agreed."

"I guess we'll have to ask Mrs. Tucker first, but I'm sure it will be OK with her."

He pinched her on the chin. "I'm already learning things about you."

"Like what?"

"You're almost as impulsive as I am."

"Don't kid yourself. I'm much more impulsive." She got up, reached down and took his hand. "We'd better get back. I haven't heard Sanford arrive yet. Mollie must be getting frantic."

Walking up the path toward the house, Sam asked, "I wonder what could have happened to him?"

"Mrs. Allen told Mollie that he went over to Brownsville yesterday."

"Is there a road between Brownsville and here?"

"None that I know of."

"Then I'll bet Sanford took off cross-country and got lost."

She took hold of his arm. "That would be terrible. He could freeze to death if he had to spend the night outside."

"I'm sure the man knows how to build a fire."

She stopped and looked at him, and her eyes widened. "The *Silver Heels* stops at Brownsville."

"What is the *Silver Heels?*"

"It's the boat we took from Saint Louis to Nebraska City when we came here."

"You think he got on the boat and left?"

"It's possible."

Sam said, "He doesn't seem like that kind of a man to me. Besides, where would he ever find anyone good enough to replace one of the Dorsey sisters?"

She laughed. "You're absolutely right. What was I thinking?"

When Sam and Dora rejoined the family and guests, a few jokes were made about how long they had been gone. Mrs. Allen exclaimed in a voice loud enough for everyone within a quarter of a mile to hear, "You two could have walked to Beatrice and back in the time you've been gone! What in the world have you been doing?"

Sam smiled. Dora looked guilty. A few of the bachelors looked jealous.

Dora glanced over at Mollie smiling and chatting with some of the neighbors and knew her sister had to be dying on the inside.

An old grandma from a couple of farms south of the Dorseys' told a story about a wedding where the bridegroom never did show up and the bride ended up in an insane asylum.

Dora grabbed Mollie's arm and steered her out toward the road. Sam followed along behind. Dora put her arms around her sister. "He's going to be here, sweetheart. Sam thinks he might know what happened." She repeated what Sam had suggested about Sanford being lost between Brownsville and the Little Nemaha.

Mollie listened, then held an arm out toward each of them. They stood on each side of her, lending comfort as well as they could.

"When he does get here, I won't know whether to kill him or kiss him," Mollie said.

"In case you're going to do both, I'd kiss him first," Sam added.

Mollie and Dora both laughed, which seemed to lessen the tension. Dora realized how much she enjoyed Sam's sense of humor.

At three o'clock a decision was made to eat the dinner that had been prepared before the food was ruined.

Around four-thirty, an evening chill began to settle in. The men built two fires outside and one in the fireplace of each of the cottages. As the time passed, people huddled around the fires and chatted. The men discussed politics and the growing unrest between the North and the South. The women reviewed a much more diversified number of topics. Children played games in the sitting room of the smaller house. People were enjoying themselves, and the time passed quickly for those outside of the family. As the hours went by, no one seemed inclined to retire for the night.

A little before eight o'clock, Sam, Dora, and Mollie were standing around a small fire that Sam had built away from the group and closer to the road. When they first heard the hoofbeats, Mollie bolted toward the sound. The bright moonlight illuminated the horse and rider. It was Byron Sanford.

As he climbed down from the horse he said, "Oh, Mollie, what must everyone think?"

"What do you suppose *I* think, Lord Byron?"

When he hugged Mollie she said, "My goodness, you're as cold as ice. Come over here by the fire."

Sanford shivered and shook until Sam got more logs and threw them onto the blaze. Even then, it took a while before he began to get warm. Sam had figured right except for the possibility of the groom stopping and building a fire. He told them that he had indeed gotten lost, but that he would have ridden all night even to the detriment of his health before he would have stopped to get warm. Looking toward the people laughing and talking around the other fire, he said, "It looks like everyone is having a good-enough time without me."

"Everyone but me," Mollie said.

Sanford pulled his bride up next to him and held her close.

Mollie rested her head on his shoulder and said, "I have an idea. Dora, you and Sam go and join the wedding guests. By and I will go into the main house and get into our wedding clothes. Then in about fifteen minutes, Dora, you say that you're tired of waiting for Mollie's faithless lover and tell everyone to come up to the house for their prayers before retiring."

As Sam and Dora walked toward the wedding guests, he asked her, "Do you think that Lord Byron will sneak a peek while they're getting dressed?"

"He'll be a fool if he doesn't. It is their wedding night."

Sam nodded his head and smiled. "I love the way your mind works."

Dora and Sam followed Mollie's instructions, and in a short time the wedding guests were marching solemnly into the house. To everyone's surprise, a smiling bride and groom awaited them there. With Uncle Milton officiating and a happy crowd and intensely relieved family watching, Byron N. Sanford and Mary E. Dorsey became husband and wife.

Kisses were exchanged all around between the excited family members, neighbors, townspeople, and a young couple who just hours before had never officially met. A few of the older ladies displayed shocked expressions as they observed the fervor with which Dora Dorsey and Sam Harris were embracing and kissing each other.

"That hardly seems proper," one frowning grandma whispered to another.

A wedding supper was quickly prepared, after which the out-of-town guests departed for their assigned sleeping quarters and the neighbors climbed into their buggies and left for home. It was a day that would be remembered by everyone for a very long time.

10

On the morning after Mollie's wedding, the guests who still remained at the Dorsey farm gathered for breakfast in the brush arbor outside of the larger Dorsey cottage. Most of them wore heavy coats and jackets. The mild weather that had lasted throughout the wedding day was deteriorating fast. Black clouds off to the north and a distinct chill in the air cautioned everyone of the threat.

Mollie and Sanford had ridden out at dawn. Nobody knew their destination, or at least if anyone did know, they weren't telling. Dora and Anna had prepared a breakfast of fried hard bread, eggs, and wild plum preserves. Because of the threatening weather everyone ate quickly, thanked the Dorseys for their hospitality, and left for their homes.

Sam and Dora still had some arrangements to make. Dora needed to secure an invitation from Mrs. Tucker to be a guest at her house. While Sam was hitching his horse to the wagon, Dora approached Deborah Tucker. She had prepared her excuses for wanting to come into town. Before she had time to speak, Deborah said, "You must be tired, my dear, after all the work you've been doing. Why don't you home with us and take some time out to rest?"

"What a wonderful idea," Dora said while wondering why everything was happening so easily.

"We'll have such fun while the men are working. The stores are already showing their new spring clothes. Go pack your bags so that we can get away before the storm hits."

Dora looked toward Sam, who had been standing close enough to overhear what his landlady had said. He shrugged his shoulders, indicating that he didn't know what was going on, either.

When Dora's bags were packed and on the wagon, her father walked up and said, "Deborah, I'm leaving for town before too long. Why don't you ride with me? There's no use for you-all to be crowded into one wagon."

When Deborah quickly accepted, Dora knew that this had gone well beyond a coincidence. It would have been more natural for her father to have asked her to ride with him. Suddenly everything clicked into place.

Sam helped Dora into the wagon, and they waved goodbye to everyone while starting down the road toward town. Before they were off the property, Dora declared, "That little brat."

"Who are you talking about?"

"I'll tell you later."

The road out of the Little Nemaha headed northeast. Sam and Dora's little buggy appeared to be heading directly into the approaching storm. They were both wearing heavy black coats, and Dora was further protected against the elements by a white wool knit cap and matching mittens and scarf. Sam's hands were covered with leather gloves, and a black felt hat protected his head. They also had a couple of wool blankets that Deborah had placed behind the seat before she and Sam had left town.

"From the looks of the weather up ahead, we'll have to do everything we can to stay warm," he said.

She leaned her shoulder against his side and asked, "Do you have any idea what that might be?"

"We have blankets. That will help somewhat."

"And after I have a blanket over my lap, what if I'm still cold?"

"I'll handle the horse and wagon. You can figure out how to keep us warm. Now, who is the little brat you were talking about as we left your house?"

"My sister Mollie. She's the one responsible for getting us together."

"Well, bless her heart. However, that does bring up another question."

"Yes, of course, you're wondering why she would do that. OK, a few days ago, I decided to share my feelings with my sister."

"You and your sister seem to be very close."

"My whole family is very close, but yes, you're right. Mollie and I have always had a special relationship."

"My family is the same way. Even though we're ending up in different parts of the country."

The wind began blowing harder and Dora reached back and pulled out the blankets and spread them across their laps.

"Tell me more about those feelings you shared with your sister."

She smiled. "It wasn't anything very important."

"Not important?"

"Not *very* important?"

"But important enough to get her to arrange to get us together?"

"I guess she must have thought so."

They rode on a little farther. He looked quizzically into her face. She grinned back. He frowned at her. She shrugged her shoulders.

"You're not going to tell me, are you?"

"Tell you what?"

"About that little, not very important, thing you told your sister."

"Of course I'm going to tell you."

He waited. She began arranging the blankets more securely around their legs.

"I think I get it. You're going to tell me about it, but not now."

"You're very perceptive, Mr. Harris."

"When?"

"Someday."

"Soon?"

"Maybe."

"Have you always been such a tease?"

She kissed him on the check. "You haven't seen anything yet."

"I think I'm going to enjoy this."

"I'm sure you will."

About an hour out of Nebraska City, it began to snow. Dora pulled her blanket up to her chin and snuggled more tightly against Sam.

He put his arm around her and looked at the white snowflakes falling into her black hair. "I don't care how it happened. I'm just glad that we're together now."

She brushed some snowflakes out of his beard, stroked the side of his face, and said, 'So am I, Sam. So am I."

Mercifully the snowfall abated somewhat as the two rode into town. When they arrived at the Tuckers' house, they shook the snow off of their outercoats and hung them out on the porch. Then Sam carried Dora's bags into the downstairs bedroom. Next he got an armful of logs from the back of the house and built a fire in the living room fireplace. Dora fixed some hot coffee, filled two mugs, and carried them over to the fireplace. They sat close together on the hearth, and soon they heard horses' hooves outside.

In a few minutes Nathan Tucker walked into the room. He looked at Sam and Dora, noticed how their shoulders were touching and said, "Well, what have we here?"

"Your wife invited Dora to spend a few days with us so she could rest up from helping Mollie with the wedding."

Tucker couldn't grasp why Sam and Dora looked so affectionate but figured that Deborah would explain everything to him. "Splendid. Where is my wife?"

"She's on her way here," Dora said.

"I understand," Tucker replied. His expression indicated that he didn't understand, but that not understanding was all right with him, too.

"She and my father are riding here together," Dora explained. "May I bring you a cup of coffee?"

"That sounds mighty good right now."

Tucker rubbed his hands briskly together in front of the fire; then when Dora had left the room, he turned to Sam. "How in the world did you pull this off?"

"It's a long story."

The sound of hoofbeats alongside the house signaled that Dora's father and Tucker's wife had arrived and got Sam out of making any lengthy explanations to his boss, at least for now.

In a few seconds, Deborah rushed into the room and up next to the fire. She stood there shivering a while before she even greeted her husband. Dorsey entered a short time later, and they all crowded around the blazing logs. It was not the type of day that anyone would have wanted to be outside.

"I'm not sure if I'm more cold or hungry," Deborah said, still shivering. "As soon as I get thawed out, Dora and I can start fixing dinner."

The storm that had moved into the Nebraska Territory set in for the next several days, with each day's activities similar to the last. After breakfast each morning, all three men left for the construction site. Snow continued to fall intermittently throughout the day, and by midafternoon they were all cold, hungry, and filing back into the warm house.

Deborah and Dora passed the early part of the days milking the cow, gathering eggs from the henhouse, grinding coffee, slicing bacon and other meats, and planning the meals. The early afternoons were spent talking and playing games. When the men arrived home they naturally assumed that the ladies had spent most of the day resting.

After dinner each night, everyone gathered around the fireplace to talk about the day's activities. Dorsey usually retired first. During this time, Deborah did most of the talking while Sam and Dora listened politely and stole glances at each other. When the others had all gone to bed, the young couple talked until after midnight and then reluctantly parted. It didn't take too many nights until the others realized that Sam and Dora wanted to be alone. The Tuckers marveled at the intense romantic involvement displayed by this couple who had known each other for only a short time.

The first few nights, the couple spent most of the time inquiring about each other. These questions and answers were liberally interspersed with clutches and tender kisses. As the nights passed by, the dialogue became more infrequent. Now the conversation, what there was of it, was directed more toward their future plans.

During dinner on Thursday of Dora's second week at the Tuckers' she announced that she was afraid she was overstaying her welcome and would be leaving for home the next day. She had made arrangements for her father to take her back to the farm.

Deborah expressed her disappointment. Sam looked shocked.

When the others had retired for the night, Sam added a couple of logs to the fire and stirred the glowing embers until the flames leaped up. Then he sat down on the couch next to Dora.

She laid her head on his shoulder. "You knew that I couldn't stay here like this much longer."

"I guess I didn't want to think about it."

They stared at the flames dancing above the logs and the dark curling smoke disappearing up the chimney.

"It's a long ways from Nebraska City to your farm," he said.

"It's too far. How often will I see you?"

He shook his head. "This isn't going to work. We have to find some way to stay closer together."

"I don't know how we could do that."

"We could get married." The words had come out so easily that he could hardly believe that he'd said them.

"But, Sam, we've known each other for such a short time."

"Not long enough for you to be sure how you feel?" he asked.

"I knew how I felt about you the day my sister got married."

"So did I. I've never been more sure of anything in my life."

"Still, it's too soon," she said.

"Why?"

"People will think we're crazy."

"They already think that. We could get married and prove it to them."

"You're silly," she declared.

"Dora, we could be engaged for a year and I wouldn't be any more certain about marrying you than I am right now. I knew it the first time I saw you."

She put her hands around the back of his neck and pulled his face toward hers until their noses were touching. "My mother is going to kill me."

He put his finger softly against her lips. "That sounded very much like a yes."

There was a wide smile on her face and her eyes were shining when she asked, "Do you realize that we've fallen in love and become engaged in less than two weeks?"

"Absolutely. That's why I think that we should wait another week before the ceremony."

Her mouth dropped open. "You want to get married in one week?"

"I do unless that's too soon for you. I seem to remember you saying something about being more impulsive than me."

"Oh, I am. I was just wondering why you wanted to wait so long?"

His eyes widened and a broad grin swept across his face. "Then, it's settled! We are going to get married as soon as we possibly can!" His voice had risen considerably in volume.

"Yes!" she shouted back. "Do you think I would roll around on the couch every night with a man I wasn't going to marry?"

"I'm marrying Dora Dorsey!"

"That's right!"

"Next week!"

"At my house!"

He grabbed her up off the couch and began dancing around the room carrying her in his arms.

She squealed, "Wheee!"

Deborah Tucker appeared at the top of the stairs in her nightgown.

"We're getting married," Sam said as he pulled Dora's mouth up against his.

"Nathan, Charles, you'd better come out here right away!" Deborah called out.

They gathered in the kitchen to toast and congratulate the delighted young couple. Deborah had slipped on a robe over her nightgown. Tucker and Dorsey wore only their long flannel nightshirts and slippers. Sam properly asked Charles Dorsey for his daughter's hand in marriage. Dorsey, who never had been happy about having someone Dailey's age for a son-in-law, promptly granted his permission.

Deborah told Dora, "Your mother will be shocked, losing both you and Mollie at almost the same time."

Tucker opened a bottle of champagne that he had been saving for a special occasion such as this, filled five wine glasses, and passed them around. "Here is wishing you two a long and happy life together. You're certainly off to a fast start."

Dora held up her glass, looked at Sam, and said, "Look at the way you're influencing me. I've only been engaged to you for a few minutes and already I'm drinking my first glass of champagne."

Deborah looked at Sam but addressed Dora: "I wouldn't be surprised if you'll be doing some other things you haven't done much of before, Dora."

"When are you going to set the date?" Tucker asked.

"We are going to be married at my house one week from Saturday."

"Oh, my goodness!" Deborah said. "Your mother is going to have a *tizzy fit*."

"I would like to make a suggestion," Dorsey interjected. "Let me go back to the farm tomorrow morning. Sam, you bring Dora the day before the wedding. I think we need to give my wife a little time to adjust to having her second daughter married off so soon."

Tucker turned to Sam and Dora. "We'll take you out to dinner at Allen's Hotel tomorrow night to celebrate your engagement."

When the celebration ended, Deborah made sure that Sam went upstairs to his own bedroom before she retired for the night.

When Sam and Dora walked into the dining room of Allen's Hotel, they received a nice surprise. Seated at their table next to Mrs. Allen were Dora's sister Mollie and her new husband, Byron Sanford.

After a great deal of hugging and congratulations, Mollie said to Sam, "You know that my mother is going to kill you."

"Actually, up until now, I had only heard about the possibility of her killing Dora. Thanks for the warning."

Dora turned to her sister and asked, "How did you know about our engagement?"

"We've been staying at the hotel ever since our wedding day. I found out about you two when Mr. Tucker came here to make arrangements for your party. I still can't believe it, though."

After everyone was seated, there was still an empty chair between Mrs. Allen and Mollie.

"Is someone else coming?" Dora asked.

"Yes," the hotel owner said. "With all of this romance in the air, I thought I should have an escort, too."

"Who is the lucky man?" Sam asked.

A fair-skinned young man wearing a baggy well-worn tweed suit walked up to their table.

"Let me introduce you to George West," Mrs. Allen said.

The men stood up and shook hands with the newcomer. Sam observed that the man had soft uncallused hands but a firm grip. The ladies remained seated and smiled as each of their names was presented.

"Mr. West is stopping at the hotel for a few days on his way to Boston on business," Mrs. Allen announced.

"What kind of business are you in, Mr. West?" Tucker asked.

The man sat down next to Mrs. Allen. "I publish a newspaper in Golden, Colorado. It's called the *Western Mountaineer*. I'm on my way to Boston to purchase some more printing equipment."

"The newspaper business must be lucrative," Sanford remarked.

"Any kind of business in and around Denver is booming right now. A miner strikes gold and he can't spend his money fast enough. Prices are of very little importance to those men."

Sam noticed that Mollie seemed to be quite interested in what West had to say.

Three waitresses came to their table, bringing large platters of beef tenderloin, bowls filled with mashed potatoes, baskets of biscuits, dishes of applesauce, and gravy boats filled with steaming hot gravy. Mrs. Allen had gone all out on the celebration dinner that she had insisted would be her treat.

During dinner, Mollie plied the newspaperman with questions about the Denver gold rush. He didn't seem at all shy about sharing information.

"Thousands of people are crossing the plains right now," he said. "I'm sure some of the wagon trains come right through Nebraska City. Most of the people are only thinking about how they can strike gold. Me, I'm happy just publishing my newspaper."

As Mr. West continued answering Mollie's questions, he was also enlightening the rest of the dinner party about all the fortunes that had been made in the mines and the streams around Pikes Peak.

Sam glanced around the table to see what degree of interest the others in this group had in the Denver goldrush. Mollie was obviously intrigued. Dora was paying more attention to pinching Sam's leg under the table than to Mrs. Allen's guest. Sanford was more difficult to figure out. He was listening closely, but his expression betrayed neither an interest nor the lack of it. Sam decided that he would be very careful if he ever got into a poker game with his future brother-in-law.

"Where would you go if you were searching for gold?" Mollie asked.

"That's a good question," West said. "I think I would try the hills northwest of a small settlement called Boulder. A few miners have made big strikes in that area."

Sam remarked, "If the miners don't care how much they pay for their goods and services, I imagine that prices are quite high."

"They're extremely high," West said.

"Then a person could go through a considerable amount of money while he's waiting and hoping to strike gold," Sam added.

Dora began to realize that both her sister and her future husband had a real interest in the Denver goldrush and began listening more attentively.

"You're absolutely right," West said. "Many people leave Denver with a lot less money than they had when they arrived."

Mollie seemed unimpressed by the warning from the newspaperman. "But if you brought enough supplies and provisisions with you, you wouldn't have to pay those exorbitant prices."

West nodded. "That would certainly help."

"However," Sam added, "wages are bound to go up along with the prices. It seems that if a man is determined to dig for gold, he would be well advised to stay employed until he makes his strike."

"As long as his job doesn't limit his opportunities," Mollie countered.

West looked back and forth between Sam and Mollie. "You people understand that I'm not selling anything, don't you?"

"Of course," Mollie said. "I've already heard a few salesmen telling people all about the goldrush. It's nice to talk to someone who will give us some honest information."

West nodded. "Well, I guess it's all about priorities. Each person needs to decide how much risk they're willing to take."

Sam and Mollie both appeared happy with that compromise.

Mrs. Allen's propensity to talk had been totally suppressed during the discussion about the Colorado goldrush. After dinner, she began to make up for lost time as a whole torrent of words poured out: "Tonight we came here to celebrate the engagement of Sam Harris to my lovely friend Dora Dorsey. I never told you this, Sam, but I've had my own eye on you ever since you came to town." She winked at Dora. "I know that I'm, let's say, more mature than you, but I'm still a very lively old girl. You could have done a lot worse, Sam. But now I'll just have to console myself thinking about what might have been. So, enough of my problems; now it's time for all of us to move on into the saloon. I just hired a piano player and a fiddler, so let's all get out on the dance floor and have some fun."

11

March 1860

Regardless of their urgent desire to become man and wife, it soon became obvious that it would be impossible for Sam and Dora to travel from Nebraska City to the Little Nemaha on one day and then get married on the next. First, there was the matter of Sam going to Temcumseh, the county seat, to procure the wedding license. Formal invitations had been ruled out, but the wedding guests still had to be notified and arrangements would need to be made in order to feed and house the guests overnight. After everything was considered, it was decided that Sam and Dora would arrive at the Dorsey farm on Saturday, the original date the wedding was scheduled, then get married on the following Thursday, March the eighth.

After Mollie and Byron's honeymoon had ended, Mollie stayed at the Dorsey farm for a short time while her husband was away on business. During the week before the wedding, she came back into town for a few days. While Mollie was there, she told Dora that she wanted to sew a wedding dress for her as soon as she got back home. The two young ladies looked at just about every bolt of material that was available to examine in the stores in Nebraska City. They finally settled on a blue merino fabric at a store on Main Street, a few doors away from Allen's Hotel. During their shopping trip, Mollie confessed to Dora that she had caught gold fever and was earnestly trying to talk her husband into going to Denver. Sanford had suggested that perhaps he should go on ahead to Denver, then send for Mollie just as soon as he could. That night, when Dora repeated what Mollie had said to Sam, he confessed that he had also been considering going to Denver, but that he would not even consider the move unless Dora agreed to go with him.

On Saturday morning, Sam packed Dora's clothes and a few of his own into his wagon and they said goodbye to the Tuckers. True to form, Tucker promised to come to the wedding if he possibly could but in case something came up that prevented his going, he would see to it that his wife had reliable transportation to the event.

On the trip from Nebraska City to the Little Nemaha, Sam and Dora were greeted first by clouds, then light rain, and finally some snowfall. After the first couple hours, they rode out from under the cloud cover into clear blue skies with a few fluffy white clouds. The happy couple held hands and looked across green fields where wild-flowers were just starting to bloom. March in the Nebraska Territory could bring rain, wind, snow, or sunshine for several days at a time, so Sam and Dora had hoped for the best but prepared themselves for the worst.

As Sam's black horse pulled the wagon on the last leg of the road from Nebraska City to the Little Nemaha, they began discussing a more urgent concern to the couple than the weather: how was Dora's mother going to react to losing two daughters at almost the same time?

"You see," Dora explained, "my mother has never been a very strong person. She doesn't want to be that way, but whenever she tries to do too much work she actually gets sick. Ever since Mollie and I were in our early teens we've taken charge of running the house for her. When my father bought our farm, we took over managing those duties, too. This has to be almost overwhelming for my mother, to lose Mollie and me."

"How old is Anna?" Sam asked.

"She's seventeen. My brother Sam is fifteen, and Ada is thirteen. Of course Will, Dent, and Charlie help where they can, but they're too young to assume much responsibility."

"So, Anna and Sam are about the age you and Mollie were when you began managing the household."

"A little older, as a matter of fact. I know they won't let her down, but I'm afraid she won't see it that way right now. She is quite a worrier."

Sam's horse and wagon had entered the Dorsey property, and he and his bride-to-be were less than a hundred yards from the main house, when they heard what sounded like two coyotes howling from behind an elm tree up ahead. Sam pulled the horse to a stop, and in a loud voice he said, "Well, my dear, it looks like we're in for some *real trouble* now! It sounds like there are at least two coyotes blocking our path to the house and I'm afraid that this is the only road we can take."

Dora raised her voice so that it could easily be heard: "Oh, my. What will we do? Do you think we should turn around and go back to town?"

Two little sets of eyes peeked out at them from behind the tree. Charlie's smiling face was only about two feet off the ground. Dent's grinning face was just above Charlie's.

"Well, look what we have here. It looks like my two little brothers, and I do believe that they've chased the coyotes away."

The two youngest Dorseys leaped from behind the tree and came running to meet them. "Sister! Sister!" Charlie shouted as he ran toward Dora with his arms outstretched.

Dent vaulted into the wagon and began hugging his sister. Charlie's shorter stature made the task more formidable. Before he was halfway up the side of the wagon, Sam grabbed the little guy, hoisted him high over his head, and plopped him down on Dora's lap. Charlie turned and thanked Sam before he, too, began showing his affection to his sister.

"Do you think it's safe to travel on to the house now?" Sam asked.

Charlie looked shyly at the tall, dark man who was going to marry his sister. "There wasn't really any coyotes. It was just Dent and me trying to scare you."

"Whoa, that's quite a relief," Sam said.

"Boys, I would like to have you meet your new uncle, Sam Harris."

"I remember you," Dent said. "You were at the other wedding."

Charlie tugged on Sam's sleeve. "You have the same name as my big brother."

"You have a brother named Harris?"

Charlie giggled. "No, his name is Sam."

Sanford, Mollie, and the rest of the Dorsey family came out of the house to greet them. Sam plucked Charlie off the seat of the wagon and placed him on the ground, then did the same with Dent. Then Sam offered his hand to Dora. She was smiling at Mollie while at the same time trying to step down from the wagon and, as she did so, caught the buckle of her shoe in the hem of her skirt. Sam

99

grabbed her under the shoulders and held her just above the ground until she got her foot untangled.

Mollie told Sam, "You're a handy man to have around the house."

Dora straightened her skirt and laughed. "It's his specialty. I still haven't gotten over the first time he prevented me from falling."

Sanford and brother Sam carried the bags into the house while Sam Harris unbridled his horse and tied him to a hitching post.

Anna brought out a pitcher of tea and some glasses, and everyone sat in chairs under the brush arbor. Mrs. Dorsey and her daughters sat in one group and immediately began chatting about the wedding and planning who all would be attending. The men and boys sat a few feet away.

Sam studied Dora's mother to see if he could detect any stress and noticed several things that he hadn't observed when he had seen her at Mollie's wedding. She was an attractive woman, whose age he estimated to be somewhere near forty. Her hair was still just as black as was her two oldest daughters'. Her vivid blue eyes weren't that different from Mollie's and Dora's, with only the dark shadows under her eyes betraying her age and state of health. She was, as Dora had described, a fragile-looking woman. However, there was no sign of self-pity, nor was she displaying any sorrow on her face. If Dora had not told him different, Sam would have thought that she was just as thrilled about the upcoming nuptials as was the rest of the family. She had been more than friendly to him when they had arrived, and now she was smiling maternally at Dora as Mollie and Anna brought their sister up-to-date on how the wedding arrangements were progressing. Sam's heart went out to his bride's mother as he watched her putting on a courageous show under circumstances that he knew had to be painful for her.

He was looking at Mrs. Dorsey and thinking about how Mollie and Dora seemed to have inherited both their mother's good looks and their father's robust health when he suddenly became aware that his future father-in-law had asked him a question. Now all of the men were looking at him and waiting for his answer. "I'm sorry," he said. "I didn't hear what you said."

Sanford laughed, "It's quite understandable. I would expect that any man who was marrying Dora Dorsey in less than a week would be more than a little distracted." He turned and looked at his own new bride, and his eyes widened. He had realized too late that the women had stopped talking and were listening to his last comment.

Mollie put her hands on her hips, raised her eyebrows, and gave him a withering look. "I beg your pardon, Lord Byron."

"Or any of the Dorsey girls, for that matter," he added.

The ladies enjoyed a laugh at Sanford's expense.

Dorsey smiled at Sam and repeated his question: "Mollie tells me that she and Sanford are thinking seriously about going to Colorado to search for gold. Has the gold fever struck you and Dora, too?"

Sam thought for a moment before he spoke. This man was not only his bride's father but also someone he had worked alongside of, eaten with, and slept down the hall from at Tucker's boardinghouse, ever since he had arrived in Nebraska City. A man he admired and liked very much. He had to be honest with Dorsey but now realized how much the truth would hurt both him and his wife. He chose his words carefully. "I can't say that I have gold fever, but there is a good chance that we'll be going to Denver, too."

Dorsey's shoulders sagged and he seemed to have difficulty clearing his throat. "There is still a lot of good land that a man can pick up at a reasonable price right around here."

"I agree with you, but I don't think that I was ever cut out to be a farmer."

"Of course not. You're planning to build houses for settlers moving to the new territories. I'm sure that there will be plenty of work for you wherever you go. How about you, Sanford? What do you plan to do in Denver if you don't strike gold?"

"I'll probably get a job as a blacksmith. The newspaperman from Boulder, that we told you about, said that almost any job out there pays anywhere from eight to ten dollars a day. We plan to buy some land whether or not we strike gold."

Dorsey sighed. "I guess you've all made up your minds. I wish that things could be different, but I understand how you feel. I'll tell you both something that you should know: Mollie and Dora look soft and pretty, but underneath they are tough young ladies. When times get difficult, they will never let you down wherever you go. Of course the girls' mother and I were hoping that it would be someplace not too far away from here."

Anna called over to the men, "Is anyone getting hungry?"

The younger Dorsey boys answered in a chorus of loud affirmatives.

On Monday morning, Sam Harris and young Sam Dorsey left for Temcumseh to get the marriage license, and they returned that evening. Mollie spent the early part of the week sewing the blue merino fabric into a wedding dress. The same bridesmaids' dresses that Dora and Anna had worn at Mollie's wedding were now slated to see service again, only this time they would be worn by Anna and Mollie. Mollie was close enough to the same size as Dora, so no alterations were necessary on the dress that she was going to wear, although Dora had some fun with her sister when she tried the dress on. "Well, Sister," she said. "It looks like my dress is a little too loose up top for you and quite snug around the hips, but I think that it will look all right if you don't bend over."

"One more remark like that and I'll slap your backside," Mollie answered.

On the days leading up to their wedding, Dora sneaked down to the river with Sam as often as possible but still found time to bake the wedding cake. Sam and Dora's sudden engagement and then such short notice about the wedding caught everyone by surprise and made it impossible to notify all of the people who might have come, so a smaller group than had attended Mollie's wedding was expected.

The day of the wedding came around quickly. Deborah Tucker, Mrs. Allen, and Dick Gregory arrived together about midmorning, and then one other wagon from town carrying some people from the community church followed about an hour later. The guests from the neighboring farms made up the balance of the wedding assembly.

From the beginning, the festivities lacked the intrigue and excitement of the wedding that had been held at the Dorsey farm just a few weeks previous. To begin with, Sam was already there. Sanford, of course, had come close to missing his own wedding. Dora was happy and relaxed. Mollie had been almost frantic. Normal jokes about what Sam and Dora might do on their wedding night replaced comments about what a fox the intended groom had turned out to be or the possibility of the bride becoming a spinster or, even worse, ending up in an insane asylum.

One thing about the wedding remained the same as the earlier one: it was held in the evening instead of at the more customary early-afternoon time.

When Dora walked out of the house into the bright moonlight, her beauty almost took Sam's breath away. Her blue wedding gown contrasted with her black hair and sun-bronzed skin and even at night made her light blue eyes look even bluer.

Dora looked at the smiling man who was towering over her father and her uncle and felt a surge of exhilaration.

Uncle Milton held his Bible in his hand and asked, "Who giveth this woman to be married?"

Her father swallowed hard and answered, "I, her father, give her."

Some weddings may proceed without a hitch. Not this one, however. Near the end of the ceremony, Uncle Milton said, "Do you, Eudora Jane Dorsey, take this man—"

It wasn't exactly a sneeze, but the sound seemed to come from his nose. Nor was it a cough. It was too high-pitched to be a cough. Everyone in the small crowd knew what had happened. Sam Harris had laughed in the middle of his own wedding ceremony. Women who had been dabbing at their eyes with their handkerchiefs suddenly smiled. Men exchanged bored expressions for wide grins.

Fortunately, Sam was marrying a woman who had a good sense of humor. She elbowed him in the ribs and said, "Behave yourself, you idiot."

"Eudora? I just never heard—"

She put her left hand over his mouth, showed him her right fist, and laughed at him.

By then, Mollie's face was crimson. Dora's mother looked puzzled. Everyone else in the room was laughing. This diversion was just what had been needed to fill the rest of the ceremony and the wedding supper that followed with a happy and relaxed spirit.

When the supper was finally over and all kissing and congratulations were completed, the neighbors departed in their wagons while the few people who had traveled in from town left for their assigned sleeping quarters. Sam had put some twigs and logs in the fireplace of the smaller house so that a fire could be prepared quickly when he and his new bride arrived.

They held hands and walked up to the door, then he picked her up and carried her across the threshold. She started kissing him before he had cleared the doorway, blocking his view of the room, which caused him to cock his head to one side to see where he was going. He laid her down on the bed, lit a lantern, and then gazed down at his new bride smiling up at him.

If anyone had been watching the chimney of Sam and Dora's honeymoon cottage that night, they would have waited for hours before they saw any smoke ascending.

12

At eight o'clock on the morning following Sam and Dora's wedding, the Dorsey family and the guests from Nebraska City were gathered in the brush arbor outside the Dorseys' main house. The question on everyone's lips was, "What's happened to the bride and groom?" An hour earlier, someone had suggested that maybe the newlyweds had departed before sunup, as Mollie and Sanford had done on the morning after their nuptials. Upon checking the stable, they confirmed that Sam's horse and buggy were still there. A woman from the church said that someone should knock on the door of Sam and Dora's honeymoon cottage to make sure that no tragedy had befallen the couple. Mrs. Allan and Deborah Tucker shook their heads vigorously, and good judgment prevailed. Everyone ate their breakfasts, drank second and third cups of coffee, and chatted. Meanwhile, the door of the cottage kept drawing their eyes like a magnet.

Finally, at eight forty-five, the door to the cottage opened a crack and a sheepish bride peeked out; then her head quickly disappeared. "No one's gone home yet!"

Sam was standing at a table, leaning over a basin of hot water, bare to the waist, and looking into a mirror. His face was fully lathered, and he was scraping off the last few whiskers from around his beard. The straight razor in his right hand looked wickedly sharp. "I guess they want to see us one more time before we leave."

She walked up behind him and put her arms around his waist.

He pulled the razor away from his neck. "Be careful, sweetheart. You don't want to become a wife one day and a widow the next."

"How shall we explain why we're so late?" she asked.

"I would be surprised if any of them need an explanation." He wiped his face off with a towel, then turned around and put his arms around her. "I'll put on my shirt and we can go have some breakfast."

She tipped her head back and smiled at him. "What's your hurry?"

It was after nine when the newlyweds finally walked out the door of the cottage. They were greeted by applause led by Mrs. Allen, with Byron Sanford, Deborah Tucker, and a few others joining in. Dora smiled shyly. Sam took a bow, which earned him a vigorous shove from his new bride.

Sam sat down at the table next to little Charlie. Dora sat down next to her husband and across from her parents. Sam noticed the team effort that was being practiced by Dora's siblings. Ada poured them each a cup of coffee, then began refilling the other family and guests' cups. Mollie and Anna were at the cookhouse busily frying bacon, eggs, and hard bread. Their brother Sam was coming up the path from the river with two buckets of water. Dora's mother gave Sam a sweet smile, but the redness around her eyes told of her grief. Dorsey was harder to read, but Sam knew him well enough to detect the sorrow he was also feeling. Sam thought back to the day he'd left Grinnell and the tears that were in his own mother's eyes. She had only asked one question: "When will we see you again, Son?"

"It won't be too long," he'd said but wondered at the time how long it might actually be before he returned.

Ada interrupted his thoughts when she set a plate of hot food in front of him and another in front of Dora. He spooned some wild plum preserves onto his fried bread and started to take a large bite when he felt some obstruction to getting his fork up to his mouth. He looked down to see if his sleeve was snagged on something and saw a little hand tugging on it. Connected to that hand was Dora's youngest brother. Charlie's concerned face looked up into his, and he said, "Uncle Sam, are you and my sister going to move a long ways away from here?"

Looking down at this small troubled face, Sam gained a clearer grasp of the strong kinship among the members of this family that he'd married into. "We're not sure yet, Charlie."

After breakfast, Dora whispered to Sam, "I think everyone is waiting for us to leave first."

Sam nodded and stood to his feet. "My new bride and I want to thank all of you good people for coming here to share this happy occasion with us, and I want to personally thank the Dorsey family for their warm hospitality, and I especially want to thank Charles and Lois Dorsey for bringing this lovely woman I married into the world. Now, I know that all of you have things you have to do today, and so do we, so Dora and I will be packing up our things and leaving very soon."

Just as Dora had predicted, no one left until all of the good-byes were said, the well wishes for the newlyweds extended, and Sam and Dora's wagon was well on its way down the road towards Nebraska City. For the first few miles Sam let Dora do all of the talking. Her dialogue covered the entire wedding day. Sam chuckled as he watched his new wife bounce up and down on the wagon seat and gesture with both hands and arms as she excitingly reviewed almost everything that had been said or done by any of the guests or her family before, during, and after the wedding.

When she calmed down a little bit, Sam confirmed to her how wonderful everything had been, then asked, "How do you feel now about moving to Denver?"

"I thought that we'd already gone over everything about going and decided that it would be the wisest thing to do."

"We have talked about it, but I just want to make sure that it's still what you want to do."

"I want to do what's best for us. Why are you bringing this up now?"

"I guess I feel sorry for your family. It's obvious how much they all love you."

For several minutes the only sounds were the horses' hooves on the road, the creak of the wagon, and an occasional bird serenading them from the trees.

Dora spoke first: "Mollie is extremely excited about going to Denver. She would be terribly disappointed if we backed out now."

"How about the disappointment your family feels about you leaving?"

Dora didn't answer.

"Are you excited about going, Dora?"

"God forgive me if I'm being selfish, but I'm absolutely thrilled about going to this new territory with you!"

He grinned at her. "OK then, it's settled."

"The Bible says that a man should leave his father and mother and cleave to his wife," she said.

"I'm all for cleaving. Does it say how often we should cleave?"

"Judging from last night, it's going to be quite often."

107

"Seriously, I do feel very bad for your family, losing you and Mollie at the same time."

"My father had to make the same type of decision when he brought us to the Nebraska Territory. We had a lot of friends and family back in Indianapolis before we came here."

Sam said, "I never thought about it that way. I've always felt bad about leaving my family, yet my father did the same thing. In fact, my grandparents Ephriam Harris and Judge McKee left their families to go to Pennsylvania."

"You told me that your Grandfather Harris founded a town."

"So did Grandpa McKee. They founded Harrisville and Mc-Keesport."

"And that never could have happened unless they had left home and opened up new territories."

"Do you think that we're trying to justify what we're doing?" he asked.

"I think that what we're doing is right."

He patted her hand. "Meeting you was the best thing that ever happened to me."

It was late in the afternoon when Sam and Dora reached the outskirts of Nebraska City. The sky was clear and blue, but a cold wind was coming in from the north. In all of the last-minute preparations for the wedding, nothing had been said about where they would spend their honeymoon. Sam drove the wagon through the center of town and turned left onto the street where the Tuckers lived.

"Where are we going?" she asked.

"I thought I would drop off a few things at the Tuckers' house first."

"And then?"

Deep furrows appeared on Sam's forehead. "Are you telling me that you haven't made any plans for our honeymoon?"

"You're being silly again. Where are we going after we leave the Tuckers?"

"Well, I have carefully researched all of the best hotels in our fair city. Then, I checked on all of the inns along the river, and in the countryside, before I made my choice."

"We are staying at Allen's Hotel?"

"Where else?"

For the next several days, the happy couple slept late, had leisurely breakfasts at the hotel, packed picnic lunches, and rode horseback to various locations. They took long walks in the country, waded in secluded creeks that they had discovered, and talked long hours about their future. It was a time to savor first intimacies, including seeing each other's head on the pillow next to them when they went to sleep and waking up wrapped in each other's arms. They were building memories to strengthen them for the difficult times that they both knew were common to their pioneer type of life.

Twice from their hotel room and once from the front porch of the hotel, they watched wagon trains rumbling down Main Street as they passed through Nebraska City on their way to Colorado for the gold rush. Each time another caravan passed, Sam and Dora's excitement grew greater.

The time went by fast, and the day came when their honeymoon had to end. They had one last leisurely breakfast at the hotel, then packed their luggage in their wagon and rode across town to the Tuckers' house. Sam had assured Nathan Tucker that he would stay until construction had been completed on the large house they were building for the prosperous but not too proper saloon owner. The newlyweds stayed in the downstairs bedroom that Dora had occupied during the couple's brief courtship.

Within a few weeks, the saloon owner's home was finished, Sam's commitment was satisfied, and the couple began finalizing their plans for their journey to Denver. Sam traded a couple of lots that he had purchased in town for a team of oxen and a larger wagon; then he had a cover installed on the wagon. They purchased a cookstove, a few housekeeping articles, and six months' worth of provisions.

They learned about a caravan of covered wagons that was planned to leave Council Bluffs, Iowa, on May 1, so they decided to join this wagon train when it reached Nebraska City.

When everything was ready for their journey, Sam and Dora took a few days out to go back to the Dorsey farm and say their goodbyes. It was a sad farewell. Denver was several weeks' journey from Nebraska City. Nobody knew when the family would be reunited, and although it was never spoken, everyone except the smaller children knew that there was no assurance that they would ever see one another again.

When Sam and Dora were ready to leave, everyone kept their sadness hidden behind smiles, well wishes, promises to write, and vows to pray for one another each day. Little Charlie was the only one who couldn't contain his grief. He sat on the dirt road and cried out after their wagon as it moved away. "Sister, sister;" then he buried his head in his hands and sobbed.

May 2, 1860

The day for Sam and Dora's departure finally arrived. Shortly before noon, Sam and Dora parked their wagon on a side street just a couple blocks east of Allen's Hotel. They were eagerly awaiting the approach of the wagon train that they were scheduled to join. They didn't have to wait very long before they began to hear a low rumble coming from the direction of the river. As the wagon train from Council Bluffs drew nearer, the sound grew louder and louder and the couple's excitement mounted. When the lead wagon was almost even with them, Sam jumped down from his wagon, ran over to the wagon leader, and checked in. Then Sam hastily ran back, swung himself up onto the seat, yelled, "Gee-haw," and, with a big smile on his face and his new bride sitting alongside of him, he pulled up alongside of the passing wagons. A few wagons rolled past them before a couple acknowledged them, pulled up on their reins, and motioned them in. Sam waved his thanks, and pulled into line in front of the gracious couple, and their long journey began. Sam's black stallion and a young bay for Dora were tied to the back of their wagon. Mollie, Mrs. Allen, Dick Gregory, and a few of their other friends stood on the steps of the hotel and waved goodbye to them as they rode past. Byron Sanford had been unable to settle all of his business matters in town in time to join them, so it was agreed that he and Mollie would meet Sam and Dora in Denver a few weeks later.

As soon as Sam and Dora had pulled their wagon into the long line of wagons, the ox team and wagon in front of them began throwing sand and dirt up into their faces.

As they reached the outskirts of Nebraska City, Dora said, "I hope this isn't the way it's going to be all the way to Colorado."

"Nobody mentioned this when they were urging us to take this trip. When we get out on the open road, I'll fall back a little further from the wagon in front of us."

"Maybe that will help," she said.

Widening the space between their wagon and the one in front of them made things more pleasant for about an hour; then a strong windstorm swept across the plains, engulfing the entire wagon train in dirt and sand.

Sam and Dora pulled their hats down as low over their eyes as they could and tied cotton scarves around their necks and over their mouths.

"What have I gotten you into, Dora?"

She looped her arm through his and leaned into the wind. "I don't remember hearing you say that the trip was going to be easy."

"Anyway, it's only about seven hundred miles. We should be there by the middle of June." He turned and grinned at her, then immediately regretted his action as the scarf blew to one side and a gust of wind blew dirt into his mouth. He pulled up the scarf, licked the dirt off of his teeth, turned away from her, spit several times, and said a few choice words under his breath.

Dora had the good sense to hold the scarf tight against her mouth as she laughed at her husband's plight.

When he had cleared most of the grit from his mouth, he said, "Your father told me that you were tough, but he never said that you were mean."

"Well, now you know."

The wind and dust continued through the rest of the day until finally at dusk they heard the lead driver shout, "Whoa!" This was followed by a chorus of men shouting, "Whoa!" as they brought their ox teams to a halt. Mercifully, Sam and Dora's first day's ride was over.

As soon as the couple climbed down from their wagon, the family in the wagon directly behind them walked over to meet them. The woman was carrying a baby boy, and two small boys were following close behind.

"Thanks for letting us in, and sorry about our dust," Sam said as he shook hands with the man.

"It can't be helped. I'm sure that you were swallowing just as much dirt from the wagon in front of you. The name's Dalton. This is my wife, Adeline."

Dalton was a rawboned man with wide shoulders and rough features. His brown hair hung down close to his shoulders. His wife was skinny, with freckles, but not unattractive. Sam figured that she couldn't have been over fourteen when she had given birth to the oldest child.

"Harris is my name. This is my wife, Dora. Where are you folks from?"

"Missouri, most recently. Are you going to test your luck digging for gold in Colorado?"

"No, I'm planning to build houses for some of the prospectors who do get lucky. How about you?"

The ladies quickly tired of the *men-talk* and moved closer to the wagon. Adeline proudly displayed her baby, and Dora went through the mandatory oohs and aahs. The other two Dalton boys played tag around the wagons, burning off some of the pent-up energy from their long hours of confinement.

"I'm in law enforcement. I figure there's going to be a shortage of peace officers in and around Denver."

A sudden gust of wind blew the women's dresses tight against their bodies and sent them scurrying behind the wagon for shelter.

"It's going to be too windy to put up a tent tonight," Dalton said. "It looks like we're going to have to sleep in the wagon."

"Yes, I was thinking the same thing," Sam said.

"My wife and I have a big tent that we put up when the weather's decent. There's enough room for all of us if you need a comfortable place to sleep."

"Thanks for the offer, Dalton, but I brought my own tent. Dora and I are newlyweds, so we'll be needing our privacy. Maybe we can cook together and eat together, though."

Dalton glanced over at Dora standing next to his wife. "I can see what you mean. I'm going to get my wife and kids out of this wind and into the wagon."

"Right. I think Dora would like to get out of the wind, too. Maybe we can meet for breakfast if the weather settles down."

Once inside the covered wagon, Sam lit a lantern and he and Dora worked together rearranging boxes of supplies and clearing enough space for them to eat their supper and sleep for the night. When they were through, Dora dug into a picnic basket and removed some cold chicken, a loaf of hard bread, and a jar of applesauce. They sat cross-legged on their makeshift bed, thanked the Lord for their food, and began eating.

When their stomachs had been satisfied, she asked, "How was your food?"

"Surprisingly good for a cold supper."

"It probably tasted better than it was because you were so hungry." She got up on her knees and pulled a chocolate cake out of the food basket. "Do you still have room for this?" she asked.

His eyes widened as he looked at the thick fudge-colored frosting making swirls across the top of the cake. "I'll find room."

After dinner, Sam propped a couple pillows against a box, clasped his hands behind his head, leaned back, and sighed. She moved over next to him and laid her head on his shoulder. The high winds swayed their wagon back and forth and fluttered their canvas cover. They could hear an occasional horse or ox registering complaints about the weather.

"It's hard to believe that we're actually on our way to Colorado," she said.

He slipped his arm around her shoulder and kissed her on the forehead. "A lot of things have happened in a very short time. Are you missing your family?"

She snuggled closer to him. "Not yet." She laid her head on his chest and felt it rise and fall. Finally, she rolled over, sat up, and looked at him. "What shall we do now?"

"I could put the lantern up on the stove and we could read for awhile."

She blinked her eyes a few times. "I don't know. With all of this sand in my eyes, that doesn't sound too good."

"Did you bring any games?"

"Yes, but I don't know where they are."

"Are you tired enough to go to sleep?"

"No."

He scratched his chin and looked at her. "I guess then the only thing left to do is to talk."

"We could start out that way, I guess."

He leaned down and kissed her, then reached over and put out the lantern.

13

The next morning dawned warm and clear, without a trace of the wind that had been so fierce during the night. Sam jumped down off of the wagon, took a hatchet from under the wagon seat, and went searching for kindling wood to build a fire. Not too far away he found a thicket containing some small dead trees. He chopped off enough wood to build their breakfast fire; then, since he had no idea what kind of terrain they would camp at that night, he chopped enough for another fire.

When he returned, his wife and the Daltons had gathered together and were waiting for him. Dora had already ground some coffee, and Dalton had somehow come up with a basket of eggs. Sam dropped the pile of wood on the ground, then turned to Dalton and asked, "How did those eggs make it through yesterday without getting broken?"

Dalton pointed to a coop tied onto the back of his wagon. "I kept them inside of the hens."

Sam looked toward where the man was pointing. A rooster was strutting around while overseeing several hens. "Makes sense to me," Sam said.

Since Sam had gathered the wood, Dalton built the fire, and soon Dora and Adeline had coffee brewing and bacon and eggs spitting grease. From the front to the back of the long wagon train, columns of smoke curled toward the sky as the travelers enjoyed their first breakfast between the Missouri River and Denver. The wagon-train leader gave everyone about forty-five minutes to prepare and eat their breakfasts; then he yelled out, "Haw-gee!" and the words resounded like a different pitched echo down the line of wagons as one by one they began moving west.

Conditions were much better on their first full day on the road as they passed through what seemed like endless prairie. The monotonous scenery was broken first by a stagecoach that passed them around noon. It was carrying passengers and mail from Saint Joseph to Denver. Then, once in the early afternoon and again closer to evening, wagon trains went by heading back east from Denver. The sun was at their back during the morning hours, then in their faces during the afternoon. When the white clouds in front of them began to turn pink, they again heard the wagon leader shout, "Whoa!" The caravan had traveled about eighteen miles that day, which enabled Sam to make a rough estimate of the ultimate duration of their trip. If this was an example of the average day's journey, then they would arrive in Denver in approximately thirty-nine days.

That night they camped near a town called Beatrice near the Big Blue. In contrast to the barren country they had seen during the day, their campsite was surrounded by farmhouses with lush green pastures and groves of trees scattered here and there. The weather was mild, so both Sam and Dalton pitched their tents not too far from their wagons and a couple hundred yards from the river.

During a supper of bacon and beans, the men agreed to go hunting as soon as they had an opportunity, to provide a better fare for their families. After supper the men sat on the ground by the campfire while the women sat in chairs by the wagon, watching the children work off their pent-up energy from their day's wagon confinement. After the children were put to bed, the men brought some wooden chairs out of the wagon and they all sat around the fire.

While they were sipping coffee and chatting, a man from the wagon in front of them joined them. Earlier in the day, they had watched this same man ride across to one of the wagon trains that had passed them heading east. He had engaged in conversation with several of the travelers and now seemed anxious to share the information he'd received. He told the Daltons and Harrises that more than seventy thousand people had traveled this route to Colorado and now almost as many were coming back. Sam asked if he'd found out why so many were leaving Denver. The man said he had heard conflicting reports: "Some men told me they were going back to get their families. Others were shaking the dust of Denver from their feet and cursing the place and the people."

"Wherever you go, you take yourself," Sam observed.

Their visitor appeared confused by Sam's remark.

Dalton immediately understood Sam's meaning and said, "That's the absolute truth."

Soon the hard day's ride began to catch up with everyone and they headed to their separate tents.

Sam and Dora had already retired for the night when she looked out through the flap of their tent and saw a big orange moon rising in the east. The evening was still warm enough for them to be comfortable, so they decided to take a walk and enjoy the view. The aroma of logs burning and assorted meats that had been cooked over open fires mixed with the scent of pine from a grove of trees just beyond their camp. As they walked along the side of the wagon train, most of the campfires had been deserted. Only a few young couples remained around the campfires. Some of them waved and called out friendly greetings as Sam and Dora strolled by.

They walked along the river for a ways, listening to the sound of moving water and feeling the cool breeze; then they walked back toward their wagons. Sam looked across the moonlit pastures and farmhouses in the distance and commented, "This is very nice country around Beatrice."

"Several men have told me that. I think it's even nicer than they described."

He looked at his wife with raised eyebrows. "When and where did this happen?"

"Men who were traveling between Beatrice and Nebraska City often stopped at our farm to spend the night. We gave them a supper and let them sleep in Bachelor's Hall."

"Bachelor's Hall?"

"They slept on the ground outside. Mollie called it Bachelor's Hall."

"That was mighty charitable of you and your family."

"Don't kid yourself. We charged them a dollar and a half just for supper, breakfast, and a place on the ground to sleep. We needed the money."

"Unless I'm mistaken, a man traveling between those two towns would have to ride at least five miles out of his way to get to Little Nemaha."

"Some of them were on foot."

"Men walked five miles out of their way, then five miles back to stay at the Dorsey farm for one night?"

"And paid us a dollar and a half once they got there."

"For two meals and Bachelor's Hall," Sam replied.

"Why are you surprised?"

"Actually, I'm not. I just don't think they came for the cooking. They came to see Mr. Dorsey's beautiful daughters."

"You think so?"

They got back to their tent, and the couple sat on their chairs in front of it. Sam leaned back in his chair and grinned mischievously. "I don't know if I myself would have walked ten miles out of my way just to see you."

"Would you like to sleep by yourself in the wagon tonight, Mr. Harris?"

"On the other hand, you did serve two good meals. A man certainly has to consider that, too."

"Mollie and I are pretty good cooks."

"And you're really not all that unpleasant to talk to."

"What makes you think I would have talked to you?"

"Ouch, now you're showing that mean streak again."

"It's the only way I have of keeping you in line. So how about now? How far would you walk to spend one night in a tent with me?"

"Ah, now you're making it much more interesting."

The moon had turned from orange to silver and the campfires were down to red-glowing coals when Sam and Dora rushed back through the flap of their tent.

For the next several weeks the wagon train plodded along averaging about twenty miles each day. One day was not too much different from the one before. The travelers forded rivers, endured long, dusty roads, and plowed through deep sand as each looked forward to resting at their next campsite. They withstood rain, hail, and wind and then were blessed by a few pleasant sunny days. They camped at places with names like Cub Creek and Little Sandy. The wagons bounced along through miles of dull terrain, broken only by an occasional farmhouse, mail station, or wagon train headed the other way. Then someone would see some cottonwood trees or willow timber up ahead and signal that they were nearing a river or lake. At each freshwater hiatus, they refilled their water barrels, rinsed out their dirty clothes, and found secluded spots to bathe or swim.

They rode past several Indian villages along their route; then one morning, their long caravan rumbled past Fort Kearney. A few soldiers waved greetings, but most of them hardly looked up. Sam and Dora supposed that it was not due to any unfriendliness on the part of the military as much as it was that so many wagon trains had passed the fort that it had become all too common an occurrence.

As May turned to June, the air turned hot and windy. Finally, one morning during the second week of June, nature smiled down on them. People awakened to find that the annoying wind had been replaced by a pleasant cooling breeze and the sky had turned to a dazzling shade of blue. Even some people who had been grumbling and complaining throughout the trip smiled and shouted greetings to each other during breakfast.

In the afternoon of that day, Dora was in her usual spot on the wagon seat next to Sam. The reins were lying carelessly across his lap as he lazily guided the ox team along. After so many days on the road, the oxen automatically followed the wagon in front of them. The only thing Sam had to do was keep enough space between the wagons to minimize the amount of dust that he and his wife had to breathe. Both of their faces had turned several shades darker from the long afternoons when their wagon had headed toward the late-day sun. Dora had woven her thick black hair into a long braid that hung below the middle of her back. Her lavender gingham dress and her light blue eyes were the only things that distinguished her from a pretty Indian girl.

It had been another day of traveling through boring terrain, but the pleasant weather made even the plains appear more attractive.

Toward late afternoon, a man from one of the wagons up front rode back along the caravan informing everyone that they would be stopping to camp earlier tonight. He never gave any explanation. When the wagon train pulled into the campsite, the reason for stopping at that spot became clear. Two other wagon trains that were heading east were already parked along a wide place in a river. The water was sparkling clear and flowing fast. Sheer cliffs lined the opposite shore. There were green pastures for the animals to graze in and fire pits that had been crafted by former travelers.

As her husband pulled the wagon to the side of the road, Dora said, "Why don't we just stop and live here, Sam?"

"It would be difficult to find a more beautiful place than this," he replied.

Sam pitched their tent under a cottonwood tree about fifty yards above the river. There were still some daylight hours left, which many of the travelers used to catch up on their rest. Sam and Dora decided to use that time to explore the area on horseback. After Sam had saddled up his black horse and the bay for Dora, he slipped his rifle into its casing behind the saddle and strapped his belt holster and his revolver on his hip.

"Planning to run into some trouble?" Dora asked.

"It's more likely that we'll run into a turkey or pheasant that we can have for our dinner."

"I heard some men talking about shooting a buffalo," she said.

"How could they get one of those monsters back to camp?" Sam thought for a moment, then answered his own question. "They would have to butcher him where he falls. No thanks, I think I'll just stick to the smaller game."

With Sam on his black horse and Dora on her bay, they rode up the river until they found an old Indian trail, then followed it upriver.

"I'll bet you were tired of getting pulled along behind the wagon," Sam said.

Dora looked puzzled. "What do you mean?"

"Oh, I'm sorry. I was talking to my horse."

"Hmm, interesting. Do you do that very often?"

"Only when I'm riding him."

"Is he a good conversationalist?"

"No, but he's a good listener."

"You're silly."

"What's silly about talking to my horse?"

"It just is."

"Whatever you say, dear."

"Were you talking to me?" Dora asked.

"Stop that."

Dora giggled.

The evening shadows highlighted the crags in the cliffs across the river, and the whole countryside took on a light reddish glow. They crossed wide sandy beaches and grassy meadows with trees and thick brush.

"This is such beautiful country it's a wonder that no one lives here," Dora remarked.

"Maybe someone does."

The trail narrowed and they rode single file through a small opening between two rocks and out into another green meadow. Three Indians on horseback seemed to appear out of nowhere. Behind the Indians was a string of six riderless ponies. It was difficult to tell who was more surprised, the white couple, or the Indians. Sam and Dora brought their horses to a halt, and Sam loosened his rifle in its leather holder.

The Indian closest to them saw Sam's action and put his hand on the handle of an ancient-looking pistol that was stuck in his belt. The other Indians had only knives.

"What are you going to do?" Dora asked.

"I'm not going to do anything. They've gotten themselves into this mess; they can get themselves out."

The young brave nearest them was quite handsome. He was well muscled, with thick black hair and chiseled features. There were only a few pieces of rawhide covering his copper-colored skin.

Sam's eyes locked with the first Indian's. Neither of them blinked or showed any expression.

The other Indians were talking to one another in their own language. No one seemed to know what to do.

"We were told that the Indians around here are peaceful," Dora said under her breath.

Sam directed his comment to Dora, but his eyes never left the Indian: "And every one of them is an individual with his own personal history."

"Do you think these Indians are friendly?" she asked.

"They might be wondering the same thing about us."

A rustling in the thicket right next to Sam caused him to grab the handle of his pistol. The Indian closest to them put his hand on top of his pistol while the others reached toward their knives.

To Sam and Dora's relief, a pretty Indian girl came walking out into the clearing. She was carrying a papoose wrapped in a blanket. Only the baby's sleeping face was visible. The child couldn't have been over a few weeks old. The girl looked alarmed when she saw the two white people and rushed over to the closest Indian.

Sam kept his eyes on the Indian and his facial cast didn't change when he said, "*Wano* papoose."

The Indian's face softened somewhat and he nodded his acceptance of what sounded to Dora like a compliment. The Indians behind him seemed to relax a little.

"*Wano* woman," the Indian said, gesturing toward Dora.

Sam nodded and put his hand on Dora's shoulder.

By now all of the men were smiling.

"*Wano* woman, papoose," the Indian said, looking at Dora and patting his bare stomach.

Sam sat up straight and tapped two fingers against his chest.

An understanding had been reached.

The two Indians farthest from Sam and Dora led the ponies away; then the brave and his woman with her papoose followed behind them.

On the way back to their camp, Sam and Dora found a wide spot in the river to watch the sunset. They tied their horses to a tree. Dora found a flat-topped rock near the water and sat down. Sam skipped a couple of flat stones across the water, then sat down next to his wife. The river reflected the reddish-orange color of the sky, and the cool evening breeze blew across the water into their faces.

Sam took a deep breath and said, "It's nice to breathe some clean air for a change."

"What does *wano* mean?" she asked.

"It means 'ugly.' "

"It does not."

"Actually, it means 'uglier than a sick jackass.' "

"You're lying."

"How do you know?"

"Because you didn't tell him that his papoose was uglier than a sick jackass."

"Yes, I did."

"And he told you that I'm that ugly, too?"

"Do you think I should have shot him?"

"I know that you're lying. It means 'pretty,' doesn't it?"

"I know that it either means 'pretty,' or it means 'good.' The Indians might use the same word for both. I took a chance."

"I guess I should have thanked him."

"He also thought that you're expecting a baby."

"I figured that out. So, what was all that patting your chest all about?"

"I just wanted him to know that if there is a baby, it's mine."

She rubbed a tear from the corner of her eye. He didn't know what to say to her, so he tipped his head back and watched the setting sun paint its portrait of crimson and gold hues across the western skies.

"Why do you think he said that?" Dora asked.

He looked at her full breasts pushing against her cotton shirt and the slight protrusion below the belt of her denim pants. He didn't know what he could say without risking hurting her feelings, so he just said, "I'm not sure, dear."

She got up and walked over to the water's edge. "You're not sure?" Tears were now running freely down her cheeks.

He fumbled over his words. "I'm not exactly sure. I . . . I was hoping that you are, but . . . I wasn't sure."

"I don't know, either. I don't know how to tell."

"Your mother had six children after you were born, and you don't know how to tell if you're going to have a baby? Didn't she explain any of those things to you?"

"She was embarrassed if someone mentioned which end of the snake the rattles were on. She wouldn't talk about things like that." Dora's shoulders began to shake as she hung her head down and cried harder. "And now you're mad at me," she said.

He covered the distance between them in two long strides and took her into his arms. "I could never be angry with you, darling! We want to have a big family. If we're going to have a baby, that's wonderful."

"I'm going to be fat and ugly," she sobbed, "and you're not going to love me anymore."

He held her in his arms and rocked her back and forth. Somewhere, in the deep recesses of his memory, he remembered his father comforting his mother under similar circumstances. He kissed her wet cheeks and said, "The day I stop loving you will be the day I die."

"You're going to have to tell me that regularly for the next few months."

A couple of squirrels scampered up the trunk of a tree, then turned and began scolding the humans who had invaded their domain.

"What do you think they're saying?" Dora asked.

"They're probably telling us to get out of their front yard. Would you like some squirrel stew for dinner?"

She shook her head. "I wouldn't have the heart to eat them."

It was starting to get dark when Sam and Dora rode back into camp. Dalton was sprinkling salt on the steaks he was grilling over the open fire.

Sam inhaled the wonderful aroma and grinned at his new friend. "What is this?"

"You could say that I got lucky, or you might say that a young antelope got very unlucky; anyway, we won't go hungry tonight."

Sam admired the extra-large steaks that Dalton had carved, then looked down the line of campfires and saw several other steak dinners being prepared and added, "Nor will about half of the wagon train, the way it looks from here."

"Well, the meat won't keep very well in this heat, and the poor animal gave up his life so that we could eat, so I didn't see any reason to be stingy."

"I'd say that you've got to be the most popular man in the camp tonight. Those steaks you're cooking look mighty good."

Adeline Dalton was peeling some potatoes a few feet beyond the campfire. Dora picked up a potato and another knife, sat down next to the woman, and began peeling it. "There is something I need to talk to you about," she said.

Adeline looked at Dora's nicely filled shirt and replied, "I figured that we might be having a talk before long."

14

It had been just over a week since Sam and Dora had first sighted the snowcapped peaks of the Rocky Mountains of Colorado. Once the mountains were in sight, each day of travel found them growing taller and more majestic. Finally, after six weeks of jolting and bouncing over the rough dirt roads, enduring all kinds of weather, not to mention breathing the sand and dirt from the wagons up ahead of them, Sam and Dora finally arrived in Denver, Colorado.

Now their covered wagon was parked next to their tent at Cherry Creek, where the towering mountains appeared to be within walking distance. However, one of their new neighbors had warned them not to attempt to go there on foot. The crisp, clean air, along with the high altitude, caused the mountain range to appear much closer than it actually was.

The estimated five thousand people in and around Denver were all living in tents, covered wagons, and shelters made from assorted materials, including carpet. The only buildings in Denver at this time were on Main Street, and they were composed of mostly saloons and gambling parlors. There was also a shanty that housed the post office, another that was an assayer's office, and a clapboard building that contained a bank. There were no schools, churches, or permanent dwelling houses. It seemed like an enormous opportunity for a home builder like Sam Harris. He heard that miners were showing up at the various saloons along Main Street carrying jars filled with impressive amounts of gold dust and calf-skin pouches bulging with gold nuggets. Just as a member of their wagon train had described, other less fortunate men were still waiting for their first strike and denouncing the town as a fraud because of their own failure to *strike it rich*. Until now, as far as Sam could determine, none of the miners had contracted anyone to build any permanent houses for them.

Dora still looked beautiful, though slightly plump. She and her husband were anxiously awaiting the birth of their first child. For that reason Sam planned to build the first house in Denver for his own family. However, even though he planned to finish his house first, he still needed to line up other construction projects for the future. It was for that purpose that Sam was riding into town on this particular day in mid-June. He had heard about the riots and shootings that had become commonplace along the strip; still, he knew that if he wanted to initiate his business in the new territory, he had to go and promote his services wherever the men congregated. Dora had also heard many stories of violence taking place at the saloons in town, and her intuition spoke to her of the possibility that her husband might run into trouble. He insisted that he would be safe and explained to her about how important it was for him to establish new business contacts.

It was eleven-thirty in the morning when Sam tied his horse to the hitching post in front of one of the larger saloons. He had chosen this time in hopes that the bartenders would more likely be serving coffee and sandwiches than liquor. As a precaution, his gun belt was strapped around his waist and his revolver was loaded. He pushed open the swinging doors, walked inside, and climbed onto a stool at the bar. The bartender, a short bald-headed man in a white shirt and a dark green vest greeted Sam with, "What'll you have, my friend?"

It occurred to Sam that the bartender probably greeted so many people each day that he couldn't remember which ones he'd seen before. It wasn't a bad idea to play it safe by calling everyone friend. "Just a cup of coffee," Sam replied.

Once Sam's eyes adjusted to the dimly lit room, he began looking around. On the wall behind the bar was a painting of a young woman of opulent charms. She was reclining on a couch, and her expression revealed no discomfort in being completely naked. Right next to the painting there was a sign that read: WHEELERS TAVERN. Three musicians were tuning up their instruments on a platform over near the wall, and four men and a girl were sitting on stools at the far end of the long bar. The tables in the center of the room, where Sam had hoped he might find some prospective customers, sat vacant. Apparently, he would have to come back later in the day if he wanted to stir up any business.

A young woman in a low-cut red dress appeared on the balcony, looked down at the sparse number of people in attendance, then started down the stairs toward the main floor. As she moved closer,

Sam could see that her hair was mussed and her heavy coat of makeup was smeared. She wasn't nearly as attractive as the girl in the painting. She appeared to have just climbed out of bed.

When the bartender set the cup of coffee in front of him, Sam asked, "Do you rent rooms here?"

The bartender glanced toward the woman in the red dress. "Just by the hour. A room with a girl will cost you two dollars for an hour, or six dollars for all night."

Sam suddenly felt like he needed to go somewhere and wash up. "No, thanks, I was just curious."

"Sorry I mentioned it. I didn't think you were the type. The owner of this place insists that I tell everyone about our services."

"I guess you have to do your job. You wouldn't happen to know of anyone who wants to have a house built around here?"

The bartender leaned over the counter and lowered his voice: "Most of the men who come in here are bachelors looking for a good time. If they've struck gold, they spend their money on gambling, liquor, and women. That's the way my boss likes it. There are some family men who've made big strikes, but you're not likely to find them in here. You'd better be off asking around some of the mining camps, or even down in Tent City."

Sam remembered the house that he'd helped Tucker build for the saloon owner in Nebraska City and asked, "How about the owner of this place?"

"He has himself a mansion somewhere above Boulder. He only comes in here a couple times a week to pick up his money."

"I understand. Thanks for the advice."

Sam took a few more sips of coffee, then felt an overwhelming desire to get out of this dark saloon and back into the fresh air. He laid a nickel on the counter, nodded to the bartender, and turned to leave. In Sam's rush to get out of the bar, he didn't see the skinny young man who was walking directly behind him, and they collided. Sam's three-to-four-inch height advantage and about forty additional pounds of bone and muscle overwhelmed the youngster, and he ended up on his backside on the nearest table. The bartender started to laugh. The frowsy-looking woman who had walked down the stairs chuckled, too. The group at the other end of the bar turned to see what had happened. The musicians were smiling.

126

The young man straightened up quickly. His face was crimson. It was obvious that he could not tolerate being the object of ridicule.

"Excuse me," Sam said. "I didn't see you coming."

"That ain't going to be even near good enough, mister. You ran into the wrong man today."

Sam looked the boy over. His angry expression and flushed face revealed his determination to salvage his dignity. The two guns in his gunbelt, hanging low on his hips, suggested that he either was or at least fancied himself to be a gunfighter. His hands were poised just inches above his guns.

"Forget it, Jimmy," the bartender said. "It was just an accident."

"If I embarrassed you, I'm sorry," Sam added.

Sam's casual attitude about what had happened seemed to make the lad even angrier.

"You're sorry all right. You're a sorry excuse for a man."

The young man took a step closer to Sam and looked up into black eyes that showed no fear. Everyone watching could tell that Jimmy's confidence was waning, but apparently he felt like he had gone too far to back off without suffering an even greater loss of self-esteem.

Sam slowly raised his right hand even with his face and out from his body in a sign that he wasn't going to draw his gun. This brought a smile to the youngster's face.

"I knew you were yellow," he said. "But that doesn't change anything. One of us ain't walkin' out of here."

Sam wiggled the fingers on his raised right hand. When Jimmy's eyes followed that movement, Sam's left fist crashed into the middle of his face. This time he landed in the middle of the table with Sam on top of him, and they both went crashing to the floor. Sam quickly pinned the young man down, then looked into his dazed face. The man's nose appeared to be severely damaged, and his face was going to be badly swollen for several days. The wounds to his ego were going to get much worse.

Sam pulled the two revolvers out of the holsters and noticed that neither of them had a trigger. He had heard that some gunfighters altered their guns this way, figuring that they could fan the hammer of the gun faster than they could pull the trigger. For the first time, he realized that this young man had actually been thinking about shooting him just to recover his own self-importance. Now

Sam felt his own anger come up to his face. He turned and laid the two revolvers on the counter in front of the bartender. "Sorry about your table," he said between gritted teeth.

The bartender looked nervously at this enraged stranger. "Don't worry about it, friend. These occurrences are common around here."

Sam nodded at him, then reached down, grabbed the front of the man's shirt, and jerked him to his feet. Sam was surprised at how light he was. He twisted a handful of material in his fist until Jimmy couldn't breathe, then pulled his beet red and bloodied face up to within inches of his own. He felt that it was important to frighten this fellow badly enough so that he wouldn't even think about coming after him later. "I don't care how fast you are with a revolver, Jimmy. I've got two rifles and a shotgun, and I know how to use them. As of right now, Tent City is forbidden territory to you. If I even see you out there, I'll cut you down before you get within fifty yards of me. I'd be interested to see how your triggerless guns would work from that range. So, if you want to die, I'll be glad to accommodate you. It's your choice." He gave the shirt one more twist and added, "Or maybe I should just hold onto your throat a little longer and save everybody around here a lot of trouble."

By now, Jimmy hadn't had a breath of air for almost a minute. His face was turning from red to purple. Every person in the bar knew that Jimmy's life depended on this big angry man releasing his grip within the next few seconds. When Sam felt certain that his point was driven home, he dropped the gasping young man on the floor, stormed out of the saloon, and vowed never to return.

Dora was sitting on a chair in front of the tent when Sam came riding back from town. "Oh, I'm so relieved that you're back here safe," she said.

He got down from his horse and hugged her. "Why would you think that I wouldn't be all right?"

"I had a horrible feeling about you going into those saloons. I'm just glad you're home. Did you find any people who want to have houses built?"

"No, I just went inside of one saloon and there were only bachelors and bar girls in there. I guess I'll have to find out where the married men can be found."

128

"That might be closer than you think. Do you remember a man from Nebraska City named Hiram Bennett? He was a member of the Territorial Legislature."

"Of course I do."

"Well, he came by here while you were gone. He and his family are living in a tent just a little ways up the hill from here. When I told him where you were and what you were doing, he said that he has a job for you. He also said that you should be real careful going into those saloons in town. He told me that they're not anything like the ones we're used to in Nebraska City."

Sam grinned. "So, you were right after all. I shouldn't have gone into town today. Does he want me to build him a house?"

"Better than that. He and Judge Holly want to build a mill to stamp gold that comes from the mines."

"Judge Holly is here in Denver, too?"

"Not yet. He told me that the judge is traveling here in the same wagon train as my sister and her husband."

"Mollie and Sanford are with Judge Holly, and you have already talked to Hiram Bennett about their project. Do you know what that means, dear?"

Dora shook her head.

"It means that everyone else knew about this project while I was wasting my time in town."

Dora frowned. "Isn't that all right? I thought that you would be happy about it."

Sam held his arms out toward his wife.

"What's this all about?" she asked as he hugged her.

"I was just thinking about something your father told me about you before we got married."

She pulled back and looked at him questioningly. "What did he tell you?"

"Let's just say that I'm finally realizing what a great business partner I have."

It was two weeks to the day after Sam and Dora had set up camp in Denver when Mollie and Sanford's wagon train rolled into town. The mile-high altitude had provided a piercingly hot sun, along with a brisk breeze on this late afternoon in mid-June; quite a bit different from anything they'd experienced in the flatlands that had been their former home. Puffy white clouds toward the Rocky Mountains were just beginning to turn pink. It looked like Denver intended to put on a good show for the new arrivals. As soon as Sam and Dora heard the rumbling of the wagon wheels and the thundering hooves of oxen, they knew that the caravan they had been waiting for had at last arrived. They hurried out to the road to greet Dora's sister and Byron Sanford.

Looking down the long line of wagons, Sam first spotted Mollie. She was sitting on the wagon seat alongside her husband, just as Dora had done when the two of them had first arrived in Denver. Mollie's thick black hair was tied back in a braid, and her light blue eyes were peering out from beneath her black eyebrows in her deeply tanned face. He was surprised at how much she resembled the way her sister had looked when he and Dora had first arrived in town. Neither Mollie nor Sanford had any dirt on their faces, indicating that they had probably taken some time to wash up in anticipation of this reunion.

Sam tapped Dora on the shoulder and pointed toward the wagon on which Mollie was riding. He had expected his wife to be excited when she first saw her sister but nothing like what happened next. As soon as Dora recognized Mollie's face, she began jumping up and down and screaming her sister's name. Tears were running down Dora's cheeks, and she wasn't even trying to wipe them away. If Sam had ever wondered how close she was to Mollie or how much she had missed her sister, all doubts were erased.

Sam waved to the new arrivals and pointed down the road toward the spot in Cherry Creek's Tent City where he had pitched two tents. Sanford steered his ox team to an open space where Sam directed, and the happy celebration was under way.

As soon as Sanford helped his wife down from the wagon, the two sisters embraced, cried, and laughed, all at the same time. When the hugs and kisses were over, Dora took Mollie's hand and led her to one of the chairs around the fire pit just outside of the tent flap. Dora settled in the chair next to her sister, and Sanford sat opposite them.

Sam picked up an empty bucket and disappeared behind the tents. In a few minutes he returned with a bucket of crystal-clear ice-cold water and filled up four tall glasses.

Sanford took a long drink and asked, "Is this water as good as it tastes or am I just that thirsty?"

"It's the best I've ever tasted," Sam answered. "It flows right down off of the melted snow almost to our back door."

Dora said, "Our place certainly isn't elegant, but we're very comfortable here."

"Sister, it looks like a mansion to me right now."

The two couples caught up on events that had happened to each of them over the last several weeks. First Mollie told Dora about the sad good-byes that had taken place when she and Sanford had visited the Dorsey farm. Then they all compared their wagon train experiences. They were pretty much the same, until Dora shared about her and Sam's experience with the Indians. Mollie had an even better story. She had ridden out ahead of the train one day and encountered Indians all by herself. They had circled her, talked in a language she didn't understand, and taken turns feeling her long hair. They had almost scared her to death. To top it off, when the wagon train caught up to them one of the Indians offered to trade a string of horses for Sanford's *wano* woman.

"What did you tell the Indians?" Sam asked.

"The Indian didn't understand much English," Sanford explained.

Mollie started pounding on her husband's shoulder. "Tell them what you said to those other men," she said.

"Well, one of them asked me if I was going to trade her to the Indian, and I replied, 'Why would I do that? He's never done anything to hurt me.' "

Sam and Dora both laughed while Mollie doubled up her fist and held it up in front of her husband's nose.

After Mollie had finished her glass of water, Dora said, "Come on inside the tent. I'm going to heat some water for you. You must be dying to take a bath."

The inside of the tent was divided by a heavy curtain. The side nearer the entrance contained a small table, some chairs, and a lamp. Behind the curtain were sleeping quarters containing a bed, a large half-barrel made into a bathtub, a chest of drawers, and another lamp.

When the bath had been prepared, Mollie settled down into the hot water and moaned in pleasure. "Oh, Dora, you don't know how wonderful this feels."

"Oh, yes, I do. I had to wait two more days after we got here before I could soak in a hot tub."

The years of living in tight quarters in Nebraska City and at the Little Nemaha had eliminated any feelings of modesty the two sisters might have had between each other. They could hear the men talking and laughing outside.

After luxuriating in the hot water for a while, Mollie took a bar of soap and a washrag and began scrubbing off the road dust from the day. Dora brought some more hot water from the stove and reheated the bath.

"I'm glad our husbands get along so well," Dora said.

"So am I. Has Sam found any work yet?"

"Hiram Bennett has a job for him, but he's going to build our house before he does any other jobs."

"Judge Holly told us about the stamp mill on our way here. He and Mr. Bennett are planning to build it somewhere near Boulder. Does Sam have enough money to build your house first?"

"Yes, thank God. Sam has worked as a carpenter for almost ten years, and he has some money saved. How about you two? Are you going to be all right?"

"By needs to get work right away. We weren't able to sell our lots in Nebraska City, so we're down to five dollars in cash. We do have a few weeks' provisions."

"What kind of work will he look for?"

"He has experience as a blacksmith."

"Oh, Mollie, there are people here working as blacksmiths right out of their tents."

"Whatever happens, I hope that we can be together for awhile."

"I'm sure we will. I'll bet our husbands are making business plans right now."

After Mollie had bathed and slipped into some clean clothes, Dora had the men carry the dining table outside next to the fire pit and she began preparing supper. She had been planning this meal for several days. She served roast pork, boiled potatoes, lettuce, radishes, and young onions. They finished up with gooseberry pie. Dora had been right about the men talking business. Sam announced during supper that he had enlisted Sanford's help in building their new house.

"How many homes are there in Denver right now?" Mollie asked.

Sam had just taken a big bite of pork, and everyone watched him chew it up while he appeared to be wrestling with a difficult equation. He swallowed and then asked, "Let me see. Do you mean counting the one your husband and I are going to build?"

Dora was smiling.

"Either way," Mollie said.

Sam put his knuckles against his chin, frowned, and began counting to himself. Finally he said, "OK, I think I've got it now. Counting our new house, I believe that would be one."

"You mean to tell me that there are no permanent dwellings in Denver?" Mollie asked.

Sam and Dora both nodded.

Sanford said, "Well then, Sam, if Denver grows up to be as big as Nebraska City, we'll be able to say we built the first dwelling house here."

Dora laughed. "That's in the unlikely event that Denver ever grows to be that big."

After dinner they positioned their chairs in a circle around the fire.

Mollie looked up into the sky. "I don't think I've ever seen so many stars in my entire life."

"I'm sure you haven't. It's the high altitude in Denver," Sam explained. "The air is thinner, so you're undoubtedly seeing stars you've never been able to see before."

Sam's comment caused everyone to look up across the milky white sky.

Finally Dora could hold her secret no longer. She sat up straight in her chair, cocked her head to one side, smiled, and asked, "Hasn't anyone noticed anything different about me?"

Her two guests looked at each other, then shook their heads.

Dora put her hand on Sam's knee. "We're going to have a baby."

Mollie shrieked. "When?"

"We figure the baby will arrive about January," Dora said.

Sanford shook Sam's hand, then began counting on his fingers and displaying the same expressions Sam had used while counting the non-existent houses.

For the next hour and a half the men talked business, politics, and the growing tension between the North and the South. Sanford was convinced that the country would be at war within a year. The women reminisced about old times, discussed how the new baby was going to affect their lives, and also shared their fears that their husbands would have to go to war.

Finally, Sanford said, "We better be going. Do you know of a good spot for me to put up our tent?"

"It's getting awfully crowded, but I can help you look," Sam replied.

Dora turned to Sam. "Don't we have room for them to spend the night in our other tent?"

"It's pretty tight with my tools and supplies in there, but if you don't mind being a little cramped, we might be able to find a place for you to sleep."

"I've been in tight quarters for about as long as I can remember," Mollie said.

Sam went into the back of their tent and came out with a lighted lantern. "Come on, everyone; let's have a look."

Sam held the lantern low until they were all inside the second tent; then he lifted it up.

Mollie gasped. The tent was at least the size of Sam and Dora's sleeping quarters, and it contained no tools or supplies. There was a bed with sparkling white sheets, pillows with white pillowcases, and a multicolored quilt. On the other side of the tent, there was a cherry-wood dresser, a small table with a lantern on it, and a wooden straight chair.

"Welcome to your new home," Sam said.

Dora pointed to the table and chair. "Those are so you can write in your precious journal."

Mollie said, "This looks heavenly to me right now." She looked questioningly at her husband, who had not registered any surprise.

"Sam told me about this while you were taking your bath," he explained.

"Then what was all that talk about having Sam help you find a place to pitch a tent?"

Sanford smiled sheepishly. "I didn't want to ruin the surprise for you."

Mollie half-closed her eyes, fell over into the bed, rolled onto her back, and laid her head on the pillow. Then she looked up at Dora and patted the spot next to her. Dora jumped onto the bed with her head on the other pillow. Glossy black hair and tanned faces rested against white linen. Blue Irish eyes shone from behind dark thick eyelashes. Two hands clasped together, while their loving smiles told of the pure joy Dora and Mollie felt about being together again.

The two men looked down at their wives, and Sanford asked Sam, "How did we ever talk these two ladies into marrying us?"

Sam just shook his head and smiled.

Sam and Byron had finished their breakfasts and were drinking their second cups of coffee and Mollie was helping Dora wash the dishes when Hiram Bennett walked up to the front of their tent. "Mind if I join the boys?" he asked.

Sam stood to his feet and held out his hand. "My name's Sam Harris."

Hiram took Sam's hand and gripped it firmly. "Yes, I remember you, Harris. I saw you a few times when you worked for Tucker back in Nebraska City."

"This is my brother-in-law, Byron Sanford."

"Oh, I know this fellow pretty well." He shook hands with Sanford, then turned to the ladies. "Hi, Mollie. Hi, Dora."

Sam pulled a chair up for their guest, then poured him a cup of coffee.

Sanford said, "I was surprised when I found out that you were in Denver, Mr. Bennett."

Bennett laughed. "Did you think that I was too old to pull up stakes and leave Nebraska?"

"Oh, no. I just knew that you had a lot of business interests back there."

"Well, you're probably right, I am too old for all of this, but I still get excited when these new territories open up, especially when there is gold involved."

"Dora told me about her conversation with you yesterday. She said that you're planning to build a gold stamping mill near here," Sam said.

"As a matter of fact, Judge Holly and I are part of a group that are going to build the mill. I've already purchased some land at Gold Hill. That's a mining camp northwest of Boulder. While I was out here locating the land, the judge went back east to buy the equipment. He just arrived here yesterday."

"Sanford and Mollie were on the same wagon train as the judge," Sam said.

"Then I guess you already know what we're doing. You boys probably don't know this, the judge never likes to blow his own horn, but he helped write the regulations for the mining district for this territory back in March of 'fifty-nine."

Both men shook their heads, indicating that it was news to them.

"Anyway, the judge and I had a meeting last night, and we want you young people to know that we're here to help you any way we can. We Nebraska folks have to stick together. I told Dora yesterday that we'll need to have some buildings constructed. You men might as well build them for us."

"We appreciate that, sir," Sam said.

"There is something else the judge wanted me to mention. Since you just got here, Sanford, you're probably not aware of this, but the lawlessness in Denver is bad and getting worse. Just last night, four men were killed at Wheelers Tavern. We want to put together a group of people and hire a sheriff. We wouldn't expect you young folks to contribute any money, but if you hear any talk around town about this, you can advocate our position. We want Denver to be a safe place for our families."

"You can count on our support, Mr. Bennett," Sanford said.

"Do you know any details about the killings?" Sam asked.

"From what I was told, it happened outside the saloon. A couple of Indians were sitting on the porch, minding their own business. I guess this white man had too much to drink and thought he was too good to be associating with Indians. He ordered them to leave. When they wouldn't oblige him, he reached for his gun and got knifed through his heart for his effort. This kid named Jimmy, who hangs out at Wheelers, fancies himself as a gunfighter. He came out on the porch, fanned his triggerless gun four times, and we had two dead Indians."

"That only adds up to three," Sam said.

136

"Three if the kid had been a better shot. One of the Indians was still alive. When the kid leaned over to take the Indian's beaded necklace for a souvenir, the Indian cut his throat from ear to ear. People that were watching said the Indian died with dignity, but the kid ran around in the street like a chicken with its head cut off."

Sam shivered noticeably. Bennett caught it and said, "I know that's pretty grisly, but it isn't that unusual around here. We've already had twelve killings this month. The worst thing about this one is that there were two Indians killed. Our relationship with the local Indians has been deteriorating anyway. If a group of renegade Indians decide to take revenge, they will more than likely kill some white settlers. Then we could have a war on our hands."

"There is a man named Dalton who drove the wagon behind us all the way from Nebraska," Sam said. "He told me that he'd had some experience in law enforcement. He has to be camped somewhere near here."

"Dalton," Bennett repeated, and nodded his head. "I'll see if I can locate him."

After Bennett left, Sam announced that he and Sanford had to take care of some business in town.

"What kind of business?" Dora asked.

"We need to purchase some lots if we're going to start building houses."

Sanford looked surprised. "You have enough money to buy lots?"

"I don't think we're going to need any money. You saw all of the wagon trains heading the other way, when you were coming here. My guess is that a few of the men who are leaving have purchased land."

"That makes sense," Byron said, "but I doubt if they'd be willing to *give* it away."

"I agree but what does a man need most if he wants to head back east?"

Mollie answered Sam's question for her husband: "A covered wagon and a team of oxen."

"That's right, Mollie, and Dora and I have both."

"So do we," Sanford added.

"But won't we need them if we decide to go home?" Dora asked.

"If we go home, I'd rather sell out and take the stagecoach. Money travels light."

Sam put his hands out in front of him, palms up, and looked questioningly back and forth from his wife to his in-laws. After a few moments of thought, they all nodded their agreement.

"OK," he said. "Come on, Sanford, we've got some swapping to do."

15

Their first year in Denver was a time of joy and optimism for Dora and Mollie. They were newlyweds, happily in love, helping their mates carve out success in the new Colorado Territory. First, their husbands finished building their new house and the two families moved in together. Next, the men built the stamp mill at Gold Hill for Hiram Bennett and Judge Holly. When the men came back to Denver, they were inundated with more new building contracts than they could handle. Various miners who had struck gold in the hills around Denver, Boulder, or the surrounding communities solicited their services.

Then Abraham Lincoln was elected president of the United States, and the town had a jubilee. Hiram Bennett gave a speech, bands played patriotic songs, and a considerable amount of food and hard liquor was consumed by the townsmen. The people in the Colorado Territory couldn't vote, but they did know how to have a party.

Then in January the anxiously awaited event took place. Dora gave birth to a healthy baby boy. They named him Frank, and he was the joy of their home. An alert, happy, laughing baby boy. A month later, Mollie discovered that she, too, was pregnant. Baby Frank was to have a playmate. Next a letter from Nebraska City announcing the marriage of their sister Anna to a man named Henry Harvey. Since the Harrises and Sanfords couldn't celebrate with the rest of the family, they had a special dinner party of their own. It appeared that nothing could go wrong for the two couples.

Then, one day when Dora and Mollie were hiking in the woods, they ran across a small cabin that looked deserted. When they went inside, they discovered a man who had been sick for several days. He was too far gone to be helped, but before he died he asked them if they would write to his young wife back east and tell her what had happened to him. Mollie, who had always been rather superstitious, said that this event was a bad omen. Dora, though saddened by the man's death, argued that it was just an isolated incident and that it held no ominous warnings for them. Whether by coincidence or by some grand and unknown scheme, Mollie turned out to be right. A series of tragic events began to occur in the two couples' lives.

One day Sam walked into the kitchen of his house to find his wife and sister-in-law sobbing uncontrollably. Neither of them seemed able to talk, but Dora pointed to a letter that was lying open on the table. It was from their father, and it told that their baby brother, Charlie, had died of diphtheria. By the time the letter had arrived in Denver, Charlie had already been buried next to his recently departed grandfather in the Nebraska City Cemetery. The last time Dora had seen her little brother alive, he was sitting in the middle of the road, crying and holding his little hands out toward his sister as she rode away. She had assured him that she would come back and see him again. She had been wrong. When Mollie was able to get out a few words, she recounted how Charlie had run after her wagon, crying, "Sister, Sister," when she had told him goodbye. The two women were inconsolable. When Sam read the letter, and listened to what Mollie said, tears began to run down his own cheeks, too. Surely a family treasure had been lost.

A few weeks later, headlines in the *Rocky Mountain News* reported the bombardment of Fort Sumter and its eventual capitulation to the Rebels. Sam and Byron were indignant. Dora and Mollie were gripped with fear that their husbands would soon go off to war and be killed. Almost immediately after the assault on Fort Sumter, people in the community began hearing reports of settlers out on the plains being attacked by marauding bands of Indians. The Indians were burning down houses and killing the occupants. The two sisters, as well as other citizens of Denver, could no longer feel safe.

It was during this time of apprehension and anxiety that Mollie had gone into labor. Neither Mollie nor her husband had expected the baby to arrive for several more weeks, so they had felt it was safe for Byron to leave town on business. He was only to be gone for a couple of days. Dora, Sam, and a midwife were the only ones with Mollie during her terrible ordeal. The first time Mollie looked into the sweet face of her newborn baby boy, he was in his coffin. Byron Sanford never saw his first son.

September 1861

When Hiram Bennett finished delivering the eulogy, Mollie and Dora clutched each other and wept openly as the tiny casket was lowered into the ground. It was hard to believe the sudden turn of events that had culminated with Mollie losing her firstborn child. Sam stood a few feet away from his wife and sister-in-law, holding his child, Frank. The little fellow twisted in his father's arms to watch a band as they marched down the street alongside of the graveyard. Since the assault at Fort Sumter, Denver had erupted into a fever pitch of patriotism. Some men wanted to go and kill the Rebels. Others wanted to go after the hostile Indians. Frank's little fists pounded on his father's shoulder as he tried to imitate the drummer who was striking both sides of the big bass drum that was strapped to the front of his body.

Sam, Dora, Mollie, and Frank were the last ones to leave the gravesite. By the time they got home, a cold wind was blowing down off the mountains. Dora nursed Frank, then put him down for the night. Sam stacked some logs into the fireplace and soon had a nice flame rising up from the dry wood. Then, not knowing what to do or what to say, he sat down by the fire with his sister-in-law. Mollie had hardly spoken to anyone since her baby's birth and immediate death.

When Dora finished putting Frank down for the night, she joined them, and they all sat quietly staring at the blazing logs. To everyone's surprise, Mollie spoke first. "We don't always understand God's will. The Good Shepherd has called my baby into his fold, and no harm can ever come to him now."

"No harm would have ever come to him in your arms, either." Dora said.

Mollie looked at the angry face of her sister and asked, "Are you mad at God?"

"Maybe I am. I just don't understand how He could have let this happen."

Dora's anger and the ensuing challenge for Mollie to defend her faith seemed to somehow energize her. "We can't question God, Dora."

"If God thinks your baby is better off with Him, then He's wrong this time."

Mollie looked shocked. "You don't mean that."

Sam had been sitting with his shoulders hunched forward and his head lowered ever since they had come home from the grave service. Now he slowly lifted his head and looked into his wife's face. "Don't you think that, perhaps, the Creator of the universe is entitled to His opinion?"

Dora's face changed from anger to grief. "Yes, of course I do, but why did he take Mollie's baby? I just don't understand it." She began to cry again.

To Sam's surprise, Mollie got up from her chair, walked over to her sister, and began comforting her. His mind went back to when he was growing up in Harrisville. If one of his younger brothers or sisters was in some way injured, Sam would get more upset than if he himself had been hurt. Maybe his wife was displaying this type of behavior now. Her sister had been so badly hurt, and Dora was angry about it, angry to the point of questioning the will of God.

"I've always trusted God," Dora said. "I just don't understand why He isn't protecting us now."

Once this discussion began, Mollie seemed to rise above her despondency. "God's people have always had troubles. He doesn't insulate us against the trials and tribulations of this life. He gives us the strength to get through them and become stronger people because of them."

"Remind me to never pray for strength, then," Dora said.

Mollie laughed. She actually laughed.

Sam looked at his wife and then at her sister. He couldn't tell if Dora's faith was at its lowest point ever, or if she was making these comments to take her sister's mind off her grief. Whatever the reason, Mollie was more animated than she had been for several days.

Mollie said. "Just think how wonderful it will be when I get to Heaven and find my baby boy waiting for me."

Sam stood up, excused himself, and walked into the bedroom up to Frank's crib. He touched the black silky hair of the head of his sleeping child and wondered how he would react if anything were to happen to his own baby.

On the first night after Byron Sanford returned to town, the two couples and baby Frank gathered in the family's kitchen for supper.

The happy babbling of the child in his high chair contrasted the somber mood of the adults.

Mollie put her fork into a bite of roast beef, then just sat looking down at it. Byron put his hand on his wife's shoulder and said, "If I'd had any idea that the baby was coming so soon, I wouldn't have left."

Mollie tried to answer, but the words wouldn't come out.

Dora said, "You had no way to know, Byron."

Mollie nodded her agreement.

They all ate in silence for awhile; then Mollie asked, "Are you planning to join the army, By?"

"Not right away. Governor Gilpin has offered me a commission if I join the First Colorado and help them recruit volunteers. That's probably what I'll eventually do. He said that he would do the same thing for you, Sam, if you're interested."

Dora looked across the table at her husband. "What about it? Are you going to enlist, too?"

"Not in Colorado. If I join up it will be in Iowa with my father and my brothers."

"Maybe the war will be over by the time we get to Iowa," Dora said. "I read in the newspaper that President Lincoln has asked for seventy-five thousand volunteers from the states that are not in rebellion."

Sam nodded. "And, they claim that they have more men wanting to enlist than they think they'll need."

Byron added, "Up in the mine country, hundreds of men are walking away from their claims. I guess everyone wants to get a crack at the Rebels for what they did at Fort Sumter. The problem here in Colorado is no one knows if our soldiers will be fighting the Rebels or the Indians."

"You'll probably be fighting both," Sam said.

"I don't think the war against the South is going to end very soon," Mollie said softly.

"Why not?" Dora asked. "If the war is only about freeing the slaves, why would anyone other than rich slave owners be willing to fight?"

"Do you remember that Southern man who I met on the *Silver Heels* when we were coming to Nebraska? The one I had so many arguments with?"

Dora nodded. "Yes."

"He didn't own any slaves, but he said that he would fight to the death anyone who tried to usurp his state's rights. He seemed to be as loyal to his state as we are to our country."

"I hope that isn't the general feeling in the South, but I'm afraid it might be," Sam added.

From a park a few blocks away they heard a band playing. Frank started beating his spoon on the tray of his high chair.

"Would anyone like to take a walk after supper?" Sam asked.

Byron looked at his wife, who shook her head. She had hardly touched her food.

Dora put her hand over her sister's. "Maybe it would do you good to get out of the house for awhile."

Mollie shrugged her shoulders. In her current state of mind, she wasn't sure what she wanted.

It was a pleasant September night in Colorado. A cool breeze off the Rocky Mountains rustled the young oak trees that had been planted in the new city park. A bright moon, along with several lanterns on picnic tables and others on the bandstand, provided light for this event. The two couples slowly strolled on the grass around the perimeter of a remarkably large crowd that had gathered for a cookout and loyalist rally. Smoke, inundated with the aroma of assorted barbecued meats, drifted around the tables laden with salads and casseroles. People sat on blankets spread out on the grass. Drums rumbled, fifes played, and the people of Denver cheered and clapped as all of the pomp and circumstance of a glorious war raged in full force. It was all Sam could do to hold onto his clapping, squirming child.

Men who had already enlisted were being feted and lionized by their friends and neighbors with as much enthusiasm as knights embarking on a crusade to the Holy Lands. Wine and other strong drinks were flowing freely. Flags were being presented and received, as if war was completely unrelated to the melancholy hue of blood and suffering. Men bragged to each other about how they intended to avenge this insult to our national pride by promptly destroying all remnants of the Rebel army. The sad realities of war had not yet penetrated the minds of the citizens of Denver. Men and women alike were still at the stage of romanticizing the impending conflict.

"This is amazing," Sam said. "You would think that these men were going to a party."

"I think it's frightening," Dora commented.

"Do you mind if we go home?" Mollie asked.

After the first few battles of the Civil War and the appalling number of casualties on both sides, it became apparent to everyone that there would be no easy conquest of the Confederate forces. The seventy-five thousand men President Lincoln had called up, which had seemed more than adequate at the time, was only a fraction of the manpower required to preserve the Union. The matter of how long it would take to smash the rebellion evolved into a frightening dispute over which side would actually win the Civil War. When the Indians in Colorado saw the white men forming a volunteer army, they went on the warpath.

Byron Sanford took Governor Gilpin up on his offer and was given a commission as second lieutenant in the First Colorado Volunteers, Company H. He was stationed at the newly established Camp Weld, on the bank of the Platte River, about two miles south of the center of Denver. He left for the mountains to recruit volunteers and returned the next day. The Federal Army didn't need to do any recruiting. Men were leaving their mines and farms in vast numbers and flooding into the Denver recruiting office. It seemed that almost every man in the territory wanted to fight for his country.

Byron had no sooner returned from the mountains than he was sent out again on another mission. His assignment this time was substantially more dangerous. He was to search out and destroy renegade bands of Indians. Mollie was still numb with pain from the loss of her grandfather, her little brother, and her own baby. Now she had to worry about the safety of her husband.

It was early in the evening at the two couples' home, and Dora was in the kitchen fixing supper. Mollie was in the next room packing her child's baby clothes to send to her sister Anna. Sam was in town on business and due to return soon.

Mollie turned toward the open kitchen door and stated. "I never thought I'd be a soldier's wife. I've listened to predictions about the coming war for several years, but I guess I didn't think it would happen during my lifetime."

145

"I know! It doesn't seem real!" Dora called back. "War doesn't make any sense at all to me!"

Mollie finished her packing and joined her sister in the kitchen. "Do you need any help?"

"Everything is just about ready, but you could fix us some tea." The sound of horses' hooves outside the house signaled that Sam had arrived home. "Better fix three cups."

Sam came through the door, kissed Dora, and dropped two envelopes on the kitchen table.

Mollie set a cup of tea in front of him. "Letters from home?" she asked.

"Invitations," he replied.

Dora stopped stirring the boiling pot that was on the stove in front of her. "Invitations to what?"

"We're invited to a regimental ball given by the governor for the officers and their wives."

"Why us? You're not in the army," Dora remarked.

Mollie held up one of the invitations. "This one is addressed to Mr. and Mrs. Harris. It's signed 'The Honorable C. M. Chilcott.' He's a member of the legislature. Maybe the governor is trying to recruit your husband, too."

Both ladies looked at Sam. He rested his boot up on the rung of a chair and took a sip of tea. He and Dora had discussed this matter several times, and she knew that he was thinking seriously about going back to Iowa to join up with his brothers. He took another envelope out of his pocket and handed it to his wife. This one was a letter from Grinnell from his younger brother John Agnew. It informed them that Sam's older brother, Dr. Ephriam Harris, had already joined the Federal Army Medical Corps. J.A. wanted to join the infantry and wanted to know what Sam was going to do before he enlisted.

Dora finished reading the one-page letter, handed it to Mollie, then turned to her husband. "Have you decided what you're going to do yet?"

Sam nodded. "I guess I've known all along. If my family is going to war, then I have to go with them."

"I guess I knew that, too." She turned back toward Mollie. There was a smile on her face, but her eyes were moist. "Hey, big sister, what are we going to wear to that ball?"

146

After Dora and Mollie had spent several hours altering their wedding dresses to wear to the regimental ball, Mollie got a severe toothache and was forced to remain at home with a poultice on her swollen jaw. She took care of Frank while Sam and Dora went to the dance.

Just as the band was beginning to play, the couple strolled into the newly built officers' club and immediately began socializing with some of Denver's most prominent citizens. Dora was asked to dance by quite a few of the newly commissioned officers of the Colorado First Volunteers. She whirled around the floor with George Sanborn, the captain of Company H, and Richard Sophris, the captain of Company C, as well as other officers and dignitaries who caught sight of the black-haired beauty in the blue merino dress.

Sam danced with some of the officers' wives, then began alternating between Captain Sophris's two attractive daughters. When Dora noticed how much attention Sam was getting from these two young ladies, she excused herself and went over and cut in on his dancing partner.

Sam and Dora hadn't been dancing long before she declared, "You seemed to be having a lot of fun dancing with these young girls."

He couldn't tell if she was kidding by the tone of her voice, so he leaned away from her to look at her face. One quick glance told him that his wife was angry at him. "What did you expect me to do? You were flirting with every officer in the place."

"I wasn't flirting; I was just trying to be pleasant. They all asked me to dance. I didn't ask them."

"So, while you're dancing and having fun, am I just supposed to sit and watch?"

"I noticed that you didn't ask any of the older ladies to dance."

"If it makes any difference, Mattie and Pamelia each asked me to dance."

"Well, aren't you the one! The pretty girls all ask you to dance with them, now."

Sam spun Dora around the floor and attempted to sort out what had happened to get his wife so upset. Maybe he had been holding the Sophris girls too close, and in all honesty, he had been enjoying it. He knew that he had felt jealous when he saw Dora dancing in the arms of other men. Perhaps, unconsciously, he was trying to get even. No matter what it was that had provoked this hostility between them, he wanted it to end. He tried to pull her closer to him, but she resisted.

"You are the most beautiful woman at the ball. I can't blame all those men for wanting to dance with you, but when I see you in someone else's arms I hate the way it makes me feel."

She moved closer to him, "Are you trying to turn this around?"

"I'm telling you how I feel."

"You were actually jealous of those men?"

"I don't know whether or not it was jealousy, but whatever it was it made me feel terrible."

Her expression progressed from a frown to a little smile. She put her hand up behind his neck. "You didn't look like you were suffering when you were dancing with the Sophris girls."

He didn't have any answer for his wife's last statement, so he just pulled her closer to him. When the band stopped playing and started arranging their music sheets for the next song, he asked, "Would you like to have a glass of punch with your husband?"

"I've heard that the punch is spiked."

He thought about asking who had told her that but rejected the idea. "Maybe that's what we need. You know it doesn't count if you're not sure what you're drinking."

On the way across the dance floor, a grinning second lieutenant asked Dora for the next dance. She politely declined.

Pamelia Sophris spied Sam and started in his direction. He grabbed Dora's arm and hurried her toward the refreshment table. He ladled out two glasses of an unknown pink beverage, handed one to Dora, and asked, "Shall we go out onto the porch and get some air?"

The night was cool, and the sky was milky white with stars. She sipped her drink.

He put his arm around her bare shoulders. "Are you cold?"

She leaned toward him. "I'm fine."

"What did I do wrong?" he asked.

"Probably nothing. I just wanted to be with you, and then all those men began asking me to dance. They gave me silly compliments that embarrassed me, and I kept praying that you would come and rescue me. Whenever I tried to catch your eye, you were too busy dancing and having fun with those younger girls."

"You certainly gave the impression that you were enjoying yourself with Captain Sanborn."

"He is a very nice gentleman," she conceded.

"When you were dancing with Captain Sophris, you were laughing at something the whole time. You hardly glanced away from him."

They sipped their drinks and gazed up at the stars. He dropped his arm from her shoulders, slipped it around her waist, and pulled her closer to him.

"When are we leaving Denver?" she asked.

"It's your decision, too," Sam replied.

"I know, but you feel like you would be letting your family down if you didn't go home and enlist with them."

"I suppose you're right. Is that the real reason that you're angry with me?"

She thought about that for a moment. "I think I'm angry about everything that's happening to us now."

He turned his face toward hers and looked down into her eyes. "Would you rather stay here with your sister until the war is over?"

"No, of course not."

"Maybe you should think about it. If I'm off fighting the Rebels, we won't be together wherever you are."

She laid her head against his chest and spoke in a voice so soft that he could hardly hear: "I'll stay with your parents, because wherever you are, I want to be just as close to you as I can."

"We have to leave for Iowa very soon," he said.

"I know we do. You just better come home to me. If you get yourself killed, I'm never going to forgive you."

He rubbed his hand up her arm and discovered she had chill bumps. "We'd better go back inside," he said.

"Not until you promise me that I can have all of the rest of the dances with you."

"I would like that very much."

"No one cuts in," declared Dora.

"Just let someone try," he replied.

16

Sam, Dora, and their one-year-old boy, Frank, traveled by stagecoach from Denver to Nebraska City, transferring from one coach to another several times along the way. It was a less complicated journey than their covered-wagon experience two years ago but still required many rough days of bouncing and jarring around. Every rut and bump along the Overland Trail was transferred from the wooden-and-steel wheels of the coach to the firm seats inside and in turn to the sore and tired backs of the passengers. They slept and ate on their seats on the stage and on benches in small mail stations. Frank was well behaved but still quite a handful. Being contained in such a small compartment for that many days was not this child's idea of how to have fun. Everyone was glad when their trip finally ended.

Once they reached Nebraska City, they stayed one night at Allen's Hotel, renewing friendships with Mrs. Allen, Dick Gregory, and several other townspeople. The reunion celebration in the hotel dining room that night included Dora's younger sister Anna, her newspaperman husband, Henry Harvey, and Sam's old employer Nathan Tucker along with his wife, Deborah. Anna brought her new baby girl, who promptly stole away a large portion of the attention that Frank was accustomed to receiving. Laughing, reminiscing, and local gossip consumed the evening for the women, while the men talked at length about the war and the shocking losses the Federal troops had suffered in some of the most recent battles.

The next morning, Sam purchased a horse and carriage and they departed for the Dorsey farm. Two happy weeks were spent with Dora's family, enjoying the picturesque countryside around the Little Nemaha. Those lazy days passed quickly as they took time off to go fishing, swim in the family swimming hole, and take long walks in the woods. After their respite in Nebraska, Sam and Dora said their sad goodbyes to her family and departed for the last leg of their journey.

August 1862

It was a hot summer afternoon when Sam, Dora, and Frank reached the outskirts of Grinnell, Iowa. Verdant pastures stretched for miles along both sides of the road. Behind split-log fences, cattle lazily grazed under large shade trees. Although it was late in the season, some species of wildflowers still dotted the landscape. They rode over a bridge that crossed a sparkling stream and passed the white church that Sam and his family had attended before he left for Nebraska City. The idyllic scene refreshed Sam's mind about how impressed he had been the first time he had ridden into Grinnell.

"I can certainly see why your family chose this town for their farm," Dora said.

A man in a one-horse buggy passed them going the opposite direction. He smiled as if he knew Sam and tipped his hat as he rode by.

"Do you know him?" Dora asked.

"Not very well, but I've met him. His name is James Hubbard. He bought the land just south of our farm right before I left town."

"I guess you'll be renewing a lot of acquaintances and restoring old friendships. Are there any of your old girlfriends that I should know about?"

"I dated the pastor's daughter for a while."

"And?"

"And then I left town and found the girl of my dreams."

"What is her name?"

"Jenny."

"I'll look out for her."

Sam had a moment of discomfort thinking about Dora meeting Jenny, then put it out of his mind.

When they pulled their wagon up in front of the two-story white farmhouse of the Harris farm, everyone rushed out onto the porch to greet them. The greeting party included Sam's parents, his sister Joanna, now a student at Grinnell College, class of 1865, and his youngest sister Mary, who was in her second year at Grinnell High School. Sam and Dora were told that Sam's brothers James Agnew and William were running errands in town but would be back in time for supper. Sam's mother cried for several seconds and held onto the son that she hadn't seen for more than two and a half years.

For the first time since the death of Mollie's baby, Dora saw tears in her husband's eyes as he put one arm around each of his parents. Dora was certain that she had never loved Sam more than she did right now. After Dora had been introduced to the family, Mama Harris hugged and kissed her daughter-in-law, then picked up her sleepy grandson and herded the women into the kitchen.

Sam and his father settled into a couple of large, comfortable chairs on the front porch.

"You don't know how great it is to see you, Son."

"Believe me, I'm mighty glad to be home."

"J.A. has been standing on one foot and then the other waiting for you to arrive. It seems he can't wait to join up and go fight the Rebels."

"I'm not looking forward to it all that much."

"You're a lot older than your brother. I'm afraid he still thinks that going off to war is going to be some glamorous adventure."

"Where has the rest of the family gone?"

"You know that three of your sisters are married?"

"Mother told me a little bit about the weddings in her letters."

"Well, Susan married a farmer named Henry Hill. They live about two days' ride from here. Jane is a preacher's wife. She and the Reverend Compton visit us every few months. Sarah married a wagon maker, Theodore Worthington. They live just a little ways outside of town. I'm sure you'll be able to see them before you leave."

"What's going on with Jenny?"

"She married a preacher, too. They pastor a church in Clinton."

"Preacher's daughter, preacher's wife. That's good."

"It's also good that Clinton is about three days' ride from here. No awkward introductions of your wife to your ex-girlfriend."

Sam smiled and nodded his agreement. "It's so great to be home. I'm sorry that I can't stay here longer, but I'm afraid that if we don't get some reinforcements to our boys soon, General Lee is going to march right into Washington, and the South is going to win the war."

"It doesn't look very good for our side right now. I'm thinking seriously about enlisting myself."

Sam's eyes widened. It hadn't even entered into his mind that his father might go off to war, although Sam had no doubt that he could keep up with most men half his age. "I think the family needs you here."

"Don't underestimate William, or your mother and sisters. They could run the farm just fine by themselves if it was necessary. There is another problem, however. This town is mostly abolitionists, but there are more than a few pro-slavery troublemakers in some counties south of here. Now that the war is looking bad for the North, these people have been organizing a secret order of disloyalists. They call themselves *The Knights of the Golden Circle*. We're pretty sure that they're storing weapons for an uprising. If the Rebel troops ever got this far north, these men would come out into the open, and every man would have to defend his own house."

Joanna walked out on the porch carrying two tall glasses of ice-cold tea. She kissed Sam on the cheek and said, "It's so nice to see you again, big brother."

"It's great to see you, too, Joanna. You've grown up to be quite an attractive lady since I've been gone. Is there any special man in your life yet?"

"I've been too busy with my studies and working on the Railroad to even think about romance." As she walked back into the kitchen, she turned and gave her brother a coy smile. "I have a lot of close friends, though."

Once she was gone, Sam asked, "What did she mean, working on the Railroad?"

"Prop up your feet and relax, Son. I've got a long story to tell you. Shortly after you left, your mother and I became outlaws."

Sam almost choked on his drink.

"Even worse than that, I've caused the whole family to get involved."

"I don't understand."

"I told you that it's going to be a long story. You know as well as anyone that your mother and I brought our family up to abide by the law, but I've found that there are times when the law is so very wrong that a person can't, in good conscience, live by the rules."

"You're involved with the Underground Railroad," Sam said.

His father smiled. "I guess you know that I've always been somewhat of a radical. I'm an engineer in the Railroad. Josiah Grinnell is a conductor. His big feed barn is one of the main railroad stations in northern Iowa."

"I'm proud of you, Papa. You took risks for something that you believe in, but why didn't you let me know what you were doing?"

"Your mother and I wanted to tell you, but we were afraid the letter could get into the wrong hands. I'm sure you know about the Federal Fugitives Act and how vigorously it's enforced. You'd be surprised how many people there are who are willing to go to war against the South for seceding from the Union, yet have no interest in whether or not the slaves are freed. We didn't tell you because we knew that you were living with another couple in Denver."

"Dora's sister and her husband are as opposed to slavery as we are, but still, that type of information shouldn't go through the mail. I presume that my brother in California doesn't know about your participation in the Railroad, either?"

"No, and I don't know how we're ever going to get the message to McKee and his family."

"Maybe when we win the war and the slaves have been freed?" Sam pushed his chair back, hoisted his boots up on the porch rail, and took a long drink from his glass of tea. "Now tell me all about your involvement with the Underground Railroad. I want to hear the whole story. Don't leave anything out."

"All right." Sam's father set his glass up on top of the porch railing and leaned toward his son. "Shortly after you left town, we began seeing a few Negroes coming through town on their way north toward Canada. They were hungry, tired, and many of them were sick. All of them were desperate. Each new group told us about some of their number who had died along the way. Anyone with any trace of compassion would have tried to help them. Most of the townspeople did what they could. We gave them food, shelter, clothing, money, anything we could do to ease their misery. A few outspoken local citizens reminded the rest of us that what we were doing was against the law and urged us to turn the escaping slaves over to the federal marshals.

"We were in a dilemma. The law of the land said that they should be sent back to their owners, but our sense of right and wrong demanded that we help them. Did the start of the war begin to change the pro-slavery sympathizers' minds?" Sam asked.

"Some rethought their positions before that. When the first slave catchers came to Grinnell, it was shocking how brutal and insensitive these men were. To people around here, these men represented the South. This convinced some of the fence-sitters of what an abomination slavery actually was."

"OK, I can understand why our family would want to help these people, but how did you get started, and how did you know what to do?"

"That's a good question, Samuel. You remember Josiah Grinnell?"

"Of course."

"Well, what I'm going to tell you happened prior to his reelection to Congress and before he left for Washington. Late one Saturday night, he happened to be reading an article in the *New York Tribune* about John Brown leading a group of Missouri slaves through Iowa to Canada. There was a ringing at his door. When he answered it, a tall, stately man with white hair and a white beard was standing here. The man identified himself as 'that awful Brown, whom you've heard about.' It was indeed Captain John Brown of Kansas, and he had a group of sixteen fugitives with him. He told Grinnell that he and his men needed food and shelter for the night. Grinnell invited Captain Brown into his home and told him that his parlor and some stalls in his barn were available. He also advised Brown that his party would be as safe as anywhere at Mrs. Reed's hotel in town.

"You know that Josiah Grinnell is just as radical an abolitionist as your father. When Brown said that he made it a habit not to travel on Sunday. Grinnell arranged a reception for him at the church that Sunday night. Several hundred people packed into the auditorium, with many of them having to stand throughout the meeting. Quite a few came just out of curiosity. Our family arrived early and sat in the front row.

"Captain Brown was calm in manner but filled with emotion as he described certain conditions that the slaves had to endure before he was able to help them escape.

"One man who was standing in the back called out, 'Tell us about your company and why you killed a slave owner in Missouri!'

"Brown answered, 'They call me a nigger thief. Am I? I delivered the poor that cried out, when there was no one else to help. My company that are with me now were to be sold. They called on me and I rescued them. I have never counseled violence, nor would I stir up insurrection which would involve the innocent or helpless. Twelve was the number I rescued out of Missouri, and they are part of our grateful company.'

"Captain Brown spoke without a spirit of revenge and like a statesman. 'Slavery is a crime, and a real lover of his race and country will put a wall around it. Some will need to die so that justice can be served. You have a college started here. Slavery cannot endure a college, nor a prayer that goes above the roof.'

"That night some other people who had previously been indifferent to slavery became converts to our cause. A collection was taken up for Brown and his company at the end of the service, and the next day they left town on their way toward the Mississippi River."

"So, was the town now united against slavery?" Sam asked.

"Many people became abolitionists during that meeting, but our town was not yet a unit. The shocking news of the attack by the Rebels at Fort Sumter brought more over to our side, but of course you realize there will always be a few holdouts. As for me and my family, we had already been sufficiently moved by Captain Brown's words in the church during that Sunday evening service."

"And when the Harris family feels strongly about something, you can bet that they will take action."

"That's right, Son. Since the war started, the Railroad hasn't been as far underground as it once was, but there are still a lot of people who need our help. The Railroad is still running. There is a network of towns in northern Iowa that is still traveled regularly by fugitive slaves. It starts in Tabor, then goes west to Lewis, then on to Fontanelle, Winterset, Mitchellville, and then right here where we put them up in Grinnell's big feed barn. From here we take them to Springdale, and then Clinton, and onto boats traveling up the Mississippi River to Canada. We generally move our cargo from one station to the next at night."

Sam frowned. "You refer to these people as cargo?"

"We certainly don't think of them as cargo, but we have to be deceptive in our messages and our conversation, or we would all be caught. That's why we use a code. Engineers have received notes saying to expect a shipment of books or a shipment of wool. Another time we heard that we were receiving some wagonloads of fodder. When you're breaking federal laws, you can't be too careful. A few times we moved slaves just a few hours ahead of an armed posse." Sam's father smiled as he recalled one incident. "One time a posse had bloodhounds who were only a few miles behind us. Your sister Joanna baked some poisoned biscuits, and by the time the posse caught up to the dogs, they had all collapsed on the ground. I hate to see animals treated that way, but after that event the slave catchers knew better than to try to sic their dogs on us again."

"We are living in turbulent times," Sam said. "Remember when the worst threat that we faced was that ragtag bunch from the saloon who wanted to run us out of Farmington?"

"It would be nice if that was the only opposition that we had now. Speaking of Farmington, several of our old neighbors have joined different Iowa regiments and are off fighting the Rebels."

"Do you think that they've become abolitionists as well?" Sam asked.

"Probably not, but anyway, they're fighting for their country."

A horse and buggy pulled up in front of the house. Sam's two brothers had come home. With them was a slender woman who appeared to be in her mid-twenties. She carried a black bag, which she swung playfully at J.A.'s head, apparently in reaction to something he had said.

"Is the woman a friend of J.A.'s?" Sam asked.

"She's your brother Ephriam's wife. She has taken over his medical practice while he's serving with the Army Medical Corps."

"A woman doctor?"

"A practicing physician, and a good one. Your brother met her at a medical seminar in New York."

"You would think that I'd been gone for ten years with all of the changes that have happened around here."

J.A. charged up the steps, grabbed Sam in a bear hug, lifted him completely off the floor, and spun him around.

"Do I know this impudent fellow?" Sam gasped. "He's too big to be my little brother."

"I thought you would never get here." J.A. said.

"Hi, Sam," William added, smiling and holding out his hand.

Sam looked up at the tall, handsome man grinning at him. "Didn't I used to be taller than you? You must already be out of high school."

"I'm a junior at Grinnell College."

"This is your sister-in-law, Dr. Rachael," Papa Harris told his son.

"Nice to meet you, Doctor."

She shook Sam's hand. He noticed that her grip was quite firm. She had soft brown eyes and a pretty face, but the set of her chin and the steady way she looked right into his eyes portrayed an inner strength. He liked her immediately.

"Everyone calls me Rachael."

The ladies came out of the kitchen, Dora was introduced to the newly arrived members of the Harris family, then everyone gathered in the sitting room. Sam and Dora were deluged with questions about how they had met and about their engagement and marriage. After the couple had answered numerous questions, Sam took Dora's hand and said, "This may sound foolish to all of you, but I fell in love with this woman the first time I ever saw her."

William, who had hardly taken his eyes off Dora since he'd met her, said, "That's not a bit hard for me to believe."

"How long was it before you fell in love with him?" Joanna asked.

"Well, I was crossing the street one day, and this tall, handsome man, whom I'd never seen before, grabbed hold of me and started hugging me in a very outrageous manner. To my surprise, I liked it, so I guess that it was love at first sight for me, too."

Mama Harris raised her eyebrows and looked disapprovingly at her son. "That's not true, is it, Samuel?"

"Wait a minute, everybody; let me tell you why I grabbed her."

J.A. laughed. "I guess it *is* true. This better be good, big brother."

Sam recounted the incident when Dora had slipped on the ice and how he had come to her aid. He ended his story with, "That was the luckiest day of my life."

"Or maybe that was God's way of bringing you two together," Joanna suggested.

When it was time to prepare supper, Mama Harris announced that two women in the kitchen at one time was enough. She said that she and her youngest daughter, Mary would prepare all of the meals on one day and then Joanna and Dora would be in charge of the next day's meals. Mama Harris would cook supper tonight.

When mother and daughter had left the room, Dora looked over at her son, who had already found a comfortable spot on his grandpa's lap and dozed off. "You people are sure making everything easy for me. I can't remember the last time I just sat and relaxed while someone fixed my supper."

"You might as well get used to it," Rachael said. "For several months after Ephriam left. I tried to help out around here, but Mama Harris wouldn't let me."

Dora took note that Rachael had addressed her mother-in-law as Mama. Dora had already called her Mary Ann a couple of times. She decided to go slow and wait for Sam's mother to tell her how she would like to be addressed.

Sam asked, "What do you hear from Ephriam, Rachael?"

"He's stationed at the hospital at Keokuk. First he was assistant surgeon of the Twenty-first Iowa, but the regiment wasn't full, so he was placed in charge of the Ninety-ninth Illinois."

"So, he's still in Iowa," Sam observed. "Does he ever get to come home?"

"I haven't seen him since he left," Rachel said. "Boatloads of wounded soldiers arrive several times a week. He's been working sixteen to eighteen hours a day."

"Rachael works long hours, too," J.A. said. "Recently there was an epidemic of spotted fever in Grinnell. A doctor from Kellogg came over to help out, and two days later he died of the disease himself."

"That happened while Ephriam was still here. We've got it pretty well under control now," Rachael said.

"I don't know much about spotted fever," Sam said.

Rachael nodded. "Unfortunately, neither do we, other than it's a malignant form of cerebrospinal fever, it's quite contagious, and if you contract it you're very likely to die."

Mr. Harris said, "Can you imagine all those boats full of wounded soldiers arriving at the hospital at Keokuk? If the tide of the war doesn't turn soon, we're going to have a lot of gloomy pessimists whining that we should never have gone to war with the South in the first place."

William, who had been sitting quietly while the older members of his family talked, spoke up: "It's already happening. We have debates at the college, and a few of the students are already arguing that the war is a mistake. They predict that Lincoln will only be in office for one term."

J.A. said. "I'm sure that those same students argue against the Emancipation Proclamation that Lincoln is trying to push through Congress."

"That's right," William said. "Last week a student said that he was willing to fight for the Union, but not for the niggers."

Papa Harris shook his head. "That's a horrible thing to say. I hope it's not the general feeling in Iowa. One thing is for sure: this is going to be a tough election year for the Republicans and the War Democrats in Congress. Newspapers in Ottumwa and Burlington have been bitterly attacking Josiah Grinnell over the way he welcomed John Brown into our town."

Sam asked his father, "What are Grinnell's chances for reelection?"

"Our congressional district is divided pretty evenly between Grinnell and his Democratic opponent, Henry Martyn. Martyn is a young lawyer from Marengo who wants to stop enlistments in what he calls a Negro war and to restore the Union as it was. With all of the casualties the Federal troops are suffering now, that argument is beginning to gain support."

"Do you think Grinnell will win his election?" Sam asked.

"There is a good chance that one of the bills Grinnell pushed through the House last year might help him defeat Martyn. It's the one that allows the soldiers to vote. Our men in the military are solidly behind Grinnell."

Sam tilted his head back and inhaled the aroma drifting in from the kitchen; then he grinned. "Fried chicken."

"Do you think that your mother would fix anything else on your first night home, Son?"

After dinner, Dora put Frank into a crib her husband had put up in Joanna's upstairs bedroom. That was where she and Sam would be sleeping until he joined the army. Dora looked down at her child's head resting on his little white pillow and wondered how old he would be before his father came home from the war. *If* his father came home. She sat in a wooden rocking chair and watched her child until he fell asleep; then she looked around the bedroom. In the dim light, she could see that the room still contained dolls left over from Joanna's childhood, mementos of her high school years, and framed certificates of achievement from Grinnell College. Everything in the room told some kind of story about Sam's sister. After Sam and J.A. left town, she, Joanna, and Frank would become roommates for the duration of the war. Dora sensed that this was a room where she

160

would feel comfortable. At least, as comfortable as it was possible to be with her husband off fighting a war. She checked once more to make sure that Frank was sleeping soundly, then joined the family back in the sitting room.

Sam had hoped that the evening would be spent reminiscing about old times and recalling family stories and incidents. It was not to be. The defeats that were being inflicted on the Union forces and the turmoil that the country would be thrown into if the South won the war were on everyone's mind.

The Harrises' teenager daughter, Mary, was frightened by the prospect of Rebel troops marching into their town and asked, "What will happen if we lose the war?"

Her father put his arm around her. "That's not going to happen, dearie."

"We can't let it happen," J.A. said.

"I have a proposal I want to make," Mrs. Harris remarked. She folded her hands on her lap and gripped them so tightly that her knuckles turned white. "This is about the prospect of two more of my boys enlisting in the army."

The questioning look on her husband's face indicated that whatever she planned to say had not been discussed between the two of them.

"I know how important it is for the Federal forces to prevail in this war, but I also think that what we're doing here is very important. John Agnew, I know how anxious you have been for Samuel to get here so you could join the army with him. I just wonder if you two have considered how much help you could be right here, working with us to help slaves escape to Canada?" She glanced quickly at her husband, then said, "That's all I have to say."

Sam looked tenderly at his mother. This wonderful woman who had loved and nursed him when he was a baby, provided care for him through his childhood diseases, and taught him the difference between right and wrong was now making one last desperate attempt to protect him and his brother from possibly being killed in a terrible and ugly war. He got up out of his chair, went over to the couch, and wedged himself in between Joanna and his mother. He put one arm around his mother and placed his other hand on top of hers. "I know how hard this is for you, Mama, but, when we win this war Negroes won't have to go to Canada to be free."

Sam climbed into Joanna's four-poster bed and moved over to the side where he always slept; then he turned onto his back. Dora got into the other side of the bed, lay on her side, and put her head on her husband's chest.

He yawned and said, "It's been a long day."

"A long day, and a wonderful day."

"How do you like my family?"

"I love them. Who wouldn't?"

"One of the worst things about going off to war is the worry it's going to cause my mother."

Dora rose up on her elbow and looked down at his face. "How about me?"

"Of course I feel bad about leaving you. You already know that. You understand why I have to go, don't you?"

"I understand, but I'm not happy about it. I don't know what I would do if I lost you."

"From the way my youngest brother was looking at you tonight, I think you'd still have your pick of whoever you wanted."

"I already have the one I want."

17

May–June 1863

On the last day of May, the Fortieth Iowa Infantry, under orders from General Grant, embarked on a steamer moving down the Mississippi River to join the Federal Army's assault against the Rebel forces entrenched at Vicksburg, Mississippi. The steam-powered cargo vessel that the regiment was traveling on was loaded far beyond its normal capacity. Each soldier had only a small space on one of the decks in which to sleep until the troops reached their final destination. It was near midnight and most of the soldiers had settled down for the night, using their knapsacks or rolled-up blankets as pillows. An assortment of different kinds of pistols was protruding from the belts of the men, while Enfield rifled muskets, polished and gleaming, were propped up next to them. Long hours of drills had taught the soldiers in the Fortieth to fire their muskets at least five times per minute, in spite of having to go through a five-step procedure between each shot. Sam had learned the process for rapid firing of the muskets but didn't intend to have to use that knowledge. Propped up next to Sam and his younger brother John Agnew were what the Rebels who had fought against these weapons called those damned Yankee rifles. These guns could be fired seven times, limited only by how fast you could aim and pull the trigger. Repeater rifles were not issued to any of the Federal troops, but men who owned them, like the Harris brothers, and just a few other men in the regiment were supplied with ammunition.

This was the third night of traveling downriver on the steamboat. There was just enough of a moon to make out the mountainous terrain of the state of Arkansas gliding past on the port side of the ship. From the starboard side, lights from one of the many Tennessee farms along the river would occasionally come into Sam's view. In the last few days, the men had watched from the decks as their ship passed numerous rivers and streams, with their sparkling clean waters flowing down and being incorporated into the muddy Mississippi River.

Sam Harris was hunkered against a wall on the top foredeck facing down the river. Next to him, his brother was sleeping soundly. Three tin mugs of strong black coffee consumed by Sam earlier in the evening plus an intensely worried mind had ruled out any sleep for him, at least until the effects of the caffeine wore off. As he sat in the dark, there was nothing for him to do but recall memories of the past and try to contemplate what his chances might be of surviving the next few weeks. From what their commanding officer had told them about the impending conflict, Sam's outlook for the future was perilous at best.

Before they had embarked on the ship, Lt. Col. Sam Cooper, a friend of the Harris family from Grinnell, had explained to the troops that the town of Vicksburg was considered by many to be an almost impregnable fortress, but one that must be captured if the North was going to win the war. President Lincoln had stated, more than once, "The army that controls Vicksburg controls the Mississippi River." With that port open to the Rebels, waterways and connecting railroads could supply food, supplies, and fresh troops to the Confederate Army. With Vicksburg under Federal control, the South would be cut in two.

The city proper was a highly cultured metropolitan center that stood on a series of bluffs high above the river. Fortifications along these promontory riverbanks reached as high as three hundred feet. The surrounding territory was a maze of bayous and bogs. East of the city, another line of bluffs abruptly fell away to hillsides and grassy plains. Batteries of heavy guns that had been built and put into place by slave labor sat atop all of the bluffs. Last summer, Adm. David Farragut's naval forces had proved inadequate to subdue the city. Cannon fire from the ships had trouble hitting their targets. Cannonballs either fell short of the Confederate batteries or went clear over them, destroying civilians' homes. At the same time, the Confederate artillery was able to shoot their guns downward, destroying some boats and setting others ablaze. Farragut was quoted as saying, "It's a sad thing to think of your ship on a mud bank, five hundred miles away from the natural element of a sailor."

Thus it was left to Gen. Ulysses S. Grant and his army to conquer the Confederacy's river bastion. The Rebel troops in the city, under the command of Gen. John C. Pemberton, had been outnumbered by Grant's Federal forces, but two attempts to seize the city had failed tragically. The Rebels had killed and wounded thousands of Union soldiers while losing only a few hundred of their own. Blue-coated soldiers, trying to climb the steep, torturous precipice, had run headlong into a deadly hail of cannonballs, volley after volley of withering musket fire, and fire grenades tossed down onto them from the fortifications above. In the end, the earth was strewn with Union soldiers, dead, dying, and in all manner of distress. Grant had the manpower, but Pemberton's position was nearly invincible. It appeared that attacking and capturing Vicksburg, if it was possible at all, was going to be done only at a dreadful cost of human life. There seemed to be a very good chance that the Harris brothers and their comrades would be part of the next wave of soldiers to attempt charging up that deadly ridge.

In one pocket Sam carried a gold pocket watch–sized locket that contained a picture of Dora. In another pocket there was a small piece of tan printed material, rolled up and tied with a cord. Sewn to the inside of the soft cotton roll was a square piece of green paisley that had been carefully cut from Dora's robe. Next to it was another piece of red-and-black cotton material that had been cut from Frank's little robe. These mementos of Sam's former life had been an early Christmas gift from Dora, given to him at Camp Pope just a few days before his regiment had left Iowa City. "This is so you can always feel close to us," Dora had said. It was too dark for him to look at either the locket or the soft materials, so he touched each of them with his hand, then closed his eyes and visualized the faces of his wife and baby boy. It had been exactly 165 days since Sam had actually seen his family. He conjured up his best recollection of how beautiful his bride's face had looked in the firelight on the night of their wedding. He tried to remember how soft her lips had felt on that wonderful evening, which now seemed another lifetime away.

The mental images he was attempting to visualize were suddenly interrupted when a sick soldier rushed past him on the way to one of the ship's railings. Several soldiers in Sam's Company B had come down with the measles in the last few weeks. He assumed that the rocking of the ship was causing those men a much greater degree of discomfort than the others. His brother began to snore, so Sam reached out and took hold of his shoulder. Then Sam took his hand away. Since he wasn't even trying to sleep, what was the difference? Sam closed his eyes again and reflected on that summer afternoon when he and Dora were tossing their laughing baby back and forth between each other in the family's swimming hole at the Little Nemaha. He remembered how Dora had won over the hearts of Sam's family almost immediately. His sisters and parents had taken her in as one of their own. J.A. enjoyed kidding and flirting with his brother's beautiful wife while young William, though more circumspect in his actions, was caught gazing dreamily at his sister-in-law on more than one occasion.

Twenty-two-year-old William was eight years younger than Sam but still one year older than Dora. In Old Testament teachings, if one brother died, another was to take the departed brother's wife. With the extreme danger lying just ahead of him, Sam wondered if there was a possibility of that very occurrence. She was so young and vibrant. If he did lose his life in the war, he couldn't even imagine his Dora spending her life as a grieving widow. Nor would he have wanted that kind of life for her.

While Sam was still stationed at Camp Pope, Dora had told him about making friends with a young former slave who was traveling toward Canada. Upon hearing the stories of the girl's hardships, Dora became outraged and was an instant convert to her cause. The woman's owner had run into financial difficulties a few years previous and had sold her alone to one slave owner, then sold her parents, brothers, and sisters to various other slave owners. The Railroad was not quite as far underground nor as dangerous as it had been before the war, and knowing his wife's nature, Sam was sure that she would not be wasting her time away while he was off fighting the war.

Sam still felt no signs of drowsiness. He ran his hand up and down the polished barrel of his rifle. Up until now, it had not been fired even once in the line of duty. It had been only a few days since the men in his company had been complaining that they had enlisted to fight, not sit and wait. Now, it looked like they would more than get their wish. It wasn't as if the regiment had not suffered losses. In fact, they had lost as many men from sickness and disease as many regiments had lost in battle.

Sam remembered the day he had joined the Fortieth Iowa Infantry, in late August of '62. He had been officially mustered into the service of the United States on the fifteenth of November, then spent more than a month at Camp Pope while both officers and enlisted men acquainted themselves with the practical duties of being a soldier. After leaving Camp Pope, the regiment spent several months in Columbus, Kentucky. This former Rebel stronghold had been in the quiet possession of Union troops for many months but was now threatened, it was supposed, by attack from the rebel, General Forrest. Here they remained throughout the winter, suffering through alarms of an attack night after night, without ever seeing one Confederate soldier. The weather was most disagreeable to men accustomed to the colder but dryer climate of Iowa. It was mud yesterday and snow today, mud today and snow yesterday, with a probability of both tomorrow. Cold, wet, and sleety nights were sandwiched in between the days. Men sometimes had to stand shivering in knee-deep water for many long hours. The only shelter the soldiers had for sleeping was their dog tents. Few were prepared for the hardships and exposure they had to endure. Many contracted diseases, and many died. It was a time of gloom for both officers and enlisted men. When orders came to move, they were received by the men with inexpressible delight.

Finally, on the third of March, the regiment boarded a steamship and traveled seventy-five miles above Columbus to the town of Paducah. Paducah was the most important commercial center between Louisville and Memphis, with all of the blessings that could be provided by civilization and a polite society. It contained churches, stores, saloons, and billiard parlors. Here the regiment was treated to every comfort and convenience that a man could want. The soldiers were entertained by the city's elite. After their ordeal in Columbus, many felt like they had escaped from Hell and entered through the gates of Heaven. However, misery and hardship were soon replaced by guilt. The newspaper in Paducah covered all major conflicts between the North and South and gave accounts of the thousands upon thousands of casualties on both sides. Men asked, "Why are my friends and brothers from Iowa fighting and dying while I'm here enjoying all these comforts? Is this any way to fight a war?"

Well, I guess we have our answer, Sam thought. Less than three months from the time they arrived in Paducah, their regiment was steaming down the Mississippi River on an assignment that could prove to be the worst bloodbath that the North would have to endure during the War of the Rebellion.

When Sam opened his eyes the next morning, he could see soldiers already lined up and waiting for their breakfast at the ship's galley. He poured a little water from his canteen onto his hands, splashed it on his face, then smoothed his hair back with his wet hands. That would be all of the grooming he'd be able to do under the circumstances.

Sam's brother J.A. and Amos Rayburn, their close friend since the day they all arrived at Camp Pope, were saving a place in the breakfast line for Sam. "Good morning, gentlemen." Sam said, and nodded his thanks to the man in back of them, who stepped back to let him in. "What do you think they'll be serving for breakfast this morning?"

The two men laughed. The only breakfasts that they had been served since leaving Paducah were some hardtack, one green apple, and all the coffee a man could drink.

"We might wish we were still eating this kind of breakfast within the next few weeks," J.A. commented.

"I wouldn't be surprised," Sam replied.

Sam looked at his brother and his friend Amos and knew beyond any doubt that he couldn't pick any other men he would feel more comfortable fighting alongside than these two. Other than his parents, who always used their children's given names, no one had addressed James Agnew by his full name since his younger sisters, unable to pronounce "Agnew," eventually shortened it to the easier to say "J.A." Sam's younger brother's features favored his mother's side of the family. He had the McKee reddish blond hair, light blue eyes, and a light complexion that contrasted with the Harrises' dark, swarthy skin. His muscular body, Irish-looking face, and agile movements made public to everyone that he was a fighter. Since he'd entered his teens, he had always been eager to challenge anyone who wasn't convinced of his manhood to a good old-fashioned brawl. This included his older and bigger brothers.

Amos was a tall, loose-jointed Iowa farmer, transplanted from New England. He constantly looked as if he were about to break out laughing. He spoke with a nasal twang and pronounced certain words altogether differently from most of the regiment. An idea was often an "idear," cows were "caows," and a horse was a "hoss." He also had favorite phrases, including "twan't so," and "do tell." Amos had worked on his vocabulary, and his New England accent was hardly noticeable at certain times, then it would spring up suddenly when he was excited. Sam was aware that many people thought that the Harris family's manner of speech was rather queer, too. He remembered the time when Joanna was a little girl and she had gotten into an argument with one of her girlfriends when she proudly told the other child that she had clum a cherry tree. Her friend corrected her in a reproving manner, saying, "You mean you clim the tree." They squabbled for some time as to which one was correct, until they found out that they both were wrong.

People often underestimated Amos's intelligence as well as his toughness. During drills at Camp Pope and during the trying ordeal near Columbus, he had demonstrated that he was lacking in neither. Once, when a soldier near Amos collapsed with a high fever, he carried the man for over two miles to their camp hospital, which very likely saved the young fellow's life. Amos Rayburn didn't own a repeater rifle, but he could fire his musket with deadly accuracy, then reload it and fire again as fast as any man in Company B. If it was in any way possible, when they went into battle Sam intended to stay just as close to his brother and his friend Amos as he possibly could.

On the evening of June 3, the officers and men in the Fortieth Iowa were experiencing various states of stress and anxiety. Their ship was nearing Vicksburg, and the booming of artillery fire could be heard in the distance. A rumor had started among the men that the ship's captain was planning to steam right past Vicksburg under the fire of cannon and artillery, then disembark on down the river. Sam discarded that idea as impractical, but his stomach was churning just the same. The steamship passed Chickasaw Bluffs, rounded Milliken's Bend, and proceeded toward Vicksburg. As far as anyone knew, there were no remaining docks where a boat could be moored before Vicksburg itself. The sounds of the battle were growing louder and louder. Sam wished now that he had talked to one of his superior officers before rejecting the possibility that the ship might actually come under fire before they had even docked.

When the ship reached the mouth of the Yazoo River, it made a wide turn north and east and started up the *River of Death*, away from Vicksburg. Everyone breathed a sigh of relief, but they all knew that this was only a temporary reprieve. They would be in harm's way very soon. The decks of the ship were unusually quiet that night. The sound of snoring that Sam had become accustomed to was absent. The Yazoo River became more and more narrow until some wondered if the boat's steam-powered screws might dig into the river bottom and leave them stranded. Just before dawn, when it looked like the ship had become too big for the body of water it was on, it slipped into a dock.

Their boat trip had ended before dawn on the fourth of June at the town of Satartia. If the regiment was to travel any farther up the Yazoo River, it would have to be done on foot. The troops disembarked and in light fighting trim began their march toward Mechanicsville, a few miles away. The regiment had received orders to reinforce General Kimball's troops, who were now in a bitter struggle against the Rebels fighting under Wirt Adams. Artillery fire up ahead sounded much louder than what they had heard from the ship. Every mile along the way was strewn with wagon wrecks and half-buried guns. A few dead Rebel soldiers were scattered here and there where they had fallen or where they had crawled behind logs or tree stumps to die. By this time, the war did not appear at all glamorous, even to the youngest soldiers who had been the most eager to go into battle.

Sgt. Joseph Klinker barked orders at the top of his lungs right into J.A.'s ear as the troops marched up a long hill toward the battleground.

Sergeant Klinker's brother, John, was marching in front of J.A. When the sergeant was out of earshot, John said, "Don't mind him. He yelled at me all the time while I was growing up. He doesn't know how to talk any other way."

As the columns passed continuing signs of the battle that had recently been fought, J.A. said, "I find this amazing."

"You mean all of the death and destruction?" Sam asked.

"Of course what we're looking at is ghastly. Even though these dead men are our enemy, they are someone's sons, husbands, or brothers. I take no joy in what I'm seeing, but that isn't what I was talking about. What I meant was, isn't it remarkable that all of these

Iowa men we are with, who are each such strong individuals, accustomed to acting on their own impulses, would so completely subordinate their wills to the will of other men, to the point of marching to their possible death?"

Sam kept marching with his eyes straight ahead as he replied, "I understand what you're saying, J.A., but it has to be that way if we intend to stay alive for the rest of this day. The only difference between an angry mob and an army is discipline."

Amos, who was marching between the two brothers, looked nonplussed. "Here we all are marching into a battle that we well mightn't survive, and you two are trying to figure out what makes our clocks tick. If you want my slant on it, I regard you both to be daft in the head."

J.A. grinned at his friend's homespun logic. "The Harrises are a strange breed, Amos."

"Do tell!" Amos said.

"Did you see that dead cow over there?" J.A. asked.

"I think that might be what they call graveside humor," Sam said.

"It's better than crying," J.A. added.

Everyone became silent as they approached the crest of the hill. When the Fortieth emerged onto open ground upon the hilltop, they were greeted by loud cheers from the Union brigade just ahead. The enemy was already in retreat.

Before anyone had time to count their blessings, a Rebel battery covering their withdrawal fired on them.

"Take cover!" one of the officers screamed as explosions erupted all around them.

Sam, J.A., and Amos ran and dived behind a ridge just as a nearby explosion sprinkled earth all over them. They stayed low as more shells whistled over their heads; then they heard an even louder roar as the Union artillery begin to answer the enemies' fire. Within a few minutes it was all over.

The troops were told to remain where they were until receiving further orders, while Lieutenant Colonel Cooper took a member of his staff and went off to find General Kimball.

"You boys think that we're going to chase after them?" Amos asked.

"We'll just have to wait and see," Sam said.

Two soldiers stood up from behind an overturned wagon a few feet away and walked over to meet them.

"Glad to see you fellows," one of the men said, extending a large dirty hand. His hand wasn't the only thing that was dirty. His clothes were filthy, and his eyelids were the only part of his face that wasn't completely smeared with soot. "We heard that the Fortieth Iowa was coming in to help us. Is that who you are?"

"That's so," Amos said.

"We're with the Twentieth Ohio," the smaller man said. "Welcome to Hell."

The big man couldn't help observing the difference between the grimy way he and his friend looked, contrasted with the relatively clean appearance of the new arrivals. He said, "Enjoy being clean while you can, men. In a few days you'll look as bad as we do."

"We spent last winter in the mud at Columbus," Sam said. "We know what it's like to be dirty. We've been reading in the newspapers what a fierce struggle you men have been through."

"I don't think there's any way they can capture in print the horror of actually being here," the big man said. "In the battle of Champions Hill alone, we lost more than twenty-four hundred soldiers, and the Rebs lost over thirty-eight hundred. When you just hear the numbers it lacks the impact that it has when you look out across the scene of the carnage." The man's eyes stared off into space. "Fields littered with the bodies of your friends and, even worse, ones that are mortally wounded, shrieking in pain and crying out for their mothers or their wives. From a distance, the ground takes on a singular crawling effect. People who a few minutes ago had been standing right next to you have lost legs, and, and . . ." His eyes focused on them again. Sam appeared to be shocked; J.A. looked like he was sick to his stomach. Amos's face had turned almost white. "I'm sorry, men; I didn't mean to sound so dispirited. When you've witnessed something like that, it's difficult to wash it out of your mind. Let's hope that the worst of the battle is over."

The smaller Ohioan said, "It looks like we're going to be waiting here for a while; why don't we build a fire and make some coffee?"

Kindling wood was gathered from a thicket and a fire started. The smaller of the two men had some coffee in his haversack, and the newcomers supplied the coffee water from their canteens. For the next couple of hours the men from Ohio gave the new men

172

some tips on how to survive in this country. The most important instruction came from the bigger man: "Don't drink the water from the Yazoo; it can kill you."

"How will we quench our thirst?" J.A. asked him.

"Try to get along on your daily allotment of water, but if that isn't enough for you, then you have a problem. You can chew on green plants, catch rainwater, if there's any rain, take canteens off of dead Rebel soldiers, or just go thirsty, but don't drink Yazoo water unless you want to be buried out here."

Finally, Sergeant Klinker walked up to a clearing about fifty yards in front of them and called out for the soldiers to gather around him. Men from the Fortieth Iowa and the Twentieth Ohio and a couple of soldiers from the Twenty-fourth Indiana soon formed a circle around the sergeant.

"Where is the rest of your regiment?" the big Ohio soldier asked a young Indiana lad.

"Out there," the man said, and pointed to a hill in the distance where they could just barely see the blue-coated bodies of men lying on the ground.

"I truly express my condolences," the Ohio soldier said.

Once the soldiers were all gathered together, the sergeant began, "We're going to set up camp down this hill, by the thicket, at least for today and tonight. The Rebels that you men saw retreating look to be heading toward Vicksburg. That's just where General Grant wants them to be. After our forces chase the last of them into that area, he aims to completely surround the town and cut off all food, supplies, and ammunition. They'll be trapped, where even a rabbit couldn't sneak in or out. We have another problem, albeit. General Joseph Johnston is reported to be raising an army of up to forty thousand men outside of Jackson. General Grant's biggest fear, I'm hearing, is that the Confederate general will make an attempt to rescue Pemberton's troops from Vicksburg, once we have them pinned down. For that reason, he wants what he described as a second line of defense facing the other way to stave off any attack from the rear. Now you men know as much as I know. Let's go down the hill and break camp."

"We're supposed to stop forty thousand troops?" the smaller Ohioan declared. "I hardly think so. Maybe slow them down long enough to step over our dead bodies."

By late that afternoon a huge camp had been set up in a clearing near a grove of trees. Tents stretched along the ground for hundreds of yards. At sunset, there were fires in front of almost every tent. The smell of coffee, bacon, and other foods permeated the atmosphere. Sam, J.A., and Amos sat on the ground and ate bacon, beans, and hardtack and drank coffee made from the water left in their canteens. When they were finished eating, J.A. excused himself to go behind a tree and take care of business, partly brought on by the daily ingestion of too many beans.

"Whatta you think about what that Ohio man told us about the Yazoo River water being pizon?" Amos asked.

"I'm sure it's true!" J.A. called out. "I just didn't know what we're going to do if it's a choice between drinking from the river or dying of thirst."

"I've read somewhere that people who live in areas where there is bad water eventually get used to it," Sam said.

"How you gonna do that?" Amos asked.

"I hope we don't have to, but if we do, maybe by just taking one or two sips of river water a day, it would be less of a shock to our systems."

J.A. walked back up to the fire carrying a couple of logs he'd picked up in the woods. "I think our regiment is cursed," he said while placing the logs on the fire. "If we're not getting sick from exposure, we're put into a place where the water is poison."

"I'm just happy we're not preparing to charge up some hill trying to get into Vicksburg," Sam said.

"That could still come later," J.A. said.

"What do you hear from your wife and kids?" Sam asked Amos.

"I gotta letter before we left Paducah. My oldest boy is getting to be quite a help to his mama, planting taters and vegetables. Even butchered himself a hog a few weeks ago. Prices are so dear back home, any food they can grow on the farm keeps them from going hungry."

"Dora said the same thing in her last letter. Sugar and coffee are the hardest items to get and the most expensive if you're lucky enough to find them."

"When's your wife's new baby due?" Amos asked.

"She thinks it will be sometime around August."

J.A. raised his eyebrows. "You left in late December and the baby is due in August?"

"That's right."

"You two must have had a good time on those cold nights at Camp Pope during the Christmas season."

"I won't deny that. I noticed that you were getting quite a few letters before we left Paducah and you haven't shown any of them to me. Does the family like you best, or is there a certain woman in your life?"

J.A. reached back and stuck his head down into his knapsack. Sam and Amos waited in anticipation of being handed a letter. What came out of the pack was even better. J.A. held up three long dark cigars. Sam handed J.A. his metal cigar pick, and he pierced the ends and passed them out.

Sam picked up a twig and held it to the fire until there was a flame. He lit his own cigar, handed the blazing piece of kindling to Amos, and said, "Thanks for the smoke, J.A., but I still want to hear if you had been wooing some young lady before we left."

"Are you asking me about *a lady* or *some ladies*?"

"Don't brag, little brother."

"OK, then, I'll just stick to the particulars. There is this girl, Esther, she has the most beautiful brown eyes you've ever seen. Then I met this other girl named Lina." He paused and rubbed his chin. "Lucy, I don't want to forget to mention Lucy, she has a form that is really quite spectacular. Also, there is a quite attractive young lady named Lina. Then there is Claire. Claire is just about as pretty a little girl that you're going to find anywhere." J.A. stopped and took a couple of puffs from his cigar. "Did I mention anything about this extraordinary young woman I met named Lina?"

"The name does sound familiar," Sam said. "Tell us more about Lina."

"I've known her ever since she was a little girl, and I've always thought she was very comely, but much too young for me. A few months ago, I went into Mr. Scott's dry-goods store on Main Street and this beautiful red-haired clerk walked up to wait on me. She kissed me on the cheek and said, 'Don't you even remember me, J.A.?' I took a closer look and said, 'You're not little Lina, are you?' She laughed and said, 'I am that one of whom you speak.' Before I left the store, she said that she had been enamoured with me since she

175

was a little girl. Can you imagine? I still thought she was too young for me, but Father told me to ignore our age difference. It might have been the best advice I've ever received."

"Ah, that's the young redhead who came to visit you at Camp Cook," Sam said. "She is *very* nice."

"How old is she?" Amos asked.

"She's sixteen."

"Seven years' age difference," Sam said. "I'm nine years older than Dora."

"I noticed that. It was quite heartening to me when you brought home a younger girl."

Sam took a long stick and stirred the fire until more flames erupted. "Did you make any long-range arrangements with Lina before we left?"

"That's an interesting question. We had talked about how close we had become, but we didn't say anything about spending the rest of our lives together until I got to Camp Pope and realized how much I missed her."

"You're pretty good at keeping a secret," Sam said.

"Not so much. We've just progressed to this point during our last few exchanges of letters."

"It happens," Amos said.

The next morning the bugle boy woke them up early and they were told to gather up all of their gear and get ready for another march. Two days later they reached Haines' Bluff, where they remained for a week. After that, they marched three miles farther to Snyder's Bluff, and there they set up a permanent camp. The following day, they began digging trenches and building fortifications to hold off the anticipated attack from General Johnston's army. Newspapers both in the North and South were now trying to guess at what point Johnston would bring his vast army against Grant's rear guard and attempt to rescue the beleaguered garrison of Vicksburg. Some members of the press from Southern cities were already beginning to chastise Johnston for taking so long.

18

July 2, 1863

Sam threw the last shovelful of dirt over his shoulder, climbed out of the last neatly dug trench, and wiped the sweat off of his forehead. J.A. and Amos, who had just climbed out of the trench seconds before, were already sitting wearily in the shade of an old elm tree. It seemed like the Mississippi sun was getting hotter every day. Sam took a sip of water from his canteen and slowly let it cool his dry throat. He still had about half a canteen full of water, and the sun was beginning to dip in the west. He liked to preserve as much water as he could during the day, so that he never had to go to bed thirsty. The advice that they had received about the poisonous effects of the Yazoo had been correct. In spite of warnings from their commanding officer, close to a third of the men from their regiment had drunk from the river. Those soldiers were now either sick in camp or had been transported to the hospital boat *Red Rover,* which was docked near Chickasaw Bluffs over on the Mississippi River.

Sam turned and looked in the direction of Vicksburg. His ears had become so accustomed to the constant boom of Grant's artillery that he heard it only when he actually thought about it.

Members of the Fortieth Iowa had worked with shovels, hammers, and saws in the weeks since the day they had set up camp, but their guns had never been more than a few feet away. Barriers, trenches, and other fortifications that they and other members of their regiment had been working on were finally completed, which, it turned out, was none too soon. Just yesterday, one of their scouts had reported that General Johnston had moved his troops and artillery to within just a few miles of the Union lines.

Shortly after the Fortieth Iowa had set up their encampment along the Yazoo River, below Snyder's Bluff, General Grant detached three divisions, under the command of General Sherman, to help guard against General Johnston's expected attack.

Just as he had planned to do, General Grant now had Pemberton's and his Rebel army completely surrounded in Vicksburg. The Confederate Army inside the city was cut off from all supplies and communications. Federal troops, however, were not only enjoying the requirements for their basic needs; they were also reading reports about the siege of Vicksburg from a variety of newspapers that were brought into their camps. The consensus among newsmen from all over the world was that the army that won the battle at Vicksburg would eventually win the war. For that reason, most Federal soldiers were convinced that what they were doing right now would be the most important thing they would do in their entire lives.

One piece of information that Grant, Sherman, and Pemberton lacked was exactly when General Johnston was going to attack the Federal Army's rear guard. For the two Federal generals, the only thing they could was just dig in and wait. The Rebel leader faced a more troublesome problem. For Pemberton to coordinate his strategy with Johnston's, he had to know when Johnston's attack would begin. Rebel couriers had been sent out repeatedly by Johnston. Some tried to cross Federal lines through gullies and woodlands. All of them were apprehended. The Rebels had to come up with some other way of skirting the Federal pickets.

After resting in the shade for a while, J.A. stood to his feet and asked, "Are you men about ready to cool off?"

As Amos pushed himself back up to a standing position, he groaned and said, "My bones hurt."

Sam said, "Hey, I don't want to hear any complaining. I'm older than either of you two boys."

The three men walked down the short hill to the river. Trees and green shrubbery lined the shore of the Yazoo, with small sandy beaches in different spots along the river's edge. The beach where they stopped was larger than most. It had a few rocks big enough to sit on and a fire ring several feet above the shoreline. The water was deeper and the current slower at this spot. Locals had obviously used this place for picnics and swimming during more peaceful times.

They laid their guns and knapsacks up by the rocks. J.A. pulled a bar of soap out of his pocket, and with much whooping and hollering the men jumped into the river, clothes and all. After they all had splashed around for a while, J.A. soaped up his hair, face, and neck, plunged under the water to rinse off, then held out the soap: "Who's next?"

Amos took the soap bar and went through the same procedure. Within their first few days at camp, the men had decided that on working days it was best to wash clothes and bodies all at the same time. When all three had washed up as best they could, they stood chest-deep enjoying the cool water and the shade of an overhanging tree.

"I'd like to ask you both a question," Sam said. "If you were on General Johnston's staff of officers, what would be your most important consideration right now?"

"To let General Pemberton in on my plans," J.A. said.

"But, at least as far as we know, every courier that has been sent out has been caught. What are you going to do now?"

J.A. nodded. "You can stop right now. I've been thinking the same thing myself."

Amos looked perplexed. "Excuse me. You brothers might be able to read each other's minds, but I can't. What are we talking about?"

Sam replied, "Amos, you remember this morning when Sergeant Klinker told us that they had captured another courier and that the man had confessed that, to his knowledge, not one of them had made it through to Vicksburg in over a month?"

"Of course, I remember."

"Then put yourself in Johnston's place. You know how desperately he needs to communicate with Pemberton. Since all else has failed, how are you going to get a courier through our lines and into Vicksburg?"

Amos only needed a few seconds to consider the options. "I would send a man in a canoe down the Yazoo to the Mississippi, then downriver into the port of Vicksburg."

"Exactly, and you would do it as soon as possible, since Pemberton is running out of time."

Sam looked back and forth between his brother and his friend. "As far as I'm concerned, it's going to be bad enough just being here on the front line when Johnston attacks. I would like to think that Pemberton won't know when it's happening. That way Grant can bring up reinforcements for us without being under attack from Vicksburg."

Sam walked out of the water, took a towel from his knapsack, and began drying off his face and hair. "Colonel Cooper has a lot on his mind right now. He might agree with us or he might not. However, there would be no reason for him to object to us moving our bedrolls to a cooler spot down by the river. If we just happen to catch a courier trying to sneak down the river, I'm certain that he would be most pleased about that, too."

After supper, the three men hung around their tent for a while, then, with about an hour of daylight left, started toward the river. Each of them carried a bedroll, knapsack, rifle, and lantern. Pistols were stuck in each of their belts.

Sergeant Klinker came out of his tent and yelled, "Where are you men going?"

"We're going to find a cooler place to sleep!" Amos called back as the men kept walking.

"Well, look out for the alligators," Klinker said, and went back into his tent.

"What did he mean by that?" Amos asked.

"I think he was just trying to be funny," J.A. said.

When they got to the river, Sam said. "I'm going to get a boat. I'll be back in about fifteen minutes."

"Do you know what this is all about?" Amos asked J.A.

"He's going to get that old rowboat we saw at the dock up the river."

"I figured that out, but why?"

"I'm not sure, but you can bet that he has a reason."

It was just getting to be twilight when Sam rowed up onto the beach.

Amos asked, "Would you like to share your plan with us?"

"Sure, of course. I've been thinking about how hard it will be to see a small canoe or rowboat once it gets dark, especially if we're out here for a few nights. I figure that if we have a man over there"—he pointed to a small beach about thirty yards upriver on the other side—"with his lantern lit and his rifle in sight, anyone who wants to stay undetected will stay close to this shore."

"Also, a courier would have to pass between whoever we have on this side of the river and our light," J.A., added. "I like that idea. Who is going to be the decoy?"

"We can trade off," Sam suggested.

Amos picked up a dry twig, broke it into three pieces, and said, "Let's draw straws."

J.A. got the shortest piece, gathered up his gear, and rowed across the river.

Sam and Amos took turns watching the river and unsuccessfully trying to sleep. No canoe or boat came down the river.

In the morning they gathered up their gear and headed back to their tent before the bugle boy blew reveille. J.A. had enjoyed a good night's sleep and appeared alert. Sam and Amos had hardly slept at all. Their eyelids were drooping, and their speech sounded listless. Fortunately, with the fortifications completed, they were given some time off in the afternoon to rest. It was the first day, with the exception of Sundays, that the regiment had not put in a hard day's work.

That night, Amos set up across the river and Sam and J.A. took up their watch. J.A. took the first watch, and weariness finally caught up with Sam and he fell asleep. At a little after one in the morning, he woke up and told his brother he would take watch for a while. This night was as calm and uneventful as the previous one. About two-thirty in the morning, Sam was sleepily trying to keep his eyes focused on Amos's lantern and J.A. was squirming around in his bedroll trying to go to sleep. Finally J.A. got up and sat on the sand next to his brother. He leaned back against a rock and said, "It sure is easier to sleep when you're across the river being a decoy."

"I wouldn't know," Sam replied.

"Tell me, Sam, is this the most stupid thing we've ever done?"

"I'm beginning to wonder that same thing myself."

They sat silently for several minutes; then Sam said, "I think it might be better if we never mentioned the real reason we're down here."

J.A. didn't answer.

"It *is* cooler by the water."

It was too dark for Sam to see his brother's face, but he began hearing his deep, steady breathing. "Thanks for getting up and keeping me company."

Sam fought off sleep, first by eating a green apple, then by trying to recall dangerous or stimulating events in his past. Next he tried remaining alert by doing some push-ups and deep knee bends.

It was sometime after three when he heard the sound of a paddle moving through the water. His drowsiness immediately left.

Although neither Sam's voice nor his exercising had interrupted J.A.'s sleep, this slightest of sounds stimulated him to immediate consciousness. "Did you hear that?" he whispered.

Sam rose quietly to his feet and stared intently toward the lantern and its reflection on the water. When the bow of the canoe cut across the lantern's reflection, it was within ten feet of Sam. He waited for the canoe to get just a few feet closer; then he took two quick strides into the water and plunged headfirst at the dark form in the canoe.

The boy in the canoe screamed, J.A. charged into the water behind his brother, Amos yelled from across the river, and the empty canoe proceeded down the Yazoo River toward the Mississippi.

Lamps were already being lit up in the camp, and men's excited voices were chattering when Sam dragged the frightened youngster up onto the beach. J.A. lit his lantern at the same time Amos was pushing the rowboat away from the opposite shore.

Instead of the gray uniform of a Rebel soldier, the boy was wearing blue overalls and a black wool coat. "I'm so . . . I'm real pleased!" the boy stammered.

"What are you talking about?" Sam demanded. "What's so good about being taken prisoner?"

"When I heard you a-comin', I thought a gator had got me for sure."

"There are no alligators around here."

"Yes, suh, my capt'n tol' me thar was. Said to look out for 'em."

"What's a boy your age doing trying to carry a message through enemy lines? Don't you know how dangerous this is?"

"Our army's got a lotta boys in it, and some grandpas, too."

"That gives me no pleasure knowing that some of the soldiers I'm going to be killing are boys and old men. How old are you?"

"I'm almost fourteen."

Sam put his hand on the lad's shoulder. "Listen to me, son, You're a prisoner of war now. You're neither going to be killing anyone nor are you going to get killed. When the war is over, you'll be going home to your mama. Do you understand that?"

"Yes, suh. I understand, suh."

"Now what was the message that you were going to deliver to General Pemberton?"

The boy pulled a water-soaked scroll out of his coat pocket and handed it to Sam. Sam read it out loud. " 'I'll be launching my attack—at most three days, can't say exact as some messages will be intercepted. Listen for my artillery.' "

Sam rolled the scroll back up and pushed it back into the youngster's pocket. "How many of you couriers did General Johnston send out tonight?"

"Don't know, but he said enuff so's, at the least, one should get through."

19

July 4, 1863

Excitement was running rampant on this summer holiday in Grinnell. Congressman Josiah Grinnell had returned from Washington, and was scheduled to speak at the Grove during the Independence Day picnic. The hotels in town were completely sold out, much to the consternation of a certain permanent lodger at the Reed House. Josephus Eastman had been forced to sleep on a bench in his law office to make room for higher-paying overnight guests. Eastman was a Harvard graduate from New England. He was a fastidious, introspective, and quite intelligent young attorney, but none too robust. He was considered by many in Grinnell to be too much of a hothouse plant to be part of such a pioneer community. His aloofness, however, seemed to give his legal advice more objectivity, resulting in a law practice that was wholly lucrative.

Grinnell had taken a liking to Eastman and on this hot day in July had called on him at his office. When the young man recounted this grievous incident at the hotel, the congressman shocked him by taking off his coat and stretching out on his back on the floor of the piazza in front of the law office. Eastman was heard to comment, "That is western style, but rather a dirty place after all."

Josiah Grinnell was still a young man, by congressional standards, and many other members of the House considered him to be less reserved than was befitting a member of their elite fraternity. Nevertheless, his fellow congressmen were well aware that this representative from Iowa was a confidant of Abraham Lincoln. Grinnell's uncompromising dedication to the causes he believed in, plus his faithful support of the harassed and long-suffering president, had put him in good standing with the current administration. However, Grinnell was not in total agreement with Lincoln on all issues. On the matters of railway expansion and the vigorous prosecution of the war, Grinnell was very much at one with the president. The congressman felt that he was more concerned with the political and social equality of the Negro than Lincoln and did not share the president's spirit of mercy and charity for the South.

One piece of the legislation that Grinnell had introduced early in this session was a bill encouraging the enlistment of Negroes in the Northern armies. Another was an income tax designed to make the rich bear a fuller burden for the war. His bill suggested a tax as high as 10 percent on those making over $10,000 a year. He also proposed a tariff on whiskey, arguing that the grain was needed to feed the soldiers and that whiskey had a demoralizing effect on our troops. Not surprisingly, this Iowa congressman and former Congregationalist minister was considered a dangerous radical by many of his fellow members of the House, especially those on the other side of the aisle.

The need for relaxation oftentimes took Lincoln to the theater. He frequently requested the company of his young friend Grinnell at these events. After one of those performances Lincoln remarked, "What did you think, Grinnell, was the best thing there tonight? I'll tell you what convulsed me." Coming from behind his desk, he raised his hand, struck an attitude of holy horror, and cried, "Lord, how this world is given to lying!" He continued, "We had some good war news yesterday, and I was glad to unbend and laugh. The acting was good, and true to the case, according to my experiences, for each fellow tells his own story and smirches his rival."

Grinnell's aggressive party spirit was held in check, somewhat, by his warm relationship with the First Family. Once, when he called on the White House carrying his written list of grievances, President Lincoln put his hand on Grinnell's shoulder and said, "Young man, forget your annoyances! They are as fleabites compared to mine! They are serious comedy, while I'm in the focus of tragedy and fire. You folks on the Hill must aid me in placating these congenital Democrats, whom we want to keep fighting for us, if we can."

Lincoln knew that it was imperative for him to maintain the support of the War Democrats, as well as the Republicans, if he was going to be able to win reelection and have any chances of bringing the war to a successful conclusion.

As newspapers nationwide reported about the Iowa congressman's emerging friendship with the president, he became a local hero for many people in northern Iowa. To some others, who disliked both Lincoln and Grinnell, it only served to increase their animosity and their opposition to everything either man stood for.

A couple hours before dusk, the Harris family arrived at the Grove and spread out their blankets and picnic baskets in the shade of a big maple tree. The spot they picked was not too far from the platform where a band was already playing patriotic songs and where Grinnell would be giving his address later in the evening. Groups of college students had already secured many of the choice spots nearest the bandstand, and crowds of people were milling around the grass, greeting friends and socializing.

Between the culinary skills of Mama Harris, her two daughters Joanna and Mary, and Dora, the picnic baskets had been packed with more food than they all could reasonably eat at one sitting. A college friend of Joanna, William Haynes, had joined the family outing. He sat on a blanket with Papa Harris, Dr. Rachael, and William. It wasn't too long before Dora noticed something curious about the young man. While he conversed with Rachael and the men, his eyes never seemed to stray far from Joanna. When she pointed out this phenomenon to her roommate, Joanna said, "He's really just a friend."

A friend who just made my sister-in-law blush, Dora observed.

Frank found some children near his own age and began running, jumping, and cavorting on the grass nearby. Two things in young Frank's life had become a great puzzle to him these days. The first was, in spite of everyone's attempts to explain where his papa was, he still couldn't understand why he didn't come home. The other was, since everyone knew that he was going to have a new brother or sister, why couldn't they tell him which one it was going to be? The children now occupying Frank's attention provided Dora and the rest of the family a respite from the child's usual myriad of questions.

William and his father were the final two men in the family who were still living at home, and it appeared that they would soon be enlisting in the army. A Graybeard Regiment was forming, and everyone knew that Papa Harris, in spite of his approaching sixtieth birthday, was very likely going to join them. The fugitive slave law was still in effect, but the slave catchers had all but disappeared when it had become apparent to them that, once the war had begun, it was virtually impossible to return captured slaves to their owners and, what was more important to these men, collect the reward money.

William, who had been studying to become a banker, had his commencement exercises at the college coming up in two days, after which he would also be free to join his brothers. It appeared that the Harris farm would soon be populated only by women.

When the family was settled, Dora and Joanna stood and looked around at the growing crowd of people. Dora had reached the point in her pregnancy where she didn't want to sit down until she intended to stay seated.

Suddenly Joanna exclaimed, "There is Aunt Polka!"

Dora looked in the direction that Joanna had indicated and saw a middle-aged Negro woman, surrounded by people who all seemed to be waiting for their turn to talk to her. Two dark-skinned children played nearby.

"This dear woman is the only escaped slave that we literally had to capture. She had witnessed such brutalities by the slave catchers that when we tried to come to her aid she ran away. She thoroughly mistrusted all white people."

Dora looked at the obviously popular woman and said, "It looks like she trusts the townspeople now."

"People in Iowa are the only white people she trusts. Once she realized that we actually wanted to help her and her two remaining children, she wouldn't leave. Until the war started, we kept moving her from one home to another. Federal marshals searched more than one house, sometimes only a few hours after she had been moved. If it hadn't been for the line of communications that the Railroad had set up, she would have been captured and sent back to her owner. Everybody that got to know Aunt Polka fell in love with her."

"I can see that. You seemed surprised when you saw her."

"We haven't seen her for over a year. The last I heard about her, she was living in Keosauqua. She must have come to the picnic to hear Mr. Grinnell."

"What do you mean by her 'remaining children'?"

"Oh, Dora, it's such a tragic story. Are you sure you want to hear it?"

"There are too many dreadful events befalling us these days, but ignorance is never bliss. Tell me what happened."

"Aunt Polka was a slave in Mississippi who had a very cruel and abusive owner. When she ran away, she took fourteen children, and only one bag of cornpone to feed them. She knew that Canada was to the north but had no idea of the great distance that she would have to travel to reach freedom. She left two boys and two girls with Negro families along the way. She buried eight of her other children before she reached Iowa. Some died from hunger, others from exposure or illness."

"How can anyone abide slavery?" Dora declared.

Joanna took Dora's hand and led her over to Aunt Polka's blanket. They waited patiently for their turn to talk her, and when there was an opening, Joanna introduced her sister-in-law to the smiling woman. Before either Joanna or Dora was able to engage Aunt Polka in conversation, others arrived who also sought her attention.

As they walked away, Joanna said, "I hope that sometime I can get you alone with her. She'll talk your leg off, but her stories are fascinating."

When it was near dusk, Mama Harris announced it was time to eat. The contents of the picnic baskets were handed out, Papa Harris said grace, and the feast began. While everyone was eating, the sky changed from blue, to orange, to black.

Lamps were lit, and women proudly brought out their carefully prepared desserts. Chocolate cake seemed to be the dessert of choice on this holiday, and almost every group at the Grove was displaying at least one of them. Dora had made herself as comfortable as possible, with a pillow underneath her and her back up against the trunk of the maple tree, as she tried to balance her cup of coffee and her slice of cake.

A big orange moon peeked up from the east just before the program started. Congressman Grinnell had waited until he saw people beginning to eat dessert before he walked up onto the lighted bandstand. It wasn't necessary for him to ask for everyone's attention or to even raise his hand. The second he stepped up to the podium, conversations stopped and all eyes turned in his direction. "My good friends," he began, "I want to thank all of the local townspeople for coming today, as well as those who have traveled from other towns to help us celebrate this day that commemorates the birth of our great nation. A nation that is now being threatened by forces that would tear our country asunder. I am here to tell you today that these Rebels will not be successful." A loud cheer arose from the crowd. "Before I give you information from some of the battlefronts, I've got some other exciting news to tell you. The Rock Island Railroad is now laying the last stretch of tracks that will lead right into our town. It's a good day for us. The rails will soon bear the steam engine and cars directly into our village." He raised both fists into the air and shouted, "Hurrah! Hurrah! The distance from New York, via Pittsburgh, is eleven hundred ninety-four miles. The time that is necessary for that trip is . . ."—He paused, leaned across the podium, looked around the large crowd, and shouted, "Fifty-one hours and twenty-four minutes!" He held both hands high in the air and yelled, "What a ride on a rail that is!" The crowd jumped to their feet and gave him a well-deserved ovation. Josiah Grinnell had fought against heavy opposition from some who thought that the railroad would not benefit the town, and he had been instrumental in seeing that the town that he had founded was now on the Rock Island Line.

"We are now just a little over two days from New York City." Grinnell's smile faded. He stood erect and looked out over the upturned sea of faces. "The war that our country is suffering through is a most terrible thing. Still and all, we are pleased as we read in the newspapers about the victories that our boys are now achieving on many battlefields. The tide has finally turned. The question is no longer, will we win this war? But, how long will it take before the South finally surrenders?" More loud cheers and whistles filled the night air.

Neither Dora nor anyone else in the Harris family had received any letters from Sam and J.A. since they had gone to Vicksburg. They waited patiently as Grinnell recited recent victories from other battlefronts. Finally, he said, "I know that many of you have sons, husbands, and brothers who are fighting in the battle of Vicksburg. You've read in the newspapers that General Grant has the city surrounded and has been bombarding it with artillery for several weeks now. I'm told that General Pemberton and his Rebel troops are running out of food, water, and ammunition. They've started eating horses, mule meat, and you can bet that there aren't as many dogs and cats wandering around town as there once was." The last remark generated laughter among the crowd assembled.

A man from the band shouted out, "The new Rebel leader is General Starvation!" His remark was followed by the sound of a snare drum and then one loud boom from a bass drum.

189

Grinnell turned toward the band and smiled. "I liked that." He looked out over the crowd, and his expression grew more serious. "If Pemberton doesn't surrender Vicksburg to our troops in the next few days, I'm told that Grant will conduct an all-out assault on the city."

Dora felt sick to her stomach. Many people in the crowd shook their heads. One man yelled out, "If the Rebels are already running out of food and water, wouldn't it be better to just wait them out and spare all of that loss of life?"

Grinnell responded, "I'm not in disagreement with you, sir, but it's not my decision to make. We know that General Johnston is building up a force of somewhere around forty thousand Rebel troops near the city of Jackson. If Johnston comes to Pemberton's aid, our boys could be caught in the cross fire. I'm sure that General Grant will do whatever he has to do. We of Iowa have more than our share of local men fighting in that area. I want each of them home by their own hearth and fire just as soon as possible."

When Grinnell's speech was concluded, he pronounced a benediction, praying for the safe return of everyone's loved ones. Then the band played while the crowd sang patriotic songs, after which a magnificent fireworks display lit up the night sky. The evening concluded when a soldier led everyone in singing the "Marseillaise."

On the way home, Dora told Joanna that this evening had been a distinct event in her life.

July 6

The sun streaming through the upstairs bedroom window warmed Dora's face. She opened her eyes and looked at the empty pillow next to her. Joanna was already up, but Frank was still sleeping in the crib. She stretched her hands as high over her head as she could reach, then moved them out to her sides, then sighed, rolled out of bed, and looked out the window at the new day. She wondered what Sam was doing and if he was all right. She walked to the mirror and for a few moments gazed at the reflection of her protruding stomach. It appeared very unlikely that Sam would be here for the birth of their new baby.

It was Mama Harris and her daughter Mary's day to do the cooking and the kitchen chores. In the eleven months that Dora had

190

been at the Harris farm, she still hadn't become accustomed to having someone cook and clean up for her every other day. During that time, Dora had fallen completely in love with her roommate. Dora missed Mollie very much, but having Joanna around had made things so much easier. She was like Mollie in many ways yet in other ways quite different. Dora's sister-in-law had a lovely face but was smaller and less voluptuous than Mollie. Joanna was a dedicated Christian, who dragged Dora off to church on many Sundays when she might have made excuses and stayed home. Dora was certain that Joanna's motives for going to church were pure, because she seemed far less enamored with the opposite sex than her sister had been at that age. Joanna was equally as strong-minded as Mollie. When Dora had accompanied her roommate to political debates at the college, Joanna expressed her strong abolitionist views in a clear and sometimes almost indisputable manner.

Dora's thoughts were interrupted when Frank opened his eyes, saw that his mother was out of bed, and sleepily held out his arms to be lifted out of his crib.

When mother and child got to the kitchen, Mary greeted Dora with, "Good morning, Mrs. Sunshine."

"Don't you dare tease her," Mama Harris said. "Wait until you have a small child to care for and another one on the way."

"It's all right," Dora replied as she plopped Frank down into his high chair. "This little guy and his mommy slept late this morning. When Sam gets home he'll wonder why I'm so spoiled."

Mary placed a bowl of cooked oatmeal and a glass of milk in front of Frank, which quickly silenced his pounding on the tray of his high chair.

"I have bacon, eggs, biscuits, and applesauce," Mama Harris said.

"I should eat one egg and half a biscuit," Dora said, patting her stomach.

Mama Harris filled up a plate for Dora. "Nonsense, you need your strength. I have a letter for you to read when you finish your breakfast."

"Did I get a letter from Sam?"

"No, I would have given that to you the first thing. It's from your sister in Denver."

After Dora had finished eating, Mama Harris handed her the letter and said, "You go out on the porch and enjoy your letter. I'll take care of my grandson."

When Dora opened the envelope, she found that it contained both a short letter and a newspaper clipping with a note attached.

The letter read:

My Dearest Sister,

This exciting life, so full of suspense and expectations, is so hard on everyone. We have received news of a severe battle between the Texas Rangers and our boys at Pigeons Creek Ranch in New Mexico. Our men had been reinforced by General Canby and marched on to meet the Rebel forces. We have come off victorious but lost at least five men. This much and no more, and now we wait three days before finding out the killed and wounded. O! I dare not think. Could the baby I'm carrying in my womb already be without a father? Some of the women are wailing and taking on dreadfully, but I am calm and hoping for the best. I find myself here and there and everywhere, condoling with one and cheering another, when all the time I may be the bereft one. My soldier may have fallen. Pray for us as I'm praying for you and Sam.

Your loving sister,
Mollie

Dora held the newspaper clipping in her hand for a few seconds, afraid to read what it might tell, then lifted it up, and read the head-line: **VICTORY AT PIGEONS CREEK.** She quickly scanned through the description of the battle until she reached a part that had been underlined: "A turning point in the battle came when Captain Lewis and Lieutenant Byron Sanford climbed a knoll and, while under heavy enemy fire, spiked a cannon, jammed a six-pound ball into the muzzle, smashed the wheels, and set the ammunition on fire. The same two men captured several Texans, but not without the Lieutenant coming dangerously close to losing his life."

The attached note said: "At last the news has come. The killed were all single men, so no widows or orphans wail will come up from this camp tonight, but yet, they were all someone's sons and brothers. Should I be proud of By for being so heroic, or angry with him for so recklessly risking his life? He has written that he will soon resign and come home, as he can now do so with honor. I need him so much, Mollie."

Dora held the envelope on her lap and looked out across the plains. Mollie's Byron and her Sam were so alike in temperament. She wondered if Sam was somewhere charging recklessly into enemy fire and, if he was doing that, would he be so fortunate.

Her thoughts were suddenly interrupted when a rider galloped up to the front of the farmhouse and shouted, "Vicksburg has surrendered! There's a meeting in the Village at ten o'clock this morning!" Then he wheeled his horse around and galloped out the gate and down the road toward the next farm.

Dora ran into the house and grabbed her startled child out of his high chair. Papa Harris was already outside helping William hook up horses to a two-seated carriage. In minutes, the wagon carrying the Harris family was racing down the road toward town.

It seemed that the whole town was gathered on Main Street near the post office. Professor Parker, from the college, stood on a box on the piazza, holding a copy of the *Davenport Gazette* and waiting until the crowd had fully assembled. Finally, in a loud voice, he began to read, " 'Two days ago, on July fourth, General Pemberton surrendered, and General Grant's Federal troops marched triumphantly into Vicksburg.' " The professor paused until the roar of the crowd had subsided, then cleared his throat and went on reading. " 'Once there was a cessation of the hostilities, Yankee and Rebel pickets shook hands, sat down together, and exchanged coffee and hardtack for tobacco. Inside the city, Federal troops are now providing food to hungry Vicksburgers, and to Rebel soldiers. Our army has effectively cut the South in half. From this day on, neither arms nor provisions to aid Rebel forces will be moved up or down the Mississippi River.' "

Parker lowered the newspaper and said, "I dislike reading this list of names, but prolonging all of our knowing about this would only make it worse. Our town and our college have lost some brave men during the intense fighting in the last few days prior to the surrender."

Papa Harris put his arm around his wife and pulled her close to him.

Dora's knees became weak, and her face turned pale. William noticed her frightened look and took hold of her elbow. "Are you going to be all right?" he asked.

She couldn't speak, so she just nodded.

In a strong clear voice, Parker began reading the names of the men who had been lost in battle. When one of the names was read, a man in front of Mama Harris staggered like he himself had been shot. Another name was called and a woman shrieked and fell to her knees weeping. As Parker continued, cries went up from various sections of the gathering. People moved in around those in anguish and tried to comfort them. Dora felt like she couldn't breathe. William put his arm around her and, with his other hand, squeezed her elbow more tightly as the names continued to be called.

Tears were streaming down the professor's cheeks. Several college students' names were on the casualty list. Finally, mercifully, he stopped. Neither Sam nor John Agnew Harris's name had been read.

20

July 7, 1863

The hot sun beating down on their necks while they were eating breakfast warned the men of the Fortieth Iowa Infantry that today would be another scorcher. As a result of dramatic events that had taken place the last few days, the biggest problem the soldiers faced now was how to survive the blistering heat. With the cool waters of the Yazoo River close by, plus the many shade trees along the riverbanks, as well as on the outskirts of the camp, there was no reason for any soldier to be uncomfortable. After so many days of hard work building trenches and barriers, preparing for an enemy attack, their commanding officer had excused the men of the regiment from any drills today. Everyone was looking forward to finally getting some well-earned rest.

The actions that had precipitated the sudden reprieve of Grant's rear-guard troops had begun early in the morning on July 3, when a picket had warned Colonel Cooper that General Johnston's Rebel troops were on the move and that an attack on their position was imminent. Sam, J.A., and Amos Rayburn had settled into one of the trenches closest to the river. With typical Iowa ingenuity, they had constructed two wooden crossbars, placed them about ten feet apart, then placed a large head-log across the top of the crossbars. This gave them the ability to rest their rifles in the space between the top of the trench and the head-log and negated the necessity of having to raise their heads above the trench. It would be unlikely for any enemy soldiers charging toward their position even to see them, let alone have any kind of a target to shoot at.

Between the trenches and a heavily wooded area, from where the Rebel troops would likely emerge, were about three hundred yards of wheat fields and pastures. The Iowa Fortieth and the other

Federal troops stretched out along the trenches snaking out from the river, had a distinct advantage in position, if not in numbers.

Sam stood up and looked out across trench after trench, as far as the eye could see, then turned to look in the direction from where the Rebels were expected to come.

J.A. said, "If they attack our position, this won't be a battle; it will be a slaughter. These Iowa farmers are used to shooting quail, wild turkeys, and prairie chickens that are trying to run away. Today they will be shooting four or five rifle balls a minute at men who are running right toward them."

"Four or five a minute except for us," Sam said, holding up his repeater rifle. "I can't believe that any general would march his men right into the kind of firepower we have."

Amos said, "Don't be counting your chickens. Grant did exactly that at Shiloh. Got thousands of our boys killed, but they finally did overrun some enemy positions. Forty thousand troops, give or take, is a lot of men to shoot down, and I'm sure they'll be bombarding us with artillery at the same time."

Sam stared out across the field in front of them. "Thanks, Amos. I feel a lot better now."

"I just thought it t'want a good idea to get too comfortable. You seeing anything out there?"

"No, I'm just trying to think about what I would do if I was General Johnston."

"Did you come up with any answers?" J.A. asked.

"Only what I wouldn't do. Think about it. If Johnston gets his army cut to pieces overrunning our position, then he still has to get what's left of them through Grant's army if he wants to get into Vicksburg. Then what?"

"Then Grant and Sherman have *him* surrounded, too," J.A. said.

"Right," Sam cried. "Maybe that's why Johnston is taking so long to mount his attack."

Amos looked out over the long barrel of his musket toward the thicket in the distance. "You boys just keep working out Johnston's problems for him. As for me, I've got no reason to disbelieve the pickets who're telling the colonel there's a big army heading right at us."

Sam and J.A. looked at each other, then took their positions alongside Amos.

Sgt. Joseph Klinker, and his brother, John, had been walking toward them for some time, stopping to visit with each group of soldiers as they went by. They finally reached their last stop.

"At ease, men," the sergeant said as he approached. "I just want you to know what to expect next. General Johnston's artillery is within firing range of us right now, so I'd keep my head down if I were you. When they start shooting, our artillery will see the smoke from their guns and start returning their fire. When the Rebels start charging out of those trees, there is going to be one hell of a lot of them. Shoot them down as if your life depended on it, because it does." Sgt. Klinker cleared his throat. "I know that I sometimes yell louder than I should. John here will tell you that I've done it all my life."

"You've always been the noisy one," John said.

"Anyway, we were all neighbors and friends before this war started, and I hope it will be that way after it's over. John and I just came down here to wish you men God's protection in the battle today."

When the Klinker brothers had left, J.A. said, "I think he was telling us that all hell is about to break loose."

The loud and constant boom of Grant's artillery bombarding Vicksburg had seemed ominous during the men's first days in camp. Now it was hardly noticed; that is, it wasn't noticed until ten-thirty that morning, when it suddenly stopped.

"Does it seem unusually quiet to either of you?" J.A. asked.

"Grant's artillery stopped shooting," Amos replied.

Men all the way down the line of trenches were standing up and looking in the direction of Vicksburg.

About three-quarters of an hour later, a picket rode into camp saying that Johnston had called his troops to a halt when he heard Grant's artillery stop firing. After that, a stream of messages began passing back and forth between pickets along Grant's lines and the second line of defense. First the troops learned that Pemberton had suggested an armistice to Grant where they would discuss terms for the capitulation of Vicksburg. This news was greeted with loud uproar and vigorous back slapping among soldiers in the regiment. Next they learned that Grant and Pemberton were meeting at three that afternoon. In the late afternoon, a messenger rode into camp with the news that Grant had refused to negotiate anything less than unconditional surrender and that Pemberton had stormed out of the meeting. The last message brought loud groans.

That night as they were all sitting around their campfires, Colonel Cooper spread the word among his soldiers that one of Pemberton's officers, General Bowen, had succeeded in arranging a meeting between himself and some of Grant's top officers. It would be the purpose of these men to attempt to overcome the stalemate between the two commanding officers. Sam, J.A., and Amos lay down on their cots that night without knowing whether or not they would be engaged in a dreadful and bloody battle the next day.

Shortly after daybreak the next morning, a picket rode through camp yelling at the top of his lungs, "Vicksburg has surrendered! Vicksburg has surrendered!" Men ran out of their tents cheering and laughing. Cigars were passed around to the celebrating soldiers, and a more abundant breakfast than normal was prepared. Sugar, which had been in short supply, was provided for the men's coffee. Pickets, who no longer had to be wary of Rebel sharpshooters and snipers sneaking up on their south flank, rode in and out of camp bringing details about how the agreement had been carved out.

The main point of controversy between General Grant and General Pemberton had revolved around allowing the Confederate soldiers to be paroled instead of held prisoner. Grant's officers, who wisely knew what a daunting and time-consuming task it would be transporting thirty thousand prisoners to Federal prison camps, suggested that the Confederate soldiers sign an oath not to fight again unless Federal prisoners were released in exchange. This proposal was delivered to Pemberton, and, sometime after midnight, Pemberton sent a message to Grant accepting his terms. In the early hours of the morning of July 4, on the forty-eighth day of the siege, Vicksburg had surrendered. By the time the men from the Iowa Fortieth had finished breakfast, Federal troops were marching down the streets of the city and wagonloads of food were being distributed to the hungry citizens of Vicksburg and to the defeated Rebel troops.

Pickets from the northeast brought news that General Johnston's troops were retreating, with German Sherman's army right behind them.

Now, two days later, with no threat from either direction, Colonel Cooper's Iowa regiment had nothing better to do than relax and stay cool. Sam, J.A., and Amos refilled their tin coffee cups, added several spoonfuls of sugar, and headed for their favorite spot along the Yazoo River. The morning sun filtered down through the willow trees, producing an assortment of dark green shadows and luminous light green ripples along the steadily moving water.

J.A. found a shady place on the sand, sat down, leaned back against a rock, and took a sip of his overly sweetened coffee. "This is certainly better than killing people and trying to keep from being killed yourself."

Sam and Amos found similar spots to relax, and Amos said, "Is our regiment going to always be around the fighting, but never in it? I want to know."

Sam and J.A. had been with Amos long enough to know that, when he ended a sentence with "I want to know" it was only his New England way of speaking and didn't infer that he thought either of them had an answer.

Sam shared his opinion anyway. "I have a feeling that we're going to have more than our share of fighting before this is over."

"Why do you think Johnston's army was moving in on us when Pemberton was preparing to surrender?" J.A. asked.

"Johnston didn't know," Amos replied.

Sam and J.A. both looked at him, wondering if he'd heard something they hadn't.

"At least that's my idear," he added.

"If that's true, then none of the couriers made it through," J.A. said.

Sam picked up a round rock, launched it into the air, and watched it splash down in the river, then turned toward the two men. "Tell me this; do you think if Johnston and Pemberton had been able to communicate, things might have ended up different?"

"I think perhaps," Amos replied.

"If you think about it," J.A. interjected. "Pemberton probably didn't know that there were thirty or forty thousand Johnnys only a few miles away."

"So maybe we helped a little when we captured that courier," Sam said.

"Do tell," Amos said. "It might not have mattered if Johnston had started firing his artillery before the surrender."

Sam threw a small stick at his brother's boot. "You know, J.A., I think Amos is right again."

Sergeant Klinker and Private Klinker came walking through the trees toward the beach.

"Don't get up, men," the sergeant said. "Do you mind if we use your swimming hole?"

"T'want ours," Amos said. "Help yourselves."

The Klinker brothers stacked their clothes on two separate rocks and started toward the water.

"This is the first time I've ever seen a naked sergeant," J.A. chuckled.

"I hope it's the last," Sam added.

The Yazoo River water was cool and an attractive shade of green, but it wasn't clear, and one could not see more than an inch or two below the surface. When John Klinker had waded out to waist-deep. J.A. warned him, "Watch out for the alligators."

Private Klinker's eyes widened as his head swiveled quickly from side to side.

For the first several weeks that the regiment had been camped near Snyder's Bluff, they had worked feverishly in the hot Mississippi sun preparing for a Rebel attack. The cool waters of the Yazoo provided too much temptation for many of the thirsty soldiers. Scores of men disobeyed orders and supplanted their daily supply of water with water from the river. There were a few men who drank only a few sips each day. This more moderate group of soldiers became quite sick, quit drinking from the river, and slowly recovered at the camp hospital. A much larger group of soldiers, seeing that the water was cool and had no foul taste, drank freely the first few days they were there. These men ended up in one of the hospital boats docked along the Mississippi Delta. They didn't recover as soon as was hoped, and by mid-July many of them had died. Some of the more seriously ill survivors were transported up the Mississippi to the hospital at Keokuk, Iowa. The inviting but deadly if ingested river water wreaked havoc on the regiment. As had happened in Columbus, Kentucky, the previous winter, illness had reduced the strength of

200

their ranks by an amount equal to the losses that might have been suffered in a hard-fought battle.

July 23, 1863

Early in the morning the regiment began breaking camp, loading their wagons, and packing their personal gear. They marched for most of the day, then in the evening boarded a ship and steamed back upriver toward Helena, Arkansas, to join twelve thousand other troops under the command of Major General Steele. They would become part of his expedition against the Rebel troops now occupying Little Rock.

They camped in Helena for seven weeks, preparing for the upcoming battle, then in early September began their advance toward Little Rock. The army marched for several days, at which time General Steele found it necessary to cross the Arkansas River. His plan was to build a pontoon bridge to bring wagons and artillery across the river at a point that he thought was below where the enemy was in force. This turned out to be a serious miscalculation, as a strong Rebel force was positioned in the timber on the opposite side of the river. Colonel Cooper's regiment was sent across the river first and posted a line to support the federal troops in the laying of the pontoons and for the subsequent crossing of the bridge.

As soon as they reached the far shore of the river, Sam, J.A., and Amos found a spot where a small log had fallen across a larger one, and that's where they dug in. There was no sign of the enemy until the Federal troops began placing the pontoons, then volleys of Rebel musket balls began hitting the Union soldiers who were down in the river working on the bridge. Federal men began disappearing under the water or floating downstream surrounded by pools of blood. Colonel Cooper shouted, "Fire at will," and the Fortieth Iowa was unexpectedly thrown into their first battle. The Rebel forces, who had been hidden by trees, bushes, and rocks, were no more than fifty yards away. The accuracy of the Iowa plainsmen, plus the months and months of practicing to increase their speed at loading and firing their muskets, produced a deadlier hail of gunfire than the Rebel forces had previously encountered.

General Steele held his men back while the battle raged across the river, and for the better part of an hour any Rebel soldier who raised his head got either a bullet or rifle ball through it, or one came so close that he feared lifting his head again. Any arm sticking out from behind a tree was soon shattered. Movement from behind a bush brought a hail of gunfire, often followed by a scream from an unfortunate Confederate soldier. The Rebel force, though superior in numbers, was well within range of the hunters and marksmen from the plains. A Rebel colonel saw Sam, J.A., and a few other soldiers in the regiment firing one accurate shot after another from their repeater rifles without having to reload. His soldiers were falling over as if the rocks and trees weren't even there. The other men were firing their muskets, reloading and firing again at the rate of about five times per minute. The Rebel commander came to a false but probably prudent conclusion. "They've all got those damned Yankee rifles!" he yelled, and told his bugle boy to sound the retreat.

From across the river, General Steele said to one of his aides, "From now on, Colonel Cooper's men will be among the first sent out during any attack and will form part of my rear guard if we're forced to retreat. Send my medical staff across the bridge to give all of the wounded men aid." He paused for a moment, then added, "Send a burial detail, too."

"Of course, sir."

The Confederacy had sustained very heavy losses, against the relatively small number of casualties suffered by the Iowa Fortieth Infantry, but the Rebels could not have been more shocked and appalled than the men from Iowa. For the first time they had seen their friends and neighbors killed or wounded in the line of duty. Fellow soldiers of the regiment were hurrying from one fallen soldier to another, administering aid or calling to someone from the medical staff to look after the more seriously wounded.

Sam, J.A., and Amos walked along the battle line looking for anyone they could help. They found four men from Poweshiek County who had fallen. J.A. saw the first one, Cary Kisor, and rushed up to him, only to find that it was too late. The young man had caught a rifle ball right through the middle of his neck and was already dead. Eli Schooley was lying a few feet away from Kisor and had also gone to meet his maker. This was the second loss the Schooley family had suffered. Eli's brother, Aaron, had been the regiment's first casualty, dying from the measles during training camp in November of '62.

When they saw the dead body of John Davis, a jovial farm boy from Grinnell, Sam looked up toward the sky and pleaded, "Please, God, no more."

There was one more man, Paschal Booze, another farmer who had resettled his family from New England to Iowa. He was leaning back against a tree with a circle of red growing in the breast of his blue uniform and a smile on his face. The three men ran to their fallen friend, with Amos getting there first.

Amos leaned over and looked at the man's wound. "You're hurt bad, Paschal. We'll get some help over here for you."

The wounded soldier lifted his hand, with the palm toward Amos. "T'want any use. I'm killed. We sure taught those Johnnys a lesson, though, didn't we?"

"We sure did, my friend."

"You tell my missus and my young'ns that I'll be waiting for them up yonder."

"No, Paschal, you're going to make it."

The man put his hand on Amos's arm. "You tell them for me, Amos."

He nodded, and the wounded man's hand slipped off his arm as his head fell forward.

Tears were in Amos's eyes as he looked up at his two best friends.

In the months following the battle at the pontoon bridge, the Fortieth Iowa Infantry was involved in two other minor skirmishes but suffered no further casualties. However, their ranks were further depleted when soldiers fell victim to dysentery, typhoid fever, and other serious illnesses. In November of 1862, the regiment that was officially mustered into the army was 900 strong. Now, less than one year later, only 219 men were still fit and able to fight. Some men were in the hospital at Duvall's Bluff. Most of those were still sick from drinking the poisonous waters of the Yazoo and were expected to return soon. Others, still too ill to continue their military service, had been sent back to Keokuk Hospital, on the Mississippi River, in eastern Iowa. Sadly, many other soldiers who had served in the regiment were in their graves at Columbus and Vicksburg and just outside of Little Rock.

For the next two months General Steele's army poured artillery fire on Little Rock and waited for the Rebels either to come out and fight or retreat. Finally the latter of the two happened.

It was late September when Colonel Cooper rode his horse at the head of his regiment, along with the twelve thousand troops under General Steele, as they rode triumphantly into the city. The Confederate Army, knowing that defeat was inevitable, had saved thousands of lives on both sides by choosing to withdraw. As the men marched along, Sam observed the trees along the side of the road. They were beautifully changing colors, oblivious to the death and destruction that had surrounded them. He contemplated how men made war while nature ignored them and went on with her business.

Colonel Cooper was much more than just a commanding officer to the men from Grinnell and the surrounding area. Most of them had known and respected the colonel prior to the outbreak of war. He had supported Josiah Grinnell in setting up the city's schools and in establishing Grinnell College. It had been largely due to the efforts of Cooper that Professor Parker and his beautiful wife had come to their town. Cooper had known them previously in Oberlin and knew of their outstanding success, not only in teaching the young but also in inspiring their students to seek higher education. They had stated their intentions of moving to Bleeding Kansas, as it was called in antislavery circles. Cooper persuaded them to come to Grinnell instead and help start the college.

It was a soul-inspiring moment as the troops marched down the street through Little Rock. The Iowa Fortieth Infantry marched toward the front of the columns, their flag bearer marching ahead and their drummer boy beating on his drum and another boy playing his fife. Sam was looking toward Colonel Cooper when he noticed him slumping in his saddle, then beginning to fall off to one side. Sam broke ranks and ran across the street and up to the colonel. Sergeant Klinker got there at the same time, and together they caught the falling officer before he could hit the ground. The two men laid him gently down, and Klinker put his haversack under Cooper's head.

Sam quickly examined him from his head down to his boots and said, "I don't see any wound."

Klinker put his hand on the unconscious colonel's head and said, "He's come down with the fever."

A junior officer riding up ahead turned and saw what had happened, wheeled his horse around, and rode back to the fallen colonel. "What are you two doing out of formation?" he demanded.

Sam and Sergeant Klinker looked up into the face of Lieutenant Roberts, a man of their acquaintance from Jasper County.

"We saw the colonel falling off his horse," Klinker said.

"This is a job for the Medical Corps, Sergeant, not for you two. Sergeant, get back into formation, and get your soldiers marching, immediately. I'll handle this."

Colonel Garrett came riding up just as Sam and Sergeant Klinker were walking away.

As the regiment marched by, they heard the colonel giving the lieutenant orders to get an ambulance and transport Colonel Cooper to the hospital immediately, then adding in a crisp, hard voice, "If there is any delay in getting him care, I'll hold you directly responsible."

Sam could see Sergeant Klinker smiling at Lieutenant Roberts, then heard him say under his breath, "Bite off a little more than you could chew, young fella?"

Major General Steele's army marched out through the other side of the city and into a ready-made army camp. The Fortieth Iowa was assigned to a group of tents on the south side of the encampment, closest to the city. A fire was still smoldering in front of the tent to which Sam, J.A., and Amos were assigned. Apparently the former occupants had left in a hurry, because inside the tent the men found food, cooking utensils, wool blankets, and even a half-filled box of cigars.

Amos picked up a cigar from the little wooden box. "This is mighty hospitable of those Rebs to leave all of these conveniences for us."

J.A. leaned over and picked up a letter from beneath a Confederate cot and said, "Look at this."

"You planning to read it?" Amos asked.

"You bet your life." His eyes moved back and forth on the top of the page. "It's from the Reb's girlfriend back in Texas."

"Don't you feel that her letter was meant to be private?" Amos asked.

"When you're right, you're right," J.A. said, and crumpled the letter in his hand. "I'll throw it into the fire."

Before he could get out of the tent, Amos and Sam almost simultaneously said, "Wait!"

"No harm is just seeing what it says," Amos suggested.

J.A. walked over toward the smoldering fire and held the crumpled letter above it.

Sam pulled it from his hand. "I'll read it. We get little-enough entertainment these days." He read silently for a few seconds. "Oh, my, this is a little bit more personal than I'd figured. I'm not going to read it aloud." He read for a time longer, then uttered a sound of disgust.

"What?" Amos said.

"Listen to this. 'Never return to me without a necklace made from Yankee ears. Your loving sweetheart, Olivia.' She does not sound like a very nice woman."

"I wonder how many women down south feel that way?" J.A. asked.

"I don't think there'd be very many," Sam replied. "This was probably some girl he met and romanced in a saloon. Do you want me to toss it in the fire?"

Amos reached out his hand. "I might as well read it, too."

That night, Amos pan-fried some fresh venison while Sam and J.A. boiled potatoes and opened a couple jars of stewed apricots. This sumptuous meal was compliments of the Rebel soldiers who had formerly occupied their tent. After dinner, Sergeant and Private Klinker strolled up to the men's fire. When they started to rise, the sergeant motioned for them to remain seated. "We've known each other for a long time. When there is no one else around, let's dispense with the formalities." With that, the Klinker brothers sat down on the ground next to Amos.

Amos lifted the coffeepot from where it was hanging over the fire and refilled the two men's tin cups.

The sergeant began, "I just got out of a meeting with Colonel Garrett, and he gave us some information you'll be happy to hear. It looks like we'll be in Little Rock for quite a spell."

John Klinker looked around him, and said, "It looks like you men have made yourselves pretty comfortable," then tipped his head back and sniffed a couple times. "What did you men have for dinner that smells so good?"

J.A. said, "Amos fried us some venison."

"We should have come here sooner," the sergeant said. "Like I was saying, the colonel told us all that he doesn't think the Rebels will be able to put together a force large enough to attack our position at anytime soon. Since the former residents of this camp have already built fortifications for us and we can only do so much drilling and marching, we should be able to have some extra time to do chores, play cards, write letters back home, and just plain have some time to yourselves. We'll also get some newspapers to you, so you can read about what some of our other armies are doing. Here is the new camp schedule. We'll have reveille at five. I know you men like to cook your own food when you can, but breakfast call will be at seven, guard mounting at nine, and dinner call at twelve. There is a good chance that we'll spend all of the fall and winter right here. Any questions?"

The men shook their heads.

When the Klinker brothers had gone, the three men sat around their fire and chatted about their new home and the events that had brought them to this place. Their tent was really nothing more than a six-foot length of canvas draped over a horizontal ridgepole and staked down at both sides. Flaps closed off both ends, allowing them some privacy. Compared to what they had endured at Columbus, Kentucky, the first winter, this tent was everything they could ask for and more. At Columbus, they had been in a Sibley tent, named after its inventor, Henry H. Sibley, a Confederate brigadier general. It was a large cone of canvas, eighteen feet in diameter, twelve feet tall, and supported by a center pole. It was tolerably comfortable for a dozen men, but the shortage of tents at their camp had forced Sam, J.A., and Amos to share this tent with seventeen other men. They slept in wheel-spoke fashion, with their feet at the center, and because of the cold, rainy weather spent a good deal of time in their tent with the flaps down. The accumulated flatulence from twenty men on a diet containing a substantial amount of beans would not be remembered with any great degree of enthusiasm.

"The first thing tomorrow morning, I'm going to write letters to Dora and my family," Sam said.

"I'll do the same," J.A. said. "The sooner they find out where we are, the sooner we can get letters from them."

"Why aren't you telling us that you'll be writing Lina, too?" Sam asked.

"I thought it was understood."

"Sam, I'll bet your wife has had your new baby by now," Amos said.

Sam stared into the dying embers of the fire. "My little boy is three years old now. I wonder if he remembers what his papa looks like?"

In the flickering firelight J.A. looked at his brother's lean, hard face, full, untrimmed beard, and skin severely weathered by the elements. "You'd probably scare the little tyke to death if he saw you now."

Sam ran his hand across his beard and face. "I don't intend to allow either him or his mother to see me the way I look right now."

Amos said, "I have an idea. Tomorrow, I'll give you both a shave and a haircut."

"Thank you, Amos. That's awfully nice of you," J.A. said.

"Don't thank me. I'm doing it for myself. I'm tired of looking at your ugly faces."

21

March 1864–Six Months Later

In the kitchen of the Harris farm, Dora poured herself a hot cup of tea and put a cookie on the saucer next to her cup. Then she picked up the two letters she had just received and walked out to the front porch. Frank was down for his afternoon nap in the crib that he had almost outgrown. Seven-month-old Kate was sleeping in her bassinet right next to him. Dora had the house to herself this afternoon, and she planned to make the most of it. Throughout her young life, moments spent alone had not come very often and therefore were to be treasured. It was a clear spring day, but the cold nights had pre-served a few remnants of snow. In contrast to the remaining vestiges of winter, patches of wildflowers were peeking their multicolored faces up out of the soil and waving greetings to the new world they had recently encountered.

Joanna was in class at the college. Mary was at high school, and William had taken his mother to town to do some shopping. Between William's two sisters-in-law, Dora, and Rachael, his two sisters, Jo-anna and Mary, and his mother, he had about as many women to look after as one man could stand. Last August, Papa Harris had been appointed the rank of captain in the Thirty-seventh Regiment, referred to as the Graybeard Regiment. The Graybeards had been through some skirmishes in Missouri and Tennessee and had per-formed quite effectively. Now, to Mama Harris's relief, they had been assigned to guard a prison camp in Indianapolis.

William had enlisted a few days after his father was mustered in and then was sent back home. The army felt that there were enough Harris men at risk and decided that William was more needed at the ranch. The young man sulked around the house for several weeks, then adjusted to and accepted his lot in life.

Dora made herself comfortable in a soft chair on the porch and placed her feet up on the footstool. She placed Mollie's letter on the table next to her, put Sam's letter on her lap, and took a sip of tea. Since Sam had arrived in Little Rock, last September, she had been able to exchange letters with him on a regular basis. She still missed him terribly, but being able to communicate was far better than when he had been in places where he could neither send nor receive mail.

The contemporaneous campaigns of General Grant at Richmond, and General Sherman against Atlanta, had so excited the attention of the country that the campaigns in the southwest were almost ignored by the nation's news correspondents. Information about battles involving local soldiers was told and retold by the families of the men, from information they had received in letters from the battlefront. Most of Sam's recent letters told about incidents around camp and contained responses to news from home that Dora had written about to him. The forever-repetitious but most treasured part of each letter told of their undying love and how much they waited for the day they would be back together again. Toward the end of Sam's letter, he wrote that his regiment would be moving out to Prairie D'Anne and Okalona to engage some Rebels in that region. He added that the officers felt that these would only be small skirmishes and that they'd be returning to Little Rock soon.

When Dora finished reading Sam's letter, she took a couple bites of her cookie and another sip of tea. She hadn't received a letter from Mollie for several weeks. This one had come from the Dorsey farm, where Mollie was visiting. It read:

My Dearest Sister,

After a tedious trip across the plains consuming over three weeks' time, I arrived in Nebraska City, where our dear father met me. Spending the night at Allen's Hotel, we came the next day to the old home on the Little Nemaha. Oh, Dora, how can I describe or tell the feelings of a returned wanderer, as I greeted parents, brothers, and sisters? All are well, and my little Bertie was voted a fine baby. He took over the house. Anna is at home with her two little ones, so we are a numerous family. The weather is delightful. The ranches are every few miles, and I could not recognize the land of our former pilgrimage. Mother is forty-three, but she is bearing her age well. Ada has grown into a tall, pretty girl. I have been telling them so many stories about Cherry Creek and the exciting times we had in Denver. There are no wooing gentlemen coming to call as there were when we were younger. I only know that I married the man of my choice. He will be here in six weeks to pick me up.

I miss you so much, dear sister, and wonder when, if ever, I'll see you again.

Love,
Mollie

Dora had no sooner laid Mollie's letter on top of Sam's when she saw two men coming up the road toward the house. She could see that the smaller man was a Negro. The taller one had black hair and the familiar gait that she hadn't seen since Sam walked up the gangplank of the steamship that took him away. She put her hand up to her mouth; it felt like her heart was up in her throat. Sam had always been impulsive, but how could he have arrived on the same day as his letter and why hadn't he told her he was coming? The two men turned into the gate. They were still a couple hundred yards away, but Dora recognized the thick black hair and wide grin that she loved so much. Somehow, some wonderful way, Sam had come home.

Dora ran down the steps toward the two men, then stopped. Could Sam have changed that much in a year and a half? As the men drew nearer, she realized that though the resemblance was striking, this man was not Sam.

The man stuck out his hand, "You must be Dora. You're as beautiful as I've been told. I'm Sam's oldest brother, Ephriam. Everybody just calls me Doc. This is my new son, James."

Dora was still trying to catch her breath. "Does Rachael know you're here?"

"Oh, yes, I surprised her at the office before I came here. I had a chance to board a boat in New Orleans and had no time to let anyone know. It was take it or leave it, and I had to get James to Grinnell."

Dora looked at the boy. He was a handsome lad, wearing a new gray tweed suit, in which he did not appear too comfortable. She could see that, in spite of his height, he was quite young. "Pardon my manners," she said. "Can I fix you two something to eat?"

"No, thank you, Rachael took us to dinner at Reed's Hotel. I would enjoy a cup of coffee, though."

Dora looked at the boy. He nodded and she heard a very soft, "Yes, ma'am."

She leaned over and smiled at him. "Or would you rather have a glass of milk and some cookies?"

He lowered his eyes, and his wide smile indicated that this was his preference, although he didn't answer.

Ephriam and James followed Dora into the kitchen and sat down at the table. When everything was prepared, she sat across from them. Ephriam explained to Dora that circumstances had forced him to make this trip, in spite of a heavy workload at the hospital in New Orleans. Therefore, the most he could stay was two days before starting the trip back.

Dora asked, "What circumstances?"

Instead of answering her, he asked, "Do we still have that old black mare in the barn?"

"She's still there."

"I see that my son has made short work of the milk and cookies. I'm going to saddle up the mare for James and let him take a ride around the property, while you and I talk."

Dora stood at the kitchen window watching the man who reminded her so much of Sam as he pointed out the area where he wanted James to ride. The Harris farm covered eighty acres, so the boy could enjoy a pleasant horseback ride without ever leaving the property. Ephriam looked and sounded so much like Sam that she had to tell her heart to stop beating so hard. She refilled her coffee cup and his, and took them both back out to the front porch. In a few minutes, he joined her.

"You referred to James as your son," Dora said.

"Yes, he's my adopted son, and he'll always be part of my family. He's a wonderful boy. I'm glad that I have this time to talk to you before everyone else gets home."

"Why would you want to talk to me?"

"Because I have an important job that I want you to do. Joanna has told me about you in her letters, and I think that you and my sister will make sure that James is taken care of until I return from the war."

Dora looked puzzled. "I would suppose that the whole family will take care of him."

"Of course they will. Let me start from the beginning, and then I'm sure that you'll understand what I'm talking about. James's father and mother did janitorial and maintenance work at the hospital where I'd been assigned. His father was self-educated and an extremely bright man. If his skin had been of a lighter hue, he could have been a doctor. He married an equally intelligent woman, and they taught their only son to read and write, among other things. Several weeks ago, James's parents decided to visit their family who were slaves in lower Mississippi. I was against it and warned them that with the war going on, the trip could be dangerous, but I agreed to take care of James while they were gone. They made it to the plantation where their family was without incident. However, while they were there, word spread around town that someone was teaching slaves how to read and write. This is against the law in Mississippi. When, after warnings from the sheriff, they persisted in trying to educate young family members, the sheriff sent three of his deputies to arrest them. James's mother was an attractive woman, and on the way to jail the deputies decided to have some fun before they turned her over to the sheriff. When they started ripping her clothes off, her husband split one of the deputies' head open with a rock. They hung both of James's parents from a tree."

"How did you find out about all of this?" Dora asked.

"The plantation owner's wife sent me a letter. James knows that his parents are dead, but I would prefer that he not find out the details, at least until he's a grown man. Once I received news about the deaths, I adopted James to keep anyone from taking him away from me. Then, the first opportunity I had, I came here."

"I think that slave owners are the most horrible people I can imagine."

"Slavery is a shameful practice, Dora, but don't judge all slave owners with the same measuring stick. Slavery allows brutal men to indulge in cruel and savage behavior. Others who are presumed to be righteous deceive themselves for comfort and profit. They substitute kind treatment and relatively nice living conditions for the freedom to which their slaves are entitled. Some of the most horrible atrocities against the black race are committed by men who are too poor to own slaves, like the deputies I told you about."

"You sound like the preacher at the church," Dora said.

Ephriam laughed, "I guess we Harris men get on our soapboxes when we feel strongly about something."

"You can include the Harris women, too. What is it that you want Joanna and me to do?"

"I want you to enroll James in school and see that he is treated well."

"That should be no problem. Most of the people in Grinnell are in favor of Negroes' rights."

"Don't be too sure about that. Many people are idealists and friends of humanity when thinking of faraway China or Africa"—he stopped and smiled—"or South Carolina. Let's see if their good works cool when the actualities come into town, and where their own kids attend school."

The couple stopped talking and watched a horse and buggy come racing down the road, through the front gate, and toward the house.

Doc Harris strode from the porch to the ground without touching a step, grabbed his mother from the carriage seat, and twirled her around in his arms. William and his brother were grinning widely, and Mama Harris was crying and hugging her oldest son.

Dora heard Kate crying. She had no doubt been awakened by the noisy reunion, but it was time for her to get up from her nap anyway. As Dora walked up the stairs, she heard Frank say, "Don't cry, Sister. Mama is coming."

Frank had learned to climb out of his crib over a year ago. When his mother walked into the bedroom, he was standing at Kate's bassinet, patting her on the back of her diaper, which did nothing to improve the odor in the room.

"Why don't you go downstairs to Grandma, dearie, while I change your sister's diaper."

Frank went down the stairs, one careful step at a time, then followed the sounds of the voices out onto the front porch. When he saw the tall black-haired man, he shrieked. "Papa, Papa!" and ran to his uncle with arms out stretched.

Ephriam scooped the child up in his arms and hugged him for several seconds before looking into Frank's face and explaining, "I'm your papa's brother. I'm Uncle Doc."

"Papa," Frank insisted, smiling and patting his uncle on the side of his cheek and his beard.

214

"We'll get it all straightened out later," he assured the boy.

True to his word, Dr. Ephriam Harris spent only two nights at home. At breakfast, Mary's eyes were red from crying. She was the baby of the family and had grown up feeling much like a daughter to her oldest brother. He had been nineteen years old when she was born and could not have loved his little sister any more if she had been his own child. The relationship between them was very special. During breakfast, she announced to everyone that she would stay home and watch Kate and Frank while the others took Doc to the train station. Mary couldn't stand to say goodbye to him again.

At the train station, Doc kissed his wife so long and hard that his maiden sister Joanna averted her eyes.

"When I get home again, I'm never going to leave," he told his teary-eyed wife and sobbing mother. Then he was gone.

The train would take him to Davenport, where he would board a ship that would take him back to the hospital in New Orleans. It was likely that he would be aboard the first boat to leave, because Federal medical doctors were given top priority whenever they traveled.

On the way back to the farm, James drove the wagon carrying Mama Harris and Rachael. In the second wagon, Dora sat in the middle between the driver, William, and Joanna. Joanna had begun to notice that William almost always found a way to sit next to his sister-in-law.

"Did Doc mention anything to you about enrolling James in school?" Dora asked Joanna.

Joanna nodded yes, and William said, "He mentioned it to me, too. I'm going with you."

"Do you really think it will cause a problem?" Dora asked.

Joanna put her arm around Dora. "Dearie, we found out when we were working for the Underground Railroad that the people whom you'd least suspect are the ones who will disappoint you."

The Grinnell Grammar and Middle School, which served Grades 1 through 9, was a plain white-frame building, with the front door opening into a hallway that went straight through to the back door. On the left side of the hall was a door leading into the classroom where Miss Louise Bixby taught Grades 1 through 6. On the right side of the hall was the room where Miss Lucy Bixby taught Grades 7 through 9. At fifteen minutes before eight in the morning, Dora, William, and Joanna took a badly frightened James up the steps, through the door, and into the classroom on the right. Miss Lucy Bixby was standing at the blackboard, writing out the day's assignments. She welcomed them with a warm smile. "Good morning. Have you brought me a new student for my class?"

A few students were already at their desks, and two of them, both boys, picked up their books and walked out of class.

Miss Bixby picked up her enrollment book and asked, "What is your name, young man?"

James's chin was almost touching his chest, and his answer was too soft for Miss Bixby to hear. He was clutching Edward Engleston's *Hoosier Schoolmaster* tightly against his side, and his hand was trembling quite visibly.

William spoke up, "His name is James Harris. He's my brother Doc's adopted son."

"So you're Doc Harris's boy. Well, James, your father is a wonderful man. I'm happy that you decided to attend school here."

When he heard these words, James lifted his eyes and looked into the pretty blue eyes of the young teacher who was smiling at him. His mouth dropped open. This was not what he had expected, nor what would have happened if he had tried to enter a school in Louisiana.

Joanna said, "He's received tutoring in New Orleans, Lucy. I believe that you'll find that he reads and writes quite well."

"I'm glad to hear that." Lucy Bixby looked at the boy's frightened face, then said, in a voice loud enough for James and his new family to hear but soft enough so that the students couldn't eavesdrop, "Do you know what I consider true bravery, James? It's when you're really scared about doing something, but you do it anyway because it's the right thing to do. It's going to be difficult being the first Negro to attend Grinnell Middle School. You probably already realize that. Some people are not going to treat you very well, but because of what you're doing, the next colored student who enrolls here will find it to be less arduous."

James looked around the room at all the children's faces and said, "Yes, ma'am."

By now the classroom had filled up, and it seemed like all of the young people were whispering at the same time.

Miss Bixby stood to her feet and looked over her class. "Ira Rayburn, will you please stand."

A freckled-faced boy about thirteen, with a mop of sun-bleached hair down across his forehead, got to his feet. "Yes, Miss Bixby."

"Since you and James both have fathers who are away at war, I want you to show him around for the next few days."

There were a few giggles around the room, which Miss Bixby's stern look quickly quelled.

"James, there is an empty desk in front of Ira and in back of Katie Grinnell. That will be your desk. You can go to your seat now, and we'll start our lesson."

William, Dora, and Joanna left James and returned to their carriage. William pulled the carriage across the school yard and over by the flagpole. There was a cool March breeze blowing the flag, but the sun warmed their faces.

"Ar we just going to leave?" Dora asked.

William shook his head. "I think we better stay around for a while. You saw the boys who walked out. One of them was Captain Clark's boy. He's not a captain in the army; he's a former sea captain. He called the War of the Rebellion a nigger war until some soldiers came home on furlough and warned him to shut his mouth. The other one was the Kellogg boy. His parents are from the South. They aren't as vocal as Clark, but there are some questions about their feelings regarding abolition. I believe we can count on those boys returning with their fathers."

Captain Clark's wagon arrived first. In the wagon next to him was his son.

"What's going on here?" Clark demanded as he pulled his wagon into the schoolyard.

William said, "Nothing for you to get upset about, Clark. We're just registering my nephew into school."

"You're telling me that you have a nigger for a nephew?"

"I'm telling you that my brother Doc's adopted son is going to be attending school in Grinnell, and if you refer to him as a nigger one more time, I'll pull you down off that wagon and give you a beating you won't soon forget."

217

Clark laughed. "That's pretty big talk, young fellow. How many of your brothers are around to help you do that?"

The warning rattles of a rattlesnake near Clark's horse caused the animal to rear up, then pull the wagon forward several feet, until the wagon was closer to the snake and the horse was out of danger. Clark instinctively leaned as far away from the reptile as he could.

William reached into a leather bag at his feet, pulled out a knife, and removed it from its sheath. The knife blade had been hewn to a razor-sharp edge.

"Please don't do this," Joanna begged.

"Why not? It's my specialty."

Dora watched William walk right up to the snake, wondering what he planned to do.

"So you think that this snake is dangerous, Captain Clark?" William suddenly grabbed the snake by the tail, then snapped it a couple times in Clark's direction, like you might crack a whip.

What happened next was almost too fast for the eye to see. The hand holding the snake flipped its body into the air while the other hand skillfully guided the knife blade, sending the snake's head right at the captain.

Clark almost knocked his boy off the wagon trying to dodge the snakeless head.

Another quick slash of the knife and William was holding only the snake's rattles in his hand. He walked up to Clark's wagon and held the rattles out to him. The long knife was still in William's hand. "I think it's important for a man to recognize real danger when he sees it, don't you? Now what was it you were asking about my brothers?"

Joanna removed her hands from in front of her eyes. "Has he finished?" she asked.

Dora said, "Yes, but how did he do that?"

"I don't know, but he's been doing it since he was a little boy. No matter how many times I see him do it, it still scares me to death."

Two more wagons pulled into the schoolyard, and others could be seen heading down the road toward them. From the direction of the college, Professor Parker emerged from a thicket and walked in their direction. Several students were following him.

"We should no longer wonder if bringing James to school is going to cause an incident," Joanna observed.

Mr. Kellogg, his son who had walked out of the classroom, and an older son pulled their wagon up alongside Captain Clark.

Professor Parker walked up to William and said, "We received news over at the college that some people might try to prevent the enrollment of a colored student in our school system. It looks like the rumor was true."

William told the professor all that had happened before he arrived, leaving out the incident of the unfortunate snake.

As the crowd grew larger, they began to form two distinct groups. Most people gathered around Professor Parker and the Harris wagon. However, the few who stood alongside Captain Clark's wagon were louder and more boisterous.

Finally, when it appeared that all those who were coming had arrived. Professor Parker climbed up into the back of the Harris wagon and stood facing the crowd. "This is an unfortunate event that we are witnessing here today. Apparently a few citizens of our town believe that equality of the races is fine just as long as it doesn't interfere with our own white holy huddle. I'm glad that Josiah Grinnell is in Washington, so he can't see this sorry exhibition of intolerance."

One man from Clark's group yelled, "Professor, we're reasonable people! We want the Negroes to be free, but it's a whole different matter, having them go to school with our own children!"

Parker directed his comment to the man who had spoken up. "Mr. Clement, you and I both know that there are no schools for Negro children, and if there were, you'd be insisting that one not be built in your neighborhood. Therefore, I find your argument to be weak and hypocritical."

"What are you going to do when one of them wants to marry your daughter?" another man called out.

"I trust my daughters to choose men of intelligence and virtue; that's all I ask."

People around the Clark wagon gasped at such an audacious statement.

"That's not the way God intended it," a woman said.

"I read the Good Book as much as any of you, and I find none of that nonsense in either of the Testaments. Enough of this foolish banter. Who among you has not, at one time or another, been helped

219

by Doc Harris? He's put his adopted son in our charge because he's out tending to the sick and wounded who are fighting for our country. This boy will attend school in Grinnell. Other children of his race will follow. Those who are good students will go on to our college. Anyone who wants to attempt removing this boy from his classroom will do so over my dead body."

Parker's last declaration brought a loud cheer from those gathered around the Harris wagon.

The professor concluded with, "I've heard enough of this matter. Let's all start practicing what we say we believe. All of you go back and tend to your farms. Let me and the faculty of the schools in this town take care of school matters."

With that Professor Parker jumped down from the wagon, and the crowd began to disperse.

As their wagon pulled out of the schoolyard, Dora saw the Kellogg boy and Captain Clark's son walking back up the steps of the schoolhouse.

"It worked out much better this time," Joanna said.

"You mean this has happened before?" Dora asked.

Joanna nodded. "A couple of years ago, a few escaped slaves decided to settle here. Josiah Grinnell ordered that the four children of school age be admitted to our primary school. Professor Parker wanted to comply with Grinnell's order, but some townspeople insisted that a meeting be held at the church prior to the children's admittance. Grinnell's order was sustained by only eight votes, but that didn't settle the matter. People who were against Negro children attending our schools would not submit to majority rule. Especially when it was so slim a majority. They showed up at the school planning to block the new students' entrance. Parker armed himself with a club and emphatically stated that he would physically defend the right of every student permitted by the directors to attend. The objectors intercepted the Negro students near the church, and we almost had a riot. One of the children's fathers mounted a woodpile and shouted, 'Gentlemen, we'uns came up north to be free! If we can't be free, we'd just as soon die here as anywhere.' "

"How was the issue resolved?" Dora asked.

Joanna replied, "I'm sure there would have been bloodshed, but cooler heads prevailed. It was near the end of the spring term, so it was agreed to close down the school early to allow the town the

220

summer to work out their differences. Before September, the Negro families had become less convinced of the open-mindedness of our town and had left for Canada."

"That is so sad," Dora said.

"I guess at least most of the dissenters have changed their attitude," William said.

"We still have a long way to go," Joanna added.

As they traveled down the road back to the Harris farm, Dora said, "William, I never saw anything like the way you handled that snake. I'm really quite impressed."

William grinned and gave the reins a shake, causing the horse to increase his speed.

Joanna frowned. "Don't encourage him, Dora."

22

March 23, 1864–Two Weeks Later

A steady rain pelted the canvas on top of their tent as Sam, J.A., and Amos packed their haversacks and made last-minute preparations for their march south. Supply wagons had been packed with food, medical equipment, ammunition, and supplies. From what their commanding officers had told them, the fiercest enemy they would have to face could very well be the weather. A series of storms coming down from the north had produced some cold, wet days, and there was no sign of it letting up anytime soon.

Major General Steele's army had been in Little Rock for seven months now, with the monotony broken only by short marches to Benton, Brownsville, Austin, and Searcy.

The Fortieth Iowa Infantry and some other Iowa regiment would form part of the Third Brigade, Third Division, commanded by Col. A. Englemann of the Forty-third Illinois Infantry. They would be part of the troops who would act as rear guard throughout this campaign. Most of the men from the Iowa Fortieth who had survived drinking the Yazoo River water had left the hospital and rejoined the regiment. However, the deadly fever that had put Colonel Cooper into the hospital had spread throughout the camp, causing a considerable amount of illness and several deaths. Colonel Cooper had survived the fever, but not sufficiently to allow him to rejoin his troops. He was now back in Grinnell, and letters from the family had reported that he was not doing well.

At daybreak, during a driving rain, ten thousand of Steele's twelve thousand troops began their march south toward the Saline River. The bills of the soldiers' caps kept their eyes dry enough to see where they were going, but the rest of their bodies were soon soaked to the skin. The road, which was muddy enough to begin with, became a vast sea of slush. Mud thrown up by each soldier's boots splattered soldiers marching behind.

That night, cold, wet, and covered with mud, the soldiers did their best to warm themselves around campfires, prepared some food and hot coffee, and retired to their dog tents. The one-man tents might possibly have kept the men dry if they were not already dripping wet before they got into them.

The next four days were much the same, except for the troops becoming wearier each day from the long marches and the miserable weather.

Finally, on the fifth day out of Little Rock, the troops reached Okalona, and Englemann's Brigade set up camp there. Sam, J.A., and Amos pitched their tent, gathered some kindling wood, and built a roaring fire close to their tent flap. An overhanging tree branch partially sheltered the men from the still-drizzling rain, but there was no possible way to dry their clothes completely. Getting their bodies warm and filling their stomachs with hot food and coffee would be the best they'd be able to manage tonight. In a couple of days, the storm passed over, allowing the men to dry out and rest for a short period of time. On their fifth day at Okalona, a scout rode into camp bringing news about a large force of Rebel troops just a few miles south of their position. Colonel Englemann commanded his troops to engage the enemy.

The enemy force was much larger than Englemann had estimated, and the men found themselves fighting for their lives in a battle where they were heavily outnumbered. A new storm had arrived, and rain was again coming down in a deluge. The fighting took place alongside the Saline River. For several hours the superior marksmanship of the soldiers from the farming communities of Iowa and Indiana kept the Rebels from overrunning their position. Then a shrill Rebel yell rang through the woods, followed by a deafening din of musketry, and hordes of Rebel soldiers came pouring out from behind trees, bushes, and rocks, running full speed toward the Federal lines. Several men from the Iowa Fortieth were hit during the Rebel volley. Lieutenant Roberts of Company B took a rifle ball in the stomach and fell to his knees gasping in pain. Sgt. David Tanner had a rifle ball completely shatter his lower leg and another one go through his neck as he toppled to the ground. Men all along the Union line had fallen during the relentless fire prior to the Rebel charge.

As he looked down the line at all the fallen soldiers, Sam felt an immense well of anger rise up inside him. All human compassion vanished, and suddenly *kill, kill, kill* was all he could think about. He heard a loud roaring growl and knew that the sound had come out of his own mouth. The charging Rebels were within eighty yards of him. He could hit a turkey in the neck from that distance. He fired all seven shots from his repeater rifle without one bullet missing its mark, then took out his pistol and shot down three more gray-coated soldiers. J.A.'s performance next to him was equally deadly, and Amos was shooting Rebels at the rate of about one every twenty seconds. The outraged men from the plains shot with lethal precision, reloading their guns rapidly and shooting again. When the pall of smoke from the Federal muskets and rifles lifted, the wet earth in front of them was littered with enemy dead and wounded. The Rebels who had not been shot were struggling to run back through the deep mud and falling over the bodies of the men already on the ground. The scene had quickly turned from a battle to a bloodbath.

Sam looked across the field at a Rebel officer on a horse looking out over the carnage. The man's face looked horrified. Sam wondered if he was the one who had ordered this ill-fated charge. Sam aimed his reloaded rifle at the man's chest, looked at him over his gun-sight for a moment, then lowered it back down. He was sickened from all the killing.

A short time later the Rebels retreated, and Colonel Englemann ordered his troops to prepare for their march back to camp. A burial detail was given the unpleasant task of burying their fallen comrades, and the wounded were carried back to camp on stretchers, then taken to the field hospital for medical care.

Sam, J.A., and Amos ate some cold beans and fell onto their cots in exhaustion.

Amos said, "If this is what it feels like to win, think how horrible it must be to lose."

The next morning Englemann's troops were ordered to make the short march to Prairie D'Anne. They remained there for seven days just trying to rest, stay warm, and dry out.

On the seventh day, Sam, J.A., and Amos were just finishing breakfast when Sergeant Klinker and his brother came to inform them that they were leaving to engage another Rebel force just a few miles away. The three men wearily packed their gear and made sure they had plenty of ammunition and enough food and water.

"Do you remember when we were wondering if we would ever get into battle?" Sam asked.

J.A. replied, "That was before General Steele watched our regiment from across the Arkansas River and decided that we could whip the whole Confederate Army."

During this battle, neither the Rebel nor the Federal forces engaged in any suicidal charges, but rather each side shot volleys at each other from their positions less than a hundred yards apart. There were some sharpshooters among the Rebels during this skirmish, and Englemann's men had to stay under cover and exercise more caution. The battle continued until nightfall, and when the sun came up the next morning the Rebel soldiers were gone. The steadily shrinking forces of the Fortieth Iowa carried another eight of their wounded back to camp.

That night around their campfire, Sam asked, "Do you men realize that we've lost over eighty percent of our regiment in less than two years?"

They all stared into the fire for a few moments.

"Less than two hundred of us are still fit and able to fight," Amos said. "The way I figger, there will only be the three of us left by the time we get back to Little Rock."

"I wouldn't be too sure of that, Amos. Did you see the way my brother jumped out from behind that tree at Okalona two weeks ago?"

Sam said. "There was no reason to stay covered when the Johnnies were running toward us. They can't run and shoot at the same time."

Amos asked, "Do you think that people from the North and South will ever be able to get along with each other after this is over?"

Sam and J.A. just shrugged their shoulders.

Amos said, "Uh-oh, here comes Klinker again. I wonder where they're going to send us to fight now?"

"Maybe they want to send Grant home and have us go whip General Lee." J.A. replied.

Without asking, Amos picked the coffeepot off the fire and filled the Klinkers' tin cups. "Sit down and stay awhile," he said.

Sergeant Klinker seemed upset about something. "I can't spare the time. I still have too many people to see tonight."

"What's the news?" J.A. asked.

"It's not good. The Rebel troops are getting some heavy reinforcements. General Kirby Smith's army is only fourteen or fifteen miles south of here. At least we hope he's still that far away. He has rounded up what we estimate to be about twenty-five thousand Rebels from Louisiana and Mississippi. They outnumber our army more than two to one. General Steele is convinced that they're going to try to recapture Little Rock."

J.A. said, "Whoa!"

Amos pursed his lips and whistled.

"So we're going back to Little Rock," Sam concluded.

The sergeant looked tired as he nodded in agreement. "Just as fast as we can get there. We'll be pulling out in a few hours and joining the rest of Steele's army, so get all the rest you can before then. We might not get any sleep the next few nights, if Smith's army is right on our tail."

"You get some rest, too," Sam said.

As the Klinker brothers walked away, Amos threw his remaining coffee on the fire, rose to his feet, and spit on the ground. " 'Just some little skirmishes at Okalona and Prairie D'Anne. You boys should be back in camp soon.' T'want so." With that he walked into the tent.

During the night another fierce storm blew into the area, turning the already-soggy ground into a mire of slush. At four-thirty in the morning, as General Steele's troops were forming to begin their retreat, a picket rode into camp and informed them that General Smith's army was within two miles of their position. Just as they had expected, Colonel Englemann's brigade of sharpshooters marched at rear guard of Steele's divisions.

They crossed the Washita River before daylight in a drenching rain. Kirby Smith's troops were closing in on them. After winning every battle against the Rebels, retreating this way was a difficult pill for Englemann's men to swallow. The wagons carrying the food and supplies slid off the road, sank in the deep mud, and had to be abandoned. Not only would Steele's soldiers go without sleep for the next few days; they would also have nothing to eat.

Friday, March 30, 1864

The march from the Saline River to the first bluffs west of Jenkin's Ferry was over a mile. It was well after midnight when the bright moonlight revealed a forest of majestic trees rising from the water-soaked earth and stretching toward the sky. To the west was a small stream called Cox's Creek. The bottom was densely wooded and contained many fallen trees.

Englemann's men were knee-deep in mud and wet through to the skin when they helped Steele's divisions across the stream on a pontoon bridge, but saw morning light come before their task was completed. When the Rebel troops attacked, regiments from Kansas, Wisconsin, Indiana, and Illinois were still on the south side of the bridge with Colonel Englemann's rear guard. The colonel had to make a quick decision between a fight against vastly superior numbers and surrender. His men had not eaten in two days. They were hungry, cold, and tired. Nevertheless, Englemann chose to fight and positioned his troops as strategically as he could. The commanding officers of the other regiments who had not made it across the stream saw Englemann's rear guard getting ready to fight and began positioning their own troops.

Colonel Mackay of the Thirty-third Iowa held the extreme rear not far from the bluffs. Mackay's troops had barely reached their position when they were attacked. They were speedily reinforced by the Fiftieth Indiana, but their lines were pushed back by the superior numbers.

The Ninth Wisconsin and the Twenty-ninth Iowa were posted in a strong position about a half-mile to the rear of this first position. The right side of their line was behind the bank of the creek, while their left side was protected somewhat by a marsh. Soon Mackay's men fell back to this second line. Colonel Englemann brought his rear guard over to the bank of the river. Their was no room left to retreat. Some reinforcements came back across the stream to assist the trapped regiments.

Sam, J.A., and Amos were leaning against a four-foot-high bluff, waiting for the next enemy attack, when to their surprise Brig. Gen. Samuel A. Rice came riding up on his horse. He had come back across the bridge to aid the trapped regiments. "You men move about ten yards to your left behind that higher bank!" he yelled. Then as he rode off he called back, "Give 'em hell!"

As the men moved into the new position, they heard Rice yelling orders, commanding men to move this way and that way and trying to get them all in the most advantageous positions.

Sheets of rain blanketed the field in front of them. Then, as if from the bowels of the earth, masses of men, in muddy gray uniforms, erupted onto the field in front of them. Shouting Rebel yells, they tried their best to slosh through the mud toward the Federal position on the bank of the stream. They were making slow progress.

General Rice yelled, "Hold your fire!"

Sam, J.A., and Amos watched the Rebels struggle through the ooze and slush until they were well within range of their guns, then heard Rice yell, "Fire!"

The trapped Federal troops fired volley after volley into the hapless Rebel soldiers. In fifteen minutes the first attack was over. The Rebels who were still on their feet were struggling back toward the thicket. General Kirby hurled two more successive divisions at the outnumbered Federal troops, and each one was repulsed with great slaughter.

When all became quiet, Sam looked at his brother and Amos and asked, "Could you see their faces?"

"I'm afraid I'll see some of them for the rest of my life," J.A. replied.

"I wish they had never come so close," Sam said. "Before, I could just see uniforms. Today I saw husbands, sons, and brothers."

"You have a wife, mother, and sisters," Amos said. "If we didn't kill them, they'd have killed us. It's a terrible thing, but we did what we had to do."

Sergeant Klinker came running toward the men. "The Rebels are overrunning our left flank!" he yelled. "If they get through, we're all finished. Englemann wants our regiment and the Forty-third Illinois to reinforce them. He said that we're the best men he has, and that he's counting on us."

Klinker moved down the line, delivering his message, and several hundred men rose up from the riverbank and moved out.

As soon as Sam, J.A., and Amos reached their new position, they ducked behind a tree just as several rifle balls whistled over their heads.

A soldier from the Thirty-third Iowa yelled, "You got here just in time! We're almost out of ammunition!"

The men rested their rifles on the top of the dead tree and surveyed the situation through the driving rain. The Rebels were still about ninety yards away. They weren't mounting an all-out charge but were slowly moving forward, from tree to rock to bush. As Sam watched, a Rebel soldier raced from one shelter toward another and then fell face down into the mud before ever reaching his destination. Several other enemy soldiers fell in succession. After a few more Rebels were knocked down by the sharpshooters from Iowa, before they began just holding their position, Colonel Mackay unexpectedly ordered the Federal troops to advance. To everyone's surprise, the Rebels' attack turned into a fast withdrawal. Within an hour the men from Iowa and Illinois, along with the other regiments that had been trapped along Cox's Creek, had advanced over a half a mile. The troops that Gen. Kirby Smith had sent into this battle had been pushed completely away from the pontoon bridge.

Just when everyone thought it was over, a Rebel artillery battery was pushed out from behind cover. A couple dozen soldiers with muskets were on each side of the artillerymen. The artillery fired once, and the soldiers each fired one musket round, both from very close range. Before either the artillerymen or the soldiers had time to reload, the Twenty-ninth Iowa and the Second Kansas Colored charged recklessly across the soaked field. Their bayonets were fixed, and they yelled at the top of their lungs as they ran. The Rebels saw that the charging Federals would be upon them before they had time to reload and were forced to withdraw.

The colored troops captured the artillery and dragged it back in triumph, amid loud cheers. This feat of bravery had put an exclamation point on what had been an unbelievably successful Federal victory.

Amos declared, "If I ever hear another man say that the Negroes are afraid to fight, I'll slap him alongside his head."

The rain was still coming down in sheets when Sam, J.A., and Amos got back to Cox's Creek. Colonel Englemann rode up to them and declared, "What happened today was the *damnedest* exhibition of marksmanship I've *ever* seen."

229

The men's faces showed that they were not in a celebratory mood.

"How many men did we lose today, sir?" Sam asked.

"It looks like we lost a total of around seven hundred. I'm afraid your regiment suffered more than its share of casualties. We estimate that the Rebels lost closer to three thousand. This is hard to believe, but we killed three of their generals. Smith underestimated us and didn't commit a big-enough force for this battle. I don't think we can expect him to make that mistake again."

Sam looked back out over the battlefield. The ground was almost covered with fallen Rebels. Many were lying still. Others seemed to be in all manner of torment. He wondered which of the dead and dying he had shot and felt sick to his stomach. "It took a great deal of bravery to keep charging our position the way they did. Who is going to help all those wounded men out there, sir?"

"Kirby Smith has put up a flag of truce. That way he can care for his wounded and bury his dead. We can gather up our wounded, cross the bridge, and rejoin General Steele."

"What about our own dead?" J.A. asked.

"I'm going to leave a burial detail here."

"General Smith will most likely take them prisoner," Amos said.

"I trust that the general is an honorable man, but either way, I have no choice. The dead must be given a decent burial, and we don't have enough ammunition to make another stand."

Suddenly a terrible realization overwhelmed Sam. "Why are you delivering this message to us in person? Where is Sergeant Klinker?"

The colonel's face became solemn. "I'm sorry, men. The sergeant and his brother were both killed in action."

The three men were stunned into silence for several moments. Then Amos asked, "Where are they, sir? We'd like to pay our last respects."

"They are over near where you first reinforced the Thirty-third Iowa. I'm truly sorry, men. The Klinker brothers were brave soldiers." With that the colonel rode away.

Sergeant Klinker was lying on his back with two holes in the front of his uniform coat. The absence of blood suggested that he had died quickly. John Klinker was sitting against a tree with his head hanging to one side. The pool of blood around him indicated that he had not been so lucky.

"They must of both got hit during that first volley," J.A. lamented.

"How terrible for the Klinker family, losing two of their men in one day," Sam said.

A bugle signaled to the three men that it was time to leave.

Amos bent down close to his fallen sergeant and said, "I'll tell your mama that you both died bravely."

Notwithstanding the decisive victory at Jenkin's Ferry, it was necessary for General Steele's army to continue its retreat. First, his food supply was gone, and second, he couldn't leave Little Rock unprotected against recapture by the Confederacy. By the middle of the second day, every man in Steele's army was close to complete exhaustion. They had not been able to stop and sleep. The horses had not had any grain, nor the men any food, since the beginning of the retreat. The soldiers subsisted on nothing but coffee. All the while, the pouring rain washed away roads, forcing men and animals to forge through mud that was up to a foot deep. It seemed almost as if nature had decided to turn her wrath against them. Horses gave out and fell down by the roadside, unable to get up. The big guns and caissons had to be pulled by men, doing the work of the fallen horses. After defeating an enemy force far more numerous than themselves, Colonel Englemann's rear guard had to endure this humiliating and demoralizing retreat, only a few miles ahead of Kirby Smith's army.

On the third night, a picket rode into camp and announced that the Confederate general had stopped to rest his own debilitated army. Apparently, Smith had realized that with Steele's army only a few hours outside of Little Rock, any chance for him to overtake the Federal forces had vanished. His heavy losses the last time he encountered Steele's rear guard might have also influenced his decision. Some more disturbing information delivered by the picket was that Gen. Kirby Smith had captured Englemann's burial detail and then declared a great Confederate victory at Jenkin's Ferry.

General Steele immediately sent out the order for his troops to halt. Ignoring the cold, drenching rain and forgetting the hunger gnawing at their stomachs, the men dropped their bedrolls in the swamps, climbed in, and slept soundly.

231

In the morning, there was a break in the rain that had been falling so steadily for the last few days. When reveille sounded, J.A. and Amos forced their tired, aching bodies out of their bedrolls. They could smell coffee and saw a large fire not too far away. Before they walked to the fire, J.A. looked at Sam still in his bedroll and said, "You rest for a while longer, Sam. I'll bring you a cup of coffee."

Some of the men in Company C of their regiment had come up with a huge kettle and were boiling coffee over their fire. Other men in the regiment were holding their tin cups and waiting in line for the only breakfast they were going to have.

When it was his turn, Amos filled his cup, took a couple of large swallows, and filled it again. J.A. did the same, then filled a cup for his brother, and the two men thanked their hosts.

Before they left, a man from Company B asked them, "Did you hear the good news?"

"What?" Amos asked.

"Kirby Smith's troops are marching south away from us. They pulled out a few hours before daylight."

As the two men walked back toward where they'd left Sam, J.A. asked, "How are you feeling, Amos?"

"Let me spell it out for you. Other than every bone and muscle in my body aching like crazy, being cold and wet from head to toe, and my stomach thinking my throat's been cut, I guess I'm bearing up pretty tolerable. How about you?"

J.A. smiled. He was too weary to laugh. "I guess I would have to echo your sentiments. I will be very glad to get back to our tent in Little Rock."

"It looks like Sam is still sleeping," Amos said.

J.A. leaned over his brother. "Come on, Sam. It's time to roll out. I've got some hot coffee for you."

Sam rolled over and looked up at the two men. It looked like they were underwater. Their faces appeared distorted. His brother's face seemed to float up in front of his, and a hand shook his shoulder.

"It's time to get up."

It sounded as if his brother's voice was coming from a tunnel. He felt an icy hand on his forehead, and he heard, "My God, Amos, he's burning up with fever."

For the next several days, Sam's dreams, visions, and reality were blended into an undecipherable puzzle. He was bouncing along on his back, with gray skies and green trees racing past, and rain falling into his eyes. Then he was back in Denver, and Dora's sweet face was looking down at him. She reached out and touched his cheek, but her hand was hard and coarse. Then her face transformed into the face of a man he didn't know.

"Is he going to make it, Doctor?" Sam knew that was J.A. talking.

"There is no way to tell at this point, but I do know that he won't be going into any more battles."

The next time Sam awakened, he was in a field hospital. He could hear wounded men all around the large tent moaning in pain. He slept most of the time, waking whenever someone helped him with a cold drink of water and again when a nurse fed him some hot soup. He couldn't remember being bathed but was conscious of the mud and dirt being absent from his face and body.

He was awake enough to know that he was being placed in an ambulance but went back to sleep and didn't awaken until he was in new quarters. The ceiling was lower, and it was darker than the field hospital. It felt like his bed was gently moving back and forth. His mouth was dry, and he felt a stifling heat. He tried to push the blankets off his body, but a hand restrained him. Then a woman's face was in front of his, a soft but strong hand lifted his head, and he felt a cup against his lips. Cold water flowed into his mouth, and he swallowed several times, soothing his sore dry throat.

"Where am I?"

He opened his eyes and saw a thin, clean-shaven young man with a receding hairline. Even in Sam's weakened condition, he could see that the man's face looked both tired and compassionate.

"I'm Dr. Hopkins, Private Harris. You're on the hospital ship, *Red Rover* on your way up the Mississippi River. We're taking you and some other Iowa soldiers to the hospital in Keokuk."

Sam nodded that he understood, then closed his eyes and fell asleep.

23

July 1864

Newspapers nationwide continued to report the activities of Generals Grant, Sherman, and Lee; detailing accounts of the battles at Richmond and Atlanta. Newspapers in Iowa reported about battles involving Federal soldiers from the Iowa regiments. Federal victories at Okalona and Prairie D'Anne were clear-cut and well defined in the printed media. After the severe engagement at Jenkin's Ferry, the newspapers gave conflicting reports. First came the news that General Steele had scored a major triumph over Gen. Kirby Smith's Confederate forces. Then, news arrived that Steele's army was retreating toward Little Rock, with Smith right behind him. The shocking report of close to four thousand casualties at Jenkin's Ferry was tempered by the news that 80 percent of the casualties were on the Confederate side. Then the *Grinnell News* printed what was the most frightening report of all: the Fortieth Iowa Infantry had been on the front line of the battle and had suffered extremely heavy losses.

The clear blue skies, lush green fields, and pleasant aroma of flowers that portrayed June in Grinnell, Iowa, could not bring any cheer to the Harris farm. Every day, Dora and the Harris family awaited a letter from Sam or J.A. Each new day brought another disappointment and increased apprehension, as no letters arrived.

Breakfast was over, and Dora was standing at the kitchen window, looking off into the distance at William as he skillfully guided the sharp blade of the breaking plow as it turned over the almost black soil. The plow was being pulled by a single ox. Earlier that morning William had hitched a horse to a wagon so Joanna could take James and Mary off to school, then go on to her own classes at Grinnell College. Mama Harris was sitting at the kitchen table, Kate was in her playpen in the corner of the kitchen, and Frank was in the backyard playing with the family dog. The canine was a gentle long-haired dog of mixed breed.

Mama Harris said, "It's hard on William being the only man in the Harris family not off fighting the war."

Dora came over and sat across from her mother-in-law. "At least we know that he's alive."

Mama Harris walked over to the stove. "Would you like a cup of coffee, dearie?"

"No, thanks. Waiting and not knowing is so hard."

Mama Harris put her hand on Dora's shoulder. "I'm sure we'll hear something soon."

Dora put her hand on top of the hand of her mother-in-law. "I'm so sorry. You shouldn't have to comfort me. I know that you're just as worried."

"William told me that he needs to pick up some bags of feed in town today. Why don't you go with him? It will help keep your mind busy."

"What about you?"

"I'm sure that my grandchildren will keep me busy enough."

It was midafternoon when William tossed the last bag of feed into the back of the wagon; then he and Dora rode over to Scott's store.

"What did you want to buy?" William asked.

"I want to get James a present for his birthday."

"I didn't know it was his birthday. I'll pick up a gift for him, too."

A pretty red-haired clerk walked over to them and said, "Hello, William; what can I help you with?"

"It's nice to see you, Lina. We're looking for a birthday present for my new little brother. Have you met my sister-in-law?"

"I've waited on her a few times, but we've never formally met."

After William took care of the introductions, Lina asked. "Have you received any letters from your brothers recently?"

"Not for several weeks."

Lina's full red eyelashes covered her eyes as she looked down. "Neither have I."

Both William and Dora looked surprised.

"You get letters from my brothers?" he asked.

"Just from J.A. I guess he hasn't told you about me."

William laughed. "So you're the one. He's told everyone in the family that there's a beautiful young lady in town that he is enamoured with, but he wouldn't give us your name."

Lina flashed a wide smile. "We have plans," she said.

"My brother is a very lucky man." William looked at Dora. "Both of my brothers are very fortunate. Lina, if we hear anything before you, we'll let you know, and maybe you can do the same. We're all pretty worried."

"So am I. What were you thinking about for James's birthday?"

"Maybe a pearl-handled pocketknife," William said. "What about you, Dora?"

"I thought I might get him a black felt hat. Ira Rayburn was wearing one when James brought him to the house, and I noticed James admiring it."

On the way back to the farm, Dora commented, "I've never seen you with a girl, William. You Harris boys are all so good-looking, it seems strange that you have no love interest."

"I've had a few girlfriends in high school and college."

"But no one now."

"While my father and brothers are in the army, I've got as many women to take care of as I can handle. There will be plenty of time for romance after the war is over."

"Isn't there even anyone you have your eye on?"

He looked at her for several seconds, then said, "No, there is no one."

Mama Harris stood at the back doorsteps waiting for them. Her eyes were red, and she was holding a letter in her hand. William lifted Dora from the wagon seat to the ground with one quick motion, and they both ran toward the house. Dora's heart was pounding wildly.

"What is it, Mama?" he asked.

"It's a letter to Dora."

"What does it say?" Dora asked.

"I don't know, but it's to you and it's from J.A."

Dora ripped open the letter and began reading. "Oh, thank God. He says that he and Sam went through all the battles without being hurt." She read on: "I know you all have been praying for us." Then she stopped and put one hand up to her face.

"What is it?" William asked.

"Sam is in the hospital!" She began reading aloud. " 'I know that you must have been alarmed getting this letter from me, but it had to be written. During our retreat from Little Rock, Sam came down with a high fever. Amos Rayburn and I carried him back to camp on a stretcher. He spent a few days in the field hospital, then was taken to the hospital ship *Red Rover*, where he has stayed up until now. The ship is leaving in two days to take their patients to the hospital at Keokuk. He should arrive there about the twentieth of the month. I would have written this letter sooner, but I wanted to wait until I could tell everyone he had begun to recover. He hasn't. At least you don't have to worry about him being wounded or killed in a battle, as I've been told that he will be mustered out just as soon as he recovers. That's all the time I have to write. Company drills start in fifteen minutes. Tell Mama that I'll be writing to her to-morrow.

Sincerely, James Agnew Harris.' "

Dora handed the letter to her mother-in-law, who read it quietly. When she was finished, she handed it to William. "My boy is coming home, but he's very ill."

William said, "I know my brother. He didn't let himself get killed in the war, and he's not going to let this fever whip him, either."

"How long will it take me to get to Keokuk?" Dora asked William.

"I'm going with you. It will take us about three days if we take a wagon, or less if we take the train."

Dora brushed her tears away from her eyes. "I want to be there when his boat comes in."

She felt something pulling at her skirt and looked down into her son's upturned face. "Is Papa coming home?"

"Yes, Frank. Papa is finally coming home."

Dora and William stood on the dock at Keokuk and watched the big steamship pull into the wharf. In the morning sun, they could see the words, *Red Rover*, on the bow and on the cover of the big sidewheel, in big letters, "U. S. HOSPITAL SHIP." Smoke poured out of two tall smokestacks towering above the aft deck. The crowd waiting on the dock contained many anxious-looking young women and some weary older couples. On the road leading up to the dock was a train of ambulances. The ambulances that were waiting for the boat were the more comfortable four-wheel wagons. Two horses were harnessed to the front of each wagon, and two ambulance attendants waited on each seat.

When the ship was securely tied down, a ramp was pushed up to the side of the ship and fastened to the lower deck.

A distinguished-looking officer stepped up to the top of the ramp and in a loud voice said, "May I have your attention, everyone? I'm Col. Douglas Bannan. I'm the head surgeon on the hospital ship *Red Rover*. I'm happy to report that not one soldier that was brought to us from the battlefields of Arkansas has died on the way to Keokuk. Some, however, are severely wounded or critically ill. I know that it has been along time since some of you have seen your loved ones, but I have to ask all of you to persevere just a short time longer. Our hospital staff, along with the hospital attendants, will be assisting our patients from the ship to the ambulances. Please stay back and let our people do their jobs. After that, they will be taken on to the hospital, where the doctors and nurses are awaiting their arrival. As soon as your husbands, sons, or brothers are at the hospital, the staff there will prepare them to see you. God bless every one of you, and may He who knows your every care and burden bring your men back to good health once again. We are now going to begin taking the patients off the ship and putting them into the ambulances."

While Dr. Bannon was talking, the ambulances had been pulled up into a long line, with the first ambulance parked at the foot of the ramp.

Dora and William watched as stretcher after stretcher was carried down the ramp to the waiting ambulance attendants. It appeared that the more seriously wounded were being removed from the ship first. Cries went up from women in the crowd as the first men were recognized. Some had lost an arm or a leg. Others appeared to have suffered life-threatening head or chest wounds. Women called out men's names, and wounded soldiers raised arms, and sometimes stumps, when they heard the voice of their wife or mother.

Most of the ambulances had carried their passengers away before Dora finally saw Sam being carried down the ramp. She screamed his name once, then, when he was only a few feet away, called out his name once more, but his eyes were closed and he did not respond.

When Sam's ambulance pulled out toward the hospital, Dora turned to William and began to weep uncontrollably. He put his arms around her and tried to say comforting words, but he was close to tears himself. Seeing his brother so pale and corpse-like had shocked him badly. Up until now William had assumed that his brother would be better by the time the boat pulled into dock. Now, for the first time, he realized that Sam could actually die. Other men from around the county had come home only to succumb from illnesses they had contracted while serving their country.

The immense size of the temporary additions to Keokuk Hospital amazed both William and Dora. They rode their wagon past row after row of white barracks-type hospital wards. The large parcel of hospital land contained a dairy, an icehouse, an ambulance repair shop, and acres upon acres of vegetable gardens. There were several stables with ambulances parked in front of each one. A long row of cottages had been built near the original hospital building, and women in hoop skirts were sitting or standing on the front verandas of the cottages. Between the hospital barracks and the cottages, Keokuk Hospital was equal to some of the largest towns in Iowa.

Wives, mothers, and sisters of the sick and wounded men waved to Dora and William.

"I wonder in which one of those cottages I'll be living?" Dora asked.

"I just hope you won't be there very long."

"I don't care how long I'm here, as long as I bring Sam home with me when I leave."

They both became silent, each visualizing the terrible prospect of Dora coming home alone.

At the old hospital they were given directions to the barrack where Sam had been placed.

When they walked into the building, the aroma of coffee blended with the smell of various medicines and ointments. Rows of bunk beds with clean white sheets and pillowcases lined each wall. There was a space of about twelve feet between the foot of one bunk and the one directly across from it. Although the bunks were only a few feet apart, the interior of the barracks did not look overcrowded.

Some men were in uniform. Others wore hospital gowns. A man who had lost a leg was playing cards with another man who was missing an arm. Some soldiers were sitting on their bunks reading. The more seriously ill lay on their backs and watched the action around them. Both the ward and the patients in it looked clean and neat. Keokuk Hospital was a vast improvement from what the men had been forced to endure in field hospitals or during the medical care some of them had received while lying on the battlefields.

When they found Sam, he was lying still and his eyes were closed. He was clean-shaven, but his hair was quite long. He was clothed in a white hospital gown, and they guessed that he had been freshly bathed.

Dora's heart was pounding. She would have thrown herself on him if it had not been for his weakened condition. Instead, she sat carefully next to him. She kissed him on the forehead, on his closed eyes, and on his lips. Her tears splashed down on his face, but he didn't move or respond. "Sam, I've waited so long for you. You promised me that you would come home, and you kept your promise. Now you have to get well. You can't leave me now."

Sam's chest rose as he took a deep breath. His eyes opened, and he smiled weakly. His voice was husky. "Is it really you, or is this just another dream?" He closed his eyes again.

She put her hand on his cheek. "Sam, it's me. I'm here."

His eyes opened, and he reached his hand up and felt her cheek. "It really is you. How did . . .?" His voice trailed off.

"I'm here in Keokuk, and I'm not leaving until you're well. Then we'll go home together."

Sam's eyes looked longingly at Dora; then he looked past her at William. He hardly made a sound, but his lips formed the words, "My little brother." He smiled at both of them; then he closed his eyes.

A young nurse walked up to Sam's bunk carrying a pan of ice water and a bottle labeled *Quinine Sulphatis*. Over her arm was a clean white towel. "I'm sorry," she said. "I have to give him his medicine and put some cold compresses on his forehead. We have to bring his fever down. Would you mind coming back later?"

"Of course," Dora said. "We'll be back soon, darling." His eyes were closed again, and his face was so white against his black hair and eyebrows that it startled her. "He will be all right, won't he?" she asked the nurse.

The young woman had dark circles under her eyes, and she looked so tired that it seemed she could easily become ill herself. "We will do everything we can. I promise you that."

William took Dora's hand, and the two of them walked away slowly.

24

Springtime in Iowa is delightful. Clear blue skies are patched here and there by white clouds, like ghosts of diverse contours. Cool breezes balance the effects of the warm sun, providing comfort for all. Miles and miles of lush green grass are splotched with numerous colors from forests of wildflowers. Birds add their zestful songs to the scene. James Russell Lowell must have been at such a place when he penned the words *"Every clod feels a stir of might, an instinct within it that reaches and towers, and groping blindly above it for light, climbs to a soul in grass and flowers."*

The war is over, slavery has been abolished, and the country remains united, although the scars will take a very long time to heal. Farmers and townspeople can finally go back to leading normal lives, yet, in a larger sense, Grinnell will never be the same as it was before. Fatherless children, grieving widows, and mothers whose sons would never come home attested to the terrible price the town had paid for the war.

Faces around the breakfast table at the Harris farm were unable to express any of the *"joy come, grief goes"* emotions expressed by the poet. Ephriam and Rachael had already prepared themselves an early breakfast, said their goodbyes and left for the office. The large number of sick and wounded war veterans who had returned from the battlefields were causing them to work extremely long hours. The rest of the family had gathered around the kitchen table. Breakfast was over, but Papa and Mama Harris, Dora, Joanna, Mary, and William were drinking coffee and talking. Kate was still in her high chair, and Frank had gone outside to play. Dora's luggage was sitting by the kitchen door.

"I can't believe that he's really gone," William said.

Papa Harris appeared several years older than he had before the war. He had not come down with any life-threatening illnesses, but it was obvious that his health had been impaired by the rigors of military duty. He placed his coffee cup down in front of him and looked around the table to see if the others were handling the loss more easily than he. "He served his country so well, and then to die like this after it's all over." He shook his head. "It's very difficult for me to accept."

Mama Harris put her hand on her husband's shoulder. "He's in a better place now, dear. God will take care of him." She glanced over at Dora. "I can't imagine what this place will be like without you and the children."

Dora looked at the people who had been her family for the last three years. She put her hand on Joanna's. "I'm going to miss you all so much. You will always be my Iowa family."

"I wish you didn't have to leave," Joanna said.

James broke the family's somber mood when he walked into the kitchen wearing a broad grin and carrying a shiny new silver dollar.

"You must have done a mighty good job loading the wagon to be paid like that," William declared.

Sam walked into the kitchen behind James. "The wagon is ready to go except for your luggage, Dora. I pulled it around to the front of the house. Why all the long faces?"

Papa Harris said, "We were talking about the assassination of President Lincoln."

"What a horrible thing to have happened. Such a good man. Such a loss for our country," Sam said. He walked over to his mother, leaned over, and kissed her. "I want you to come visit us soon, Mama."

Papa Harris got up from his chair, walked around the table, and embraced his son. "Is it all right if I come too?"

"You'll be in trouble if you don't!"

Sam hugged his father so tightly that the elder Harris emitted a low groan. "It appears that you have your strength back. You also look a lot better than you did when Dora brought you home. You had us worried there for a while."

"Believe me, Papa, I feel a lot better."

Mama Harris turned toward Kate in her high chair. "What am I going to do without my precious grandchildren?"

Kate responded by smiling and waving her spoon.

"It won't be long before you'll be able to board a train and get to Nebraska City in only eight hours," Dora advised everyone.

"I understand they intend to have the train run both ways," Joanna reminded Dora.

Dora took a clean wet washcloth, wiped off Kate's face, took off the child's bib, picked her up, and kissed her on the cheek. "You little bundle of energy. You're going to give your mommy all kinds of trouble between here and Nebraska City, aren't you?"

When they were all outside, Sam lifted Frank up onto the wagon seat, placed Kate in a small playpen he'd rigged up behind the seat, and climbed up next to his son.

On the other side of the wagon, Dora was hugging and kissing each member of the family. When she got to Joanna both women cried. William was waiting to help Dora up onto the wagon seat, so she saved him for last. She hugged him tightly and kissed him on the cheek. "William, I'll always remember all the things you've done for me."

Dora squealed, then laughed, when William grabbed both hands around her waist, lifted her high over his head, and placed her feet on the floor of the wagon seat. "I am going to miss you, too, Dora."

Sam smiled at his brother. "Now that you don't have all of these women to take care of, I'll bet you'll be romancing some lucky young lady soon."

William nodded. "That's my plan."

"Tell J.A. that I want him and his new bride to come and see Dora and me just as soon as he gets out of the hospital." Sam said.

The Harris family stood in their front yard and watched the wagon go all the way down the drive, pull through the gate, and turn onto the road. Sam and Dora turned and waved one more time, and then they headed west.

Epilogue

Sam and Dora remained in Nebraska City for fifteen years, during which time Sam built houses for affluent townspeople. While in Nebraska City, Dora gave birth to two more boys and five more girls. The family moved back to Denver in 1890, and Dora was reunited with her beloved sister Mollie. Dora and Mollie remained close for the remainder of their lives. Sam first built a large brick house for his family in South Denver; then his construction company built and sold numerous other houses in the same part of town. Some of these homes are still occupied even to this day. Not satisfied with just raising her nine children, the always-active Dora became a midwife and delivered many babies who were born in Denver around the turn of the century. The couple remained patriots throughout their lives. Their children and grandchildren could always count on an exciting Independence Day celebration and picnic hosted by Grandma Dora and Grandpa Sam in the immense backyard of their home. Sam and Dora's home contained a spacious dining room with a large dining table. Anyone arriving at the Harrises' during the afternoon was automatically invited to stay for dinner. One of Sam and Dora's granddaughters, Phyllis Tasker, recalls sitting on her grandpa's lap and brushing his full gray beard. She stated to me that she believes that her grandfather was the most handsome man she had ever seen. In 1910, the *Denver Post* devoted the whole front page of their society section to Sam and Dora's fiftieth anniversary celebration, including a picture of the still-attractive couple. They stood up in front of the crowd that had assembled, held hands, and assured everyone that they had indeed both fallen in love at first sight. Sam died in 1919 at the age of eighty-seven and was buried at the Fairmount Cemetery in Denver. Dora died a short time later and was buried next to her husband.

Two of Sam and Dora's children were born during the years depicted in this book. The first one, Frank Harris, who was born shortly after the couple arrived in Denver, became a railroad detective. Kate Harris, who was born in Grinnell while Sam was off fighting in the war, became a schoolteacher. Frank and Kate both lived out their lives in Denver.

James, Papa Harris, spent the remainder of his life on his farm in Grinnell, Iowa. He never completely regained his health after the war and died in 1872 at the age of sixty-seven. Sam's mother, Mary Ann, Mama Harris, went to live with her daughter Joanna and remained there until her death in 1892.

James Agnew Harris and Amos Rayburn survived one more skirmish near the Arkansas River, then finished out their time in the army performing duties about which their military records state: "The labor and value of these duties is more appreciated by people who are in, or have at one time been in, the military than by civilians."

In 1866 a book titled *Iowa and the Rebellion* was written by a scholarly Iowan named Norton Ingersol. In this book he describes the battles and experiences of all the Iowa regiments during the Civil War. When he came to the chapter about the Fortieth Iowa Volunteers, Ingersol wrote: "Their marvelous victory at Jenkin's Ferry was against vastly superior numbers," and then regarding the subsequent retreat, he said: "I think that the retreat from Jenkin's Ferry to Little Rock was one of the saddest episodes of the war." In another place Ingersol reported, "The fighting they did at Jenkin's Ferry must be pronounced wonderful." The author concluded with, "The Iowa Fortieth was one of the finest regiments ever seen, east or west."

Amos went through his tour of duty unscathed and mustered out of the army at Fort Gibson in August of 1865. He spent the remainder of his life working his farm in Poweshiek County not far from Grinnell.

J.A. also avoided any injuries in combat but was stricken with a severe illness during his last days in the army. After the war, he spent some time in the hospital at Keokuk, Iowa, then went back to Grinnell and married his sweetheart Lina. The young couple went out west to join J.A.'s brother Thomas McKee, who was a hotel owner in Lake County, California. One reason for the couple moving to California was to allow J.A. to regain the robust health he had enjoyed before the war. J.A. owned farms in Lake County up until his retirement. He died in Los Gatos, California, in 1921, shortly after the death of his wife.

Sam's sister Joanna's friendship with her college classmate Robert Haines blossomed into a romance, and the couple were married in 1867, two years after their graduation from Grinnell College. They both taught at the Troy Academy in David County. After their marriage, Joanna taught at the Grinnell College Academy and Grinnell High School while at the same time raising seven children. One of her sons became a doctor, who practiced medicine in Stillwater, Minnesota. Another son became an attorney in Denver. Joanna's husband, Robert, died in 1902, and Joanna died in 1931, three months before she would have celebrated her eighty-eighth birthday. At the time of her death, the *Grinnell Herald* wrote: "For many years Joanna Haines has been an object lesson in growing old gracefully. The alertness of her mind has always been a distinguishing characteristic and did not lessen as the years rested more heavily on her. The whole town of Grinnell mourns the passing of this marvelous pioneer woman. A plaque hanging above the door of a hall at Grinnell College bears the name Joanna Harris Haines. Students refer to it as 'Haines Hall.' "

Ephriam, Doc Harris, and Rachael Hamlin Harris remained in Grinnell. They raised four sons, two of whom became medical doctors. Their adopted son, James, was already an adult by the time their younger sons began to arrive. Rachael died in 1889 at the age of fifty-six. Ephriam continued on with his medical practice well into his later years and at one time was the oldest practicing physician in the county. He lived until 1909 and was eighty-one years old before he passed away. Rachael was buried in Grinnell, and twenty years later her husband was buried next to her.

William Harris left Grinnell soon after the war had ended and became a banker in Fullerton, Iowa. Twelve-years later he married a young woman from Malcom, Iowa, Ida Dodge. The couple had five children. After forty years as a banker, William retired to Long Beach, California. Ida died in 1927. William died in 1932 at the age of ninety-one. His death certificate lists a surviving wife named Lucy.

Dora's father, Charles Dorsey, sold the family farm on the Little Nemaha in 1865 and moved to Nebraska City, where he plied his trade as a building contractor. He helped build the Otoe County Courthouse, then, in 1878, was superintendent of construction on the new state capital building in Lincoln. Dora's mother died in 1880, and her father lived with his daughter Ada, the wife of a Nebraska City soapmaker, Bradner Slaughter. Mr. Dorsey remained there until his death in 1888.

Mollie Dorsey Sanford became somewhat of a celebrity in Denver in 1895 when she made a holograph copy of her journal. It became a document of outstanding social and historical importance, and excerpts from her journal were published in many magazines and newspapers. She willed her journal to her grandson Mr. Albert N. Williams, Sr., and it was published by the University of Nebraska Press in 1959. The title of the book is *Mollie*. To this day it is considered to be one of the finest depictions of the life and times of the pioneers in the Nebraska and Colorado territories. Because of her journal, Mollie is as well known in Nebraska City today as she was almost 150 years ago. There is even a Mollie Museum in one of the Nebraska City homes where she lived. Mollie's husband, Byron Sanford, worked for the United States Mint for forty years and was a member of the comission that selected the site for the State University at Boulder. Throughout their lives, Mollie and Byron remained charming and active members of their community. Byron Sanford died in 1914, at the age of eighty-eight. Mollie died just three months later, at the age of seventy-six.